# WITHDRAWN

## DATE DUE

D1020120

DEMCO, INC. 38-2931

# STAINLESS
# STEEL
# VISIONS

# STAINLESS
# STEEL
# VISIONS

**HARRY HARRISON**

ILLUSTRATED BY
BRYN BARNARD

PRODUCED BY BYRON PREISS VISUAL PUBLICATIONS, INC.

**TOR** ®

A Tom Doherty Associates Book
New York

STAINLESS STEEL VISIONS

Copyright © 1993 by Harry Harrison

This book is printed on acid-free paper.

A Tor Book
Published by Tom Doherty Associates, Inc.
175 Fifth Avenue
New York, N.Y. 10010

Tor ® is a registered trademark of Tom Doherty Associates, Inc.

Library of Congress Cataloging-in-Publication Data

Harrison, Harry.
    Stainless steel visions / Harry Harrison.
        p.   cm.
    "A Tom Doherty Associates book."
    ISBN 0-312-85245-2
    1. Science fiction, American.    I. Title.
PS3558.A667S74   1993
813'.54—dc20                                                    92-43879
                                                                    CIP

First edition: March 1993

Printed in the United States of America

0 9 8 7 6 5 4 3 2 1

# CONTENTS

*Introduction*                                    7

The Streets of Ashkelon                          13

Toy Shop                                         33

Not Me, Not Amos Cabot!                          41

The Mothballed Spaceship                         53

Commando Raid                                    73

The Repairman                                    87

Brave Newer World                               105

The Secret of Stonehenge                        149

Rescue Operation                                155

Portrait of the Artist                          175

Survival Planet                                 187

Roommates                                       205

The Golden Years of The Stainless Steel Rat     235

# INTRODUCTION

t was wonderful to grow up in the world of the pulp magazines. Brassy and colorful they were, filled with adventure and wondrous machines. Some of the many categories invented in the thirties still exist today, in book if not magazine form; love and romance, Western and detective. Many categories have slipped away—air war and battle stories—while many heroes are now forgotten. In what lonely grave does Operator Number 5 lie? Close to The Spider, Cash Gorman, G8 and his Battle Aces no doubt.

Give science fiction that; although its magazine existence has tottered, down from around sixty titles a month to three or four, it never died. SF magazines still publish more short stories in a year than magazines dedicated to any other kind of fiction.

At the age of seven or eight I did not notice the deficiencies of this particular art form. Yes, I did read all kinds of pulps—except Western or romance. (Particularly loathsome was that hybrid, *Rangeland Romances.*) But my attention strayed more and more to science fiction until I was reading all that was being published. It was exciting, that was what counted. Having no critical standards, I did not notice the banality of the writing, the repetition and the hackwork. Excitement was what mattered, emotional and intellectual—that was the double-barreled attraction of SF. Still is. Where else can you get the machine as hero? This was good stuff, still is good stuff. When written well nothing can better it.

I sharpened my literary teeth on the short story. It is a concise art form with a beginning, middle, and end. The reader must be attracted by the opening, get involved with the middle—and be surprised by the ending. Surprised not only by the sharp twist of an O. Henry ending, but captured by the surprise of a laugh or smile, sharp contrast or relief.

(An O. Henry ending is best exemplified by his "Gift of the Magi." Where the poverty-stricken couple exchange presents. He sells his watch to buy a set of combs for her beautiful hair—but she has had her hair cut and sold it to buy a fob for his watch. . . .)

The opening must charm and entice the reader. In the pulp days this was known as a narrative hook. Something to hook the editor into turning to the second page. The first page of a story manuscript—double-spaced, of course—has the author's name and address in the upper left corner, word-length in the upper right. The title is halfway down the page, leaving a lot of white space for editorial typesetting advice. The word "by" takes up a line, as does the name or pseudonym under which the story is to be published. Which leaves only about eight lines of copy. Since pulp editors were faced with a mountain of unsolicited dreck every day, anything that got them to turn to the second page would probably get them to buy the story. This first-page copy was the narrative hook.

I once practiced writing these narrative hooks, wrote a great bundle of them. One of them hooked me so much that I went on to write a story to find out what happened next. This is what I wrote:

> "James Bolivar diGriz I arrest you on the charge—"
> I was waiting for the word "charge," I thought it
> made a nice touch that way. As he said it I pressed the

button that set off the charge of black powder in the ceiling. The crossbeam buckled and the three-ton safe dropped through right on top of the cop's head. He squashed very nicely, thank you. The cloud of plaster dust settled and all I could see of him was one hand, slightly rumpled. It twitched a bit and the index finger pointed at me accusingly. His voice was a little muffled by the safe and sounded a bit annoyed.

The story was titled "The Stainless Steel Rat." It was later incorporated into a novel of the same name—the first in the series. Writing narrative hooks had proven a profitable exercise.

Every science-fiction writer has been asked, more than once, where those crazy ideas come from. (I know one writer whose response is that he buys them from a man in Reading, Pennsylvania.) There is no single answer. I know another writer who kept a small shelf of works by what he termed original story writers. When he needed a story fast he would pick a story at random, glance through it—then turn the plot on its head.

Then there is the greed-and-glory ploy. It is always a pleasure to sell a story to a magazine; an even greater pleasure when it is the cover story. Illustrated by the cover painting. Fred Pohl, then editor of *Galaxy,* had a publisher who could not resist a bargain. Fred worked from home most days a week. When he wasn't in the office the publisher would see all the budding painters who wanted to be cover artists. If their samples of artwork had some tiny degree of talent, and were suitably cheap, he would buy them. And leave them in the office as a rude shock for Fred when next he appeared.

After a bit the editorial office began to look like an exhibition of the totally incompetent. There were as many bad artists as there were bad writers. Very rarely one of these smears would be of cover quality. When I visited *Galaxy* and one of them caught my eye, Fred would force a photocopy of the cover upon me—or any other visiting author. Because if he could get a story that matched the painting he would have a free cover, which did wonders for the editorial budget. It was a challenge to fit all the strange elements of the art into a story; a challenge I rose to a number of times. Money and fame, a cover story the hard way.

Occasionally a story would be commissioned, a practice more common today. Isaac Asimov roughed out some possible world futures, each one brought about by a different advance in biology. Bob Silverberg edited an anthology of stories that fleshed out these futures. One of these intrigued me, and you will read "Brave Newer World" here.

When the great editor John W. Campbell died, I edited an anthology of original stories done in his memory. A last tribute by his authors. It turned into a sort of end-of-series tribute with Poul Anderson writing a last Van Rijn space trader story, Clifford Simak doing a last City story. Others did the same. I wrote the story "The Mothballed Spaceship" featuring the characters from my "Deathworld" trilogy.

Looking at the stories here triggers some interesting memories—often a history longer than the story itself. I had the plot of "The Streets of Ashkelon" cooking on the back burner of the mind for many years. I did not write it, because I knew that no editor would dare buy it in those years of prudery and self-censorship. It wasn't until Judy Merril decided to edit a book of taboo-breaking stories that I actually wrote the story. It was accepted for the anthology titled, I think, *The Thin Edge,* and paid for. The book never appeared, for publishing reasons now completely forgotten. With some difficulty I regained the rights to the story and watched while it was rejected by every magazine in the United States. Unlike the USA, Great Britain admits that atheists exist and do not eat children; there are even professed atheists in Parliament. So this story appeared in the English magazine *New Worlds* and was anthologized as well by Brian Aldiss. After a great many years it did cross the ocean and even appeared in an anthology of teenage science fiction.

Writing short stories is good training for the novelist. Among other things, it teaches economy of language. Every word must count in the short story, must be important and essential. Or it must be thrown out. Writers who practice this dictum are Brian Aldiss, Thomas M. Disch, and Robert Sheckley. Their stories move and sing and captivate.

Would there were more like them. I have read too many short stories that just didn't work. Because, like many others in the early days of SF, I wore many different hats. I have edited magazines, edited alone or in collaboration over fifty anthologies, illustrated SF magazines and done SF book jackets. I feel that I have learned from this process and my stories have profited.

One thing I did learn was that too many stories do not start at the beginning. Once the plot has been established there is a natural and logical place for the story to begin. Before I ever published a story I pointed out any weaknesses to the author. If they agreed they would do a rewrite. (In all the years of editing only one author ever refused to consider a rewrite.) No name, no pack drill, so I shall not reveal who these eminent authors really are. Author A always started his story on the third page of the manuscript. After grumbling, he would reluctantly agree and throw away the surplus pages. Author B submitted a lovely story that I published—only after he accepted the fact that the first twenty pages had nothing to do with the plot. They were replaced by one sentence.

You can educate yourself about the craft of short-story writing by reading closely and learning from the process. But you can learn a lot more by editing. For nine years Brian Aldiss and I edited *The Year's Best Science Fiction.* I read all of the American magazines, Brian all of the English—and we both skimmed the non-SF publications for stories that we might be able to use. It was an education indeed. Brian, far stronger than I, persevered in his reading right to the very end. My throat began to close after about the fifth year. For the last few years I couldn't face the magazines cold and had Bruce McAllister act as a first reader. He did a wonderful job, and about one out of every three stories he passed on appeared in the anthology.

I find bits and pieces of my life in this collection. My years of slavery as a comic-book artist are reflected in "Portrait of the Artist." Soon after the end of the Second World War I met a member of the Indian Communist Party. Who suggested that I could make money and be a national savior if I exported condoms to his country. This was the first time I had my attention drawn to the growing evils of overpopulation and the need for stringent birth control. Many years later, after a good deal of research, I wrote *Make Room! Make Room!*, the first nontechnical book—fiction or nonfiction—that addressed itself to this problem. The story "Roommates" also grew out of this.

Out of mutual interest, the anthropologist Leon E. Stover and I developed a realistic theory that explains why Stonehenge was built, which became the basis for our novel *Stonehenge: Where Atlantis Died.* Spin-off from this work was the story "The Secret of Stonehenge."

I am happy with these stories. I have carefully gone through them all and taken out all the typographical errors and infelicities that have crept into them through the years. I discovered—with great shock—that some editor, unbeknownst to me, had changed the name of the lead character in "The Streets of Ashkelon" and had bowdlerized the religious discussions. If I ever discover who did this I will tear his, her or its heart out.

But I am satisfied. These stories work. They entertain, occasionally amuse, are didactic at times but never, I firmly believe, boring. I enjoyed writing them and hope that you will have pleasure as well in reading them.

Harry Harrison
Dublin, Ireland

# THE
# STREETS OF
# ASHKELON

Somewhere above, hidden by the eternal clouds of
Wesker's World, a muffled thunder rumbled and
grew. Trader Garth stopped suddenly when he heard
it, his boots sinking slowly into the muck, and cupped
his good ear to catch the sound. It swelled and waned in the
thick atmosphere, growing louder.

"That noise is the same as the noise of your sky-ship," Itin
said, with stolid Wesker logicality, slowly pulverizing the idea
in his mind and turning over the bits one by one for closer
examination. "But your ship is still sitting where you landed
it. It must be, even though we cannot see it, because you are
the only one who can operate it. And even if anyone else could
operate it we would have heard it rising into the sky. Since we
did not, and if this sound is a sky-ship sound, then it must
mean . . ."

"Yes, another ship," Garth said, too absorbed in his own
thoughts to wait for the laborious Weskerian chains of logic
to clank their way through to the end. Of course it was another
spacer, it had been only a matter of time before one appeared,
and undoubtedly this one was homing on the S.S. radar re-
flector as he had done. His own ship would show up clearly on

the newcomer's screen, and they would probably set down as close to it as they could.

"You better go ahead, Itin," he said. "Use the water so you can get to the village quickly. Tell everyone to get back into the swamps, well clear of the hard ground. That ship is landing on instruments and anyone underneath at touchdown is going to be cooked."

This immediate threat was clear enough to the little Wesker amphibian. Before Garth had finished speaking, Itin's ribbed ears had folded like a bat's wings as he slipped silently into the nearby canal. Garth squelched on through the mud, making as good time as he could over the clinging surface. He had just reached the fringes of the village clearing when the rumbling grew to a head-splitting roar and the spacer broke through the low-hanging layer of clouds above. Garth shielded his eyes from the down-reaching tongue of flame and examined the growing form of the gray-black ship with mixed feelings.

After almost a standard year on Wesker's World he had to fight down a longing for human companionship of any kind. While this buried fragment of herd-spirit chattered for the rest of the monkey tribe, his trader's mind was busily drawing a line under a column of figures and adding up the total. This could very well be another trader's ship, and if it was his monopoly of the Wesker trade was at an end. Then again, this might not be a trader at all. Which was the reason he stayed in the shelter of the giant fern and loosened his gun in its holster. The ship baked dry a hundred square meters of mud, the roaring blast died, and the landing feet crunched down through the crackling crust. Metal creaked and settled into place while the cloud of smoke and steam slowly drifted lower in the humid air.

"Garth—you native-cheating extortionist—where are you?" the ship's speaker boomed. The lines of the spacer had looked only slightly familiar, but there was no mistaking the rasping tones of that familiar voice. Garth had a twisted smile when he stepped out into the open and whistled shrilly through two fingers. A directional microphone ground out of its casing on the ship's fin and twisted in his direction.

"What are you doing here, Singh?" he shouted toward the mike. "Too crooked to find a planet of your own so you have to come here to steal an honest trader's profits?"

"Honest!" the amplified voice roared. "This from the man who has been in more jails than cathouses—and that is a goodly number in itself, I do declare. Sorry, friend of my youth, but I cannot join you in exploiting this aboriginal pesthole. I am on course to a more fairly atmosphered world where a fortune is waiting to be made. I only stopped here since an opportunity presented itself to turn an honest credit by running a taxi service. I bring you friendship, the perfect companionship, a man in a different line of business who might help you in yours. I'd come out and say hello myself, except I would have to decon for biologicals. I'm cycling the passenger through the lock, so I hope you won't mind helping with his luggage."

At least there would be no other trader on the planet now, that worry was gone. But Garth still wondered what sort of passenger would be taking one-way passage to an un-developed world. And what was behind that concealed hint of merriment in Singh's voice? He walked around to the far side of the spacer where the ramp had dropped, and looked up at the newcomer in the cargo lock, who was wrestling ineffectu-ally with a large crate. The man turned toward him and Garth saw the clerical dog collar and knew just what it was Singh had been chuckling about.

"What are you doing here?" Garth asked, and in spite of his attempt at self-control he snapped out the words. If the man noticed this he ignored it, because he was still smiling and putting out his hand as he came down the ramp.

"Father Mark," he said, "of the Missionary Society of Brothers. I'm very pleased to meet . . ."

"I said, what are you doing here." Garth's voice was under control now, quiet and cold. He knew what had to be done, and it must be done quickly or not at all.

"That should be obvious," Father Mark said, his good nature still unruffled. "Our missionary society has raised funds to send spiritual emissaries to alien worlds for the first time. I was lucky enough . . ."

"Take your luggage and get back into the ship. You're not wanted here—and you have no permission to land. You'll be a liability and there is no one on Wesker to take care of you. Get back into the ship."

"I don't know who you are, sir, or why you are lying to me," the priest said. He was still calm but the smile was gone. "But I have studied galactic law and the history of this planet very closely. There are no diseases or beasts here that I should have any particular fear of. It is also an open planet, and until the Space Survey changes that status I have as much right to be here as you do."

The man was of course right, but Garth couldn't let him know that. He had been bluffing, hoping the priest didn't know his rights. But he did. There was only one distasteful course left for him, and he had better do it while there was still time left.

"Get back in that ship," he shouted, not hiding his anger now. With a smooth motion his gun was out of the holster and the pitted black muzzle only inches from the priest's stomach. The man's face turned white, but he did not move.

"What the hell are you doing, Garth?!" Singh's shocked voice grated from the speaker. "The guy paid his fare and you have no right at all to throw him off the planet."

"I have this right," Garth said, raising his gun and sighting between the priest's eyes. "I give him thirty seconds to get back aboard the ship or I pull the trigger."

"Well, I think you are either off your head or playing a joke," Singh's exasperated voice rasped down at them. "If this is a joke it is in bad taste. But either way you're not getting away with it. Two can play at that game—only I can play it better."

There was the rumble of heavy bearings and the remote-controlled four-gun turret on the ship's side rotated and pointed at Garth. "Now—down gun and give Father Mark a hand with the luggage," the speaker commanded, a trace of humor back in the voice now. "As much as I would like to help, old friend, I cannot. I feel it is time you had a chance to talk to the father; after all, I have had the opportunity of speaking with him all the way from Earth."

Garth jammed the gun back into the holster with an acute feeling of loss. Father Mark stepped forward, the winning smile back now. A Bible, taken from a pocket of his robe, in his raised hand. "My son—" he said.

"I'm not your son" was all Garth could choke out as the bitterness and the defeat welled up within him. His fist drew back as the anger rose, and the best he could do was open the fist so he struck only with the flat of his hand. Still the blow sent the priest crashing to the ground and hurled the white pages of the book splattering into the thick mud.

Itin and the other Weskers had watched everything with seemingly emotionless interest. Garth made no attempt to answer their unspoken questions. He started toward his house, but turned back when he saw they were still unmoving.

"A new man has come," he told them. "He will need help with the things he has brought. If he doesn't have any place for them, you can put them in the big warehouse until he has a place of his own."

He watched them waddle across the clearing toward the ship, then went inside and gained a certain satisfaction from slamming the door hard enough to crack one of the panes. There was an equal amount of painful pleasure in breaking out one of the few remaining bottles of Irish whiskey that he had been saving for a special occasion. Well, this was special enough, though not really what he had had in mind. The whiskey was good and burned away some of the bad taste in his mouth, but not all of it. If his tactics had worked, success would have justified everything. But he had failed, and in addition to the pain of failure there was the acute feeling that he had made a horse's ass out of himself. Singh had blasted off without any goodbyes. There was no telling what sense he had made of the whole matter, though he would surely carry some strange stories back to the traders' lodge. Well, that could be worried about the next time Garth signed in. Right now he had to go about setting things right with the missionary. Squinting out through the rain, he saw the man struggling to erect a collapsible tent while the entire population of the village stood in ordered ranks and watched. Naturally none of them offered to help.

By the time the tent was up and the crates and boxes stowed inside of it, the rain had stopped. The level of fluid in the bottle was a good bit lower and Garth felt more like facing up to the unavoidable meeting. In truth, he was looking forward to talking to the man. This whole nasty business aside, after an entire solitary year any human companionship looked good. *Will you join me now for dinner? John Garth,* he wrote on the back of an old invoice. But maybe the guy was too frightened to come? Which was no way to start any kind of relationship. Rummaging under the bunk, he found a box that was big enough and put his pistol inside it. Itin was of course waiting outside the door when he opened it, since this was his tour as Knowledge Collector. He handed him the note and box.

"Would you take these to the new man," he said.

"Is the new man's name New Man?" Itin asked.

"No, it's not!" Garth snapped. "His name is Mark. But I'm only asking you to deliver this, not get involved in conversation."

As always when he lost his temper, the literal-minded Weskers won the round. "You are not asking for conversation,"

Itin said slowly, "but Mark may ask for conversation. And others will ask me his name, if I do not know his na—" The voice cut off as Garth slammed the door. This would not work in the long run either, because next time he saw Itin—a day, a week, or even a month later—the monologue would be picked up on the very word it had ended with, while the concept would be dragged out to its last frayed end. Garth cursed under his breath and poured water over a pair of the tastier concentrates that he had left.

"Come in," he said when there was a quiet knock on the door. The priest entered and held out the box with the gun.

"Thank you for the loan, Mr. Garth. I appreciate the spirit that made you send it. I have no idea what caused the unhappy affair when I landed, but I think it would be best forgotten if we are going to be on this planet together for any length of time."

"Drink?" Garth asked, taking the box and pointing to the bottle on the table. He poured two glasses full and handed one to the priest. "That's about what I had in mind, but I still owe you an explanation of what happened out there." He scowled into his glass for a second, then raised it to the other man. "It's a big universe and I guess we have to make out as best we can. Here's to Sanity."

"God be with you," Father Mark said, and raised his glass as well.

"Not with me or with this planet," Garth said firmly. "And that's the crux of the matter." He half-drained the glass and sighed.

"Do you say that to shock me?" the priest asked with a smile. "I assure you that it doesn't."

"Not intended to shock. I meant it quite literally. I suppose I'm what you would call an atheist, so revealed religion is no concern of mine. While these natives, simple and unlettered Stone Age types that they are, have managed to come this far with no superstitions or traces of deism whatsoever. I had hoped that they might continue that way."

"What are you saying?" The priest frowned. "Do you mean that they have no gods, no belief in the hereafter? They must die . . . ?"

"Die they do, and to dust returneth. Like the rest of the animals. They have thunder, trees, and water without having thunder gods, tree sprites, or water nymphs. They have no ugly little gods, taboos, or spells to hagride and limit their lives. They are the only primitive people I have ever encountered that are completely free of superstition—and appear to be much happier and sane because of it. I just wanted to keep them that way."

"You wanted to keep them from God—from salvation?" The priest's eyes widened and he recoiled slightly.

"No," Garth said. "I wanted to keep them from superstition until they knew more and could think about it realistically. Without being absorbed and perhaps destroyed by it."

"You're being insulting to the Church, sir, to equate it with superstition. . . ."

"Please," Garth said, raising his hand. "No theological arguments. I don't think your society footed the bill for this trip just to attempt to convert me. Just accept the fact that my beliefs have been arrived at through careful thought over a period of years, and no amount of undergraduate metaphysics will change them. I'll promise not to try and convert you—if you will do the same for me."

"Agreed, Mr. Garth. As you have reminded me, my mission here is to save these souls, and that is what I must do. But why should my work disturb you so much that you try and keep me from landing? Even threaten me with your gun, and . . ." The priest broke off and looked into his glass.

"And even slug you?" Garth said, frowning. "There was no excuse for that, and I would like to say that I'm sorry. Plain bad manners and an even worse temper. Live alone long enough and you find yourself doing that kind of thing." He brooded down at his big hands where they lay on the table, reading memories into the scars and calluses patterned there. "Let's just call it frustration, for lack of a better word. In your business you must have had a lot of chance to peep into darker places in men's minds and you should know a bit about motives and happiness. I have had too busy a life to ever consider settling down and raising a family, and right up until recently I never missed it. Maybe leakage radiation is softening up my brain, but I have begun to think of these furry and fishy Weskers as being a little like my own children, that I am somehow responsible to them."

"We are all His children," Father Mark said quietly.

"Well, here are some of His children that can't even imagine his existence," Garth snapped, suddenly angry at himself for allowing gentler emotions to show through. Yet he forgot himself at once, leaning forward with the intensity of his feelings. "Can't you realize the importance of this? Live with these Weskers awhile and you will discover that they have a simple and happy existence that matches the state of grace you people are always talking about. They get 'pleasure' from their lives— and cause no one pain. By circumstance they have evolved on an almost barren world, so they never had a chance to grow out of a physical Stone Age culture. But mentally they are our match—or perhaps better. They have all learned my language so I can easily explain the many things they want to know. Knowledge and the gaining of knowledge gives them real satisfaction. They tend to be exasperating at times because every new fact must be related to the structure of all other things, but the more they learn the faster this process becomes. Someday they are going to be man's equal in every way, perhaps surpass us. If—would you do me a favor?"

"Whatever I can."

"Leave them alone. Or teach them if you must—history and science, philosophy, law, anything that will help them face the realities of the greater universe they never even knew existed before. But don't confuse them with your hatreds and pain, guilt, sin and punishment. Who knows the harm . . ."

"You are being insulting, sir!" the priest said, jumping to his feet. The top of his gray head barely came to the massive spaceman's chin, yet he showed no fear in defending what he believed was right. Garth, standing now himself, was no longer the penitent. They faced each other in anger, as men have always stood, unbending in the defense of that which they believe is right.

"Yours is the insult," Garth shouted. "You have the incredible egotism to believe that your derivative little mythology, differing only slightly from the thousands of others that still burden men, can do anything but confuse their still fresh minds. Don't you realize that they believe in truth—and have never heard of such a thing as a lie. They have not been trained yet to understand that other kinds of minds can think differently from theirs. Will you spare them this . . . ?"

"I will do my duty, which is His will, Mr. Garth. These are God's creatures here, and they have souls. I cannot shirk my duty, which is to bring them His word so that they may be saved and enter into the Kingdom of Heaven."

When the priest opened the door, the wind caught it and blew it wide. He vanished into the storm-swept darkness and the door swung back and forth and a splatter of raindrops blew in. Garth's boots left muddy footprints when he closed the door, shutting out the sight of Itin sitting patiently and uncomplaining in the storm, hoping only that Garth might stop for a moment and leave with him some of the wonderful knowledge of which he had so much.


By unspoken consent that first night was never mentioned again. After a few days of loneliness, made worse because each knew of the other's proximity, they found themselves talking on carefully neutral grounds. Garth slowly packed and stowed away his stock and never admitted that his work was finished and he could leave at any time. He had a fair amount of interesting drugs and botanicals that would fetch a good price. And the Wesker artifacts were sure to create a sensation in the sophisticated galactic market. Crafts on the planet here had been limited before his arrival, mostly pieces of carving painfully chipped into the hard wood with fragments of stone. He had supplied tools and a stock of raw metal from his own supplies, nothing more than that.

In a few months the Weskers had not only learned to work with the new materials, but had translated their own designs and forms into the most alien—but most beautiful—artifacts that he had ever seen. All he had to do was release these on the market to create a primary demand, then return for a new supply. The Weskers wanted only books and tools and knowledge in return. Through their own efforts he knew they would pull themselves into the galactic union.

This is what Garth had hoped. But a wind of change was blowing through the settlement that had grown up around his ship. No longer was he the center of attention and the focal point of the village life. He had to grin when he thought of his fall from power; yet there was very little humor in the smile. Serious and attentive Weskers still took turns of duty as Knowledge Collectors, but their stale recording of dry facts was in sharp contrast to the intellectual hurricane that surrounded the priest.

Where Garth had made them work for each book and machine, the priest grave freely. Garth had tried to be progressive in his supply of knowledge, treating them as bright but unlettered children. He had wanted them to walk before they could run, to master one step before going on to the next.

Father Mark simply brought them the benefits of Christianity. The only physical work he required was the construction of a church, a place of worship and learning. More Weskers had appeared out of the limitless planetary swamps and within days the roof was up, supported on a framework of poles. Each morning the congregation worked a little while on the walls, then hurried inside to learn the all-promising, all-encompassing, all-important facts about the universe.

Garth never told the Weskers what he thought about their new interest. This was mainly because they never asked him. Pride or honor stood in the way of his grabbing a willing listener and pouring out his grievances. Perhaps it would have been different if Itin had on collecting duty, he was the brightest of the lot, but Itin had been rotated the day after the priest had arrived and Garth had not talked to him since.

It was a surprise then, after seventeen of the trebly-long Wesker days, he found a delegation at his doorstep when he emerged after breakfast. Itin was their spokesman, and his mouth was opened slightly. Many of the other Weskers had their mouths open as well, one even appeared to be yawning, clearly revealing the double row of sharp teeth and the purple-black throat. The mouths impressed Garth as to the seriousness of the meeting: this was the one Wesker expression he had learned to recognize. An open mouth indicated some strong emotion; happiness, sadness, anger, he could never be really sure which. The Weskers were normally placid and he had never seen enough open mouths to tell what was causing them. But he was surrounded by them now.

"Will you help us, Garth," Itin said. "We have a question."

"I'll answer any questions you ask," Garth said, with more than a hint of misgiving. "What is it?"

"Is there a God?"

"What do you mean by 'God'?" Garth asked in turn. What should he tell them? What had been going on in their minds that they should come to him with this question?

"God is our Father in Heaven, who made us all and protects us. Whom we pray to for aid, and if we are Saved will find a place . . ."

"That's enough," Garth said. "There is no God."

All of them had their mouths open now, even Itin, as they looked at Garth and thought about his answer. The rows of pink teeth would have been frightening if he hadn't known these creatures so well. For one instant he wondered if perhaps they had been already indoctrinated and looked upon him as a heretic, but he brushed the thought away.

"Thank you," Itin said, and they turned and left.

Though the morning was still cool Garth noticed that he was sweating, and he wondered why.

The reaction was not long in coming. Itin returned that same afternoon. "Will you come to the church?" he asked. "Many of the things that we study are difficult to learn, but none as difficult as this. We need your help because we must hear you and Father Mark talk together. This is because he says one thing is true and you say another is true and both cannot be true at the same time. We must find out what is true."

"I'll come, of course," Garth said, trying to hide the sudden feeling of elation. He had done nothing, but the Weskers had come to him anyway. There could still be grounds for hope that they might yet be free.

It was hot inside the church, and Garth was surprised at the number of Weskers who were there, more than he had seen gathered at any one time before. There were many open mouths. Father Mark sat at a table covered with books. He looked unhappy but didn't say anything when Garth came in. Garth spoke first.

"I hope you realize this is their idea—that they came to me of their own free will and asked me to come here?"

"I know that," the priest said resignedly. "At times they can be very difficult. But they are learning and want to believe, and that is what is important."

"Father Mark, Trader Garth, we need your help," Itin said. "You both know many things that we do not know. You must

help us come to religion, which is not an easy thing to do."
Garth started to say something, then changed his mind. Itin
went on. "We have read the Bibles and all the books that
Father Mark gave us, and one thing is clear. We have discussed this and we are all agreed. These books are very different from the ones that Trader Garth gave us. In Trader
Garth's books there is a universe which we have not seen, and
it goes on without God, for He is mentioned nowhere, we have
searched very carefully. In Father Mark's books He is everywhere and nothing can go on without Him. One of these must
be right and the other must be wrong. We do not know how
this can be, but after we find out which is right perhaps we will
know. If God does not exist . . ."

"Of course He exists, my children," Father Mark said in a
voice of heartfelt intensity. "He is our Father in Heaven who
has created us all. . . ."

"Who created God?" Itin asked, and the murmur ceased
and every one of the Weskers watched Father Mark intensely.
He recoiled a bit under the impact of their eyes, then smiled.

"Nothing created God, since He is the Creator. He always
was . . ."

"If He always was in existence—why cannot the universe
have always been in existence? Without having a creator?" Itin
broke in with a rush of words. The importance of the question
was obvious. The priest answered slowly, with infinite patience.

"Would that the answers were that simple, my children. But
even the scientists do not agree about the creation of the
universe. While they doubt—we who have seen the light *know*.
We can see the miracle of creation all about us. And how can
there be creation without a creator? That is He, Our Father,
Our God in Heaven. I know that you have doubts and that is
because you have souls and free will. Still the answer is simple.
Have faith, that is all you need. Just believe."

"How can we believe without proof?"

"If you cannot see that this world itself is proof of His existence, then I say to you that belief needs no proof—if you have faith!"

A babble of voices arose in the room and more of the Wesker mouths were open now as they tried to force their thoughts through the tangled skein of words and separate the thread of truth.

"Can you tell us, Garth?" Itin asked, and the sound of his voice quieted the hubbub.

"I can tell you to use the scientific method which can examine all things—including itself—and give you answers that can prove the truth or falsity of any statement."

"That is what we must do." Itin said. "We had reached the same conclusion." He held a thick book before him, and a ripple of nods ran across the watchers. "We have been studying the Bible as Father Mark told us to do, and we have found the answer. God will make a miracle for us, thereby proving that He is watching us. And by this sign we will know Him and we will go to Him."

"This is a sign of false pride," Father Mark said. "God needs no miracle to prove his existence."

"But *we* need a miracle!" Itin shouted, and though he wasn't human there was still the cry of need in his voice. "We have read here of many smaller miracles, loaves, fishes, wine, snakes—many of them, for much smaller reasons. Now all He need do is make a miracle and He will bring us all to Him—the wonder of an entire new world worshipping at His throne, as you have told us, Father Mark. And you have told us how important this is. We have discussed this and find that there is only one miracle that is best for this kind of thing."

His boredom and amused interest in the incessant theological wrangling drained from Garth in a single instant. He had not been really thinking or he would have seen where all this was leading. By turning slightly he could see the illustration in the Bible where Itin held it open, and knew in advance what picture he would see. He rose slowly from his chair, as if stretching, and turned to the priest behind him.

"Get ready!" he whispered. "Get out the back and get to the ship, I'll keep them busy here. I don't think they'll harm—"

"What do you mean . . . ?" Father Mark asked, blinking in surprise.

"Get out, you fool!" Garth hissed. "What miracle do you think they mean? What miracle is supposed to have converted the world to Christianity?"

"No," Father Mark said, "it cannot be. It just cannot—"

"GET MOVING!" Garth shouted, dragging the priest from the chair and hurling him toward the rear wall. Father Mark stumbled to a halt, turned back. Garth leaped for him, but it was already too late. The amphibians were small, but there were so many of them. Garth lashed out and his fist struck Itin, hurling him back into the crowd. The others came on as he fought his way toward the priest. He beat at them but it was like struggling against the waves. The furry, musky bodies washed over and engulfed him. He struggled until they tied him, and he still struggled until they beat on his head until he stopped. Then they pulled him outside, where he could only lie in the rain and curse and watch.

Of course the Weskers were marvelous craftsmen and everything had been constructed down to the last detail following the illustration in the Bible. There was the cross, planted firmly in the top of the small hill, the gleaming metal spikes, the hammer. Father Mark had been stripped and draped in a carefully pleated loincloth. They led him out of the church, and at the sight of the cross he almost fainted. After that he held his head high and determined to die as he had lived, with faith.

Yet this was hard. It was unbearable even for Garth, who only watched. It is one thing to talk of crucifixion and look at the gently carved bodies in the dim light of prayer. It is another to see a man naked, ropes cutting into his skin where he hangs from a bar of wood. And to see the needle-tipped spike raised and placed against the soft flesh of his palm, to see the hammer come back with the calm deliberation of an artisan's measured stroke. Then to hear the thick sound of metal penetrating flesh.

Then to hear the screams.

Few are born to be martyrs and Father Mark was not one of them. With the first blows the blood ran from his lips where his clenched teeth met. Then his mouth was wide and his heart strained back and the awful guttural horror of his screams sliced through the susurration of the falling rain. It resounded as a silent echo from the masses of watching Weskers, for whatever emotion opened their mouths was now tearing their bodies with all its force, and row after row of gaping jaws reflected the crucified priest's agony.

Mercifully he fainted, and the last nails were driven home. Blood ran from the raw wounds, mixed with the rain to drip faintly pink from his feet as the life ran out of him. At this time, somewhere at this time, sobbing and tearing at his own bonds, numbed from the blows on the head, Garth lost consciousness.

He awoke in his own warehouse, and it was dark. Someone was cutting away the woven ropes they had bound him with. The rain still dripped and splashed outside.

"Itin," he said. It could be no one else.

"Yes," the alien voice whispered back. "The others are talking in the church. Lin died after you struck his head, and Inon is very sick. There are some that say you should be crucified too, and I think that is what will happen. Or perhaps killed by striking on the head. They have found in the Bible where it says . . ."

"I know." With infinite weariness. "An eye for an eye. You'll find lots of things like that once you start looking."

"You must go, you can get to your ship without anyone

seeing you. There has been enough killing." Itin as well spoke with a newfound weariness.

Garth experimented, pulling himself to his feet. He pressed his head to the rough wall until the nausea stopped.

"He's dead." He said it as a statement, not a question.

"Yes, some time ago. Or I could not have come away to see you."

"And buried, of course, or they wouldn't be thinking about starting on me next."

"And buried!" There was almost a ring of emotion in the alien's voice, an echo of the dead priest's. "He is buried and he will rise on High. It is written and that is the way it will happen. Father Mark will be so happy that it has happened like this." The voice ended in a sound like a human sob, but of course it couldn't have been that since Itin was alien, and not human at all. Garth painfully worked his way around the wall toward the door, leaning against the wall so he wouldn't fall.

"We did the right thing, didn't we?" Itin asked. There was no answer. "He will rise up, Garth, won't he rise?"

Garth was at the door and enough light came from the brightly lit church to show his torn and bloody hands clutching at the frame. Itin's face swam into sight close to his, and Garth felt the delicate, many-fingered hands with the sharp nails catch at his clothes.

"He will rise, won't he, Garth?"

"No," Garth said, "he is going to stay buried right where you put him. Nothing is going to happen because he is dead and he is going to stay dead."

The rain runneled through Itin's fur and his mouth was opened so wide that he seemed to be screaming into the uncaring night. Only with effort could he talk, squeezing out the alien thoughts in an alien language.

"Then we will not be saved? We will not become pure?"

"You were pure," Garth said, in a voice somewhere between a sob and a laugh. "That's the horrible ugly dirty part of it. You were pure. Now you are . . ."

"Murderers," Itin said, and the water ran down from his lowered head and streamed away into the darkness.

# TOY SHOP

Because there were few adults in the crowd, and Colonel "Biff" Hawton stood over six feet tall, he could see every detail of the demonstration. The children—and most of the parents—gaped in wide-eyed wonder. Biff Hawton was too sophisticated to be awed. He stayed on because he wanted to find out what the trick was that made the gadget work.

"It's all explained right here in your instruction book," the demonstrator said, holding up a garishly printed booklet opened to a four-color diagram. "You all know how magnets pick up things and I bet you even know that the Earth itself is one great big magnet—that's why compasses always point north. Well . . . the Atomic Wonder Space Wave Tapper hangs on to those space waves. Invisibly all about us, and even going right through us, are the magnetic waves of the Earth. The Atomic Wonder rides these waves just the way a ship rides the waves in the ocean. Now watch. . . ."

Every eye was on him as he put the gaudy model rocket ship on top of the table and stepped back. It was made of stamped metal and seemed as incapable of flying as a can of ham—which it very much resembled. Neither wings, propellers, nor jets broke through the painted surface. It rested on three rub-

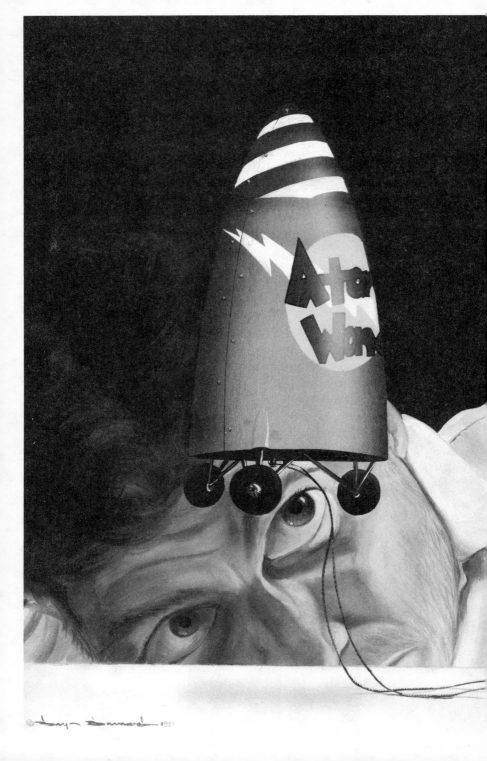

ber wheels. Emerging out through the bottom was a double strand of thin insulated wire. This white wire ran across the top of the black table and terminated in a control box in the demonstrator's hand. An indicator light, a switch, and a knob appeared to be the only controls.

"I turn on the power switch, sending a surge of current to the wave receptors," he said. The switch clicked and the light blinked on and off with a steady pulse. Then the man began slowly to turn the knob. "A careful touch on the wave generator is necessary as we are dealing with the powers of the whole world here. . . ."

A concerted *ahhh* swept through the crowd as the Space Wave Tapper shivered a bit, then rose slowly into the air. The demonstrator stepped back and the toy rose higher and higher, bobbing gently on the invisible waves of magnetic force that supported it. Ever so slowly the power was reduced and it settled back to the table.

"Only seventeen dollars and ninety-five cents," the young man said, putting a large price sign on the table. "For the complete set of the Atomic Wonder, the Space Tapper control box, battery, and instruction book. . . ."

At the appearance of the price card the crowd broke up noisily and the children rushed away toward the operating model trains. The demonstrator's words were lost in their noisy passage, and after a moment he sank into a gloomy silence. He put the control box down, yawned, and sat on the edge of the table. Colonel Hawton was the only one left after the crowd had moved on.

"Could you tell me how this thing works?" the colonel asked, coming forward. The demonstrator brightened up and picked up one of the toys.

"Well, if you will look here, sir . . ." He opened the hinged top. "You will see the space-wave coils at each end of the ship." With a pencil he pointed out the odd-shaped plastic forms about an inch in diameter that had been wound—apparently at random—with a few turns of copper wire. Except for these coils the interior of the model was empty. The coils were wired together and other wires ran out through the hole in the bottom of the control box. Biff Hawton turned a very quizzical eye on the gadget and upon the demonstrator, who completely ignored this sign of disbelief.

"Inside the control box is the battery," the young man said, snapping it open and pointing to an ordinary flashlight battery. "The current goes through the power switch and power light to the wave generator . . ."

"What you mean to say," Biff broke in, "is that the juice from this fifteen-cent battery goes through this cheap rheostat to those meaningless coils in the model and absolutely nothing happens. Now tell me what really flies the thing. If I'm going to drop eighteen bucks for six bits' worth of tin, I want to know what I'm getting."

The demonstrator flushed. "I'm sorry, sir," he stammered. "I wasn't trying to hide anything. Like any magic trick this one can't be really demonstrated until it has been purchased." He leaned forward and whispered confidentially, "I'll tell you what I'll do, though. This thing is way overpriced and hasn't been moving at all. The manager said I could let them go at three dollars if I could find any takers. If you—"

"Sold, my boy!" the colonel said, slamming three bills down on the table. "I'll give that much for it no matter how it works. The boys in the shop will get a kick out of it." He tapped the winged rocket on his chest. "Now really—what holds it up?"

The demonstrator looked around carefully, then pointed. "Strings!" he said. "Or rather a black thread. It runs from the top of the model, through a tiny loop in the ceiling, and back down to my hand—where it is tied to this ring on my finger. When I back up—the model rises. It's as simple as that."

"All good illusions are simple," the colonel grunted, tracing the black thread with his eye. "As long as there is plenty of flimflam to distract the viewer."

"If you don't have a black table, a black cloth will do," the young man said. "And the arch of a doorway is a good site; just see that the room in back is dark."

"Wrap it up, my boy, I wasn't born yesterday. I'm an old hand at this kind of thing."

Biff Hawton sprang it at the next Thursday-night poker party. The gang were all missile men and they cheered and jeered as he hammed up the introduction.

"Let me copy the diagram, Biff. I could use some a those magnetic waves in the new bird!"

"Those flashlight batteries are cheaper than lox—is this the power source of the future!"

Only Teddy Kaner caught wise as the flight began. He was an amateur magician and spotted the gimmick at once. He kept silent from professional courtesy, and smiled ironically as the rest of the bunch grew silent one by one. The colonel was a good showman and he had set the scene well. He almost had them believing in the Space Wave Tapper before he was through. When the model had landed and he had switched it off, he couldn't stop them from crowding around the table.

"A thread!" one of the engineers shouted, almost with relief, and they all laughed along with him.

"Too bad," the head project physicist said, "I was hoping that a little Space Wave Tapping could help us out. Let me try a flight with it."

"Teddy Kaner first," Biff announced. "He spotted it while you were all watching the flashing lights, only he didn't say anything."

Kaner slipped the ring with the black thread over his finger and started to step back.

"You have to turn the switch on first," Biff said.

"I know," Kaner smiled. "But that's part of illusion—the spiel and the misdirection. I'm going to try this cold first, so

I can get it moving up and down smoothly, then go through it with the whole works."

He moved his hand back smoothly, in a professional manner that drew no attention to it. The model lifted from the table—then crashed back down.

"The thread broke," Kaner said.

"You jerked it, instead of pulling smoothly," Biff said, and knotted the broken thread. "Here, let me show you how to do it."

The thread broke again when Biff tried it, which got a good laugh that made his collar a little warm. Someone mentioned the poker game.

This was the only time that poker was mentioned or even remembered that night. Because very soon after this they found that the thread would lift the model only when the switch was on and one and a half volts flowed through the joke coils. With the current turned off the model was too heavy to lift. The thread broke every time.


"I still think it's a screwy idea," the young man said. "I have spent one week getting fallen arches, demonstrating those toy ships for every brat within a thousand miles. Then selling the things for three bucks when they must have cost at least a hundred dollars apiece to make."

"But you did sell the ten of them to people who would be interested?" the older man asked.

"I think so. I caught a few air force officers and a colonel in missiles one day. Then there was one official I remembered from the Bureau of Standards. Luckily he didn't recognize me. Then those two professors you spotted from the university."

"Then the problem is out of our hands and into theirs. All we have to do now is sit back and wait for results."

"What results?! These people weren't interested when we were hammering on their doors with the proof. We've patented the coils and can prove to anyone that there is a reduction in weight around them when they are operating."

"But a very small reduction. And we don't know what is causing it. No one can be interested in a thing like that—a fractional weight decrease in a clumsy model. Certainly not enough power to lift the weight of the generator. No one wrapped up in massive fuel consumption, tons of lift, and such is going to have time to worry about a crackpot who thinks he has found a minor slip in Newton's laws."

"You think they will now?" the young man asked, cracking his knuckles impatiently.

"I know they will. The tensile strength of that thread is correctly adjusted to the weight of the model. The thread will break if you try to lift the model with it. Yet you can lift the model—but only after a small increment of its weight has been removed by the coils. This is going to bug these men. Nobody is going to ask them to solve the problem or concern themselves with it. But it will nag at them because they know this effect can't possibly exist. They'll see at once that the magnetic-wave theory is nonsense. Or perhaps true? We don't know. But they will all be thinking about it and worrying about it. Someone is going to experiment in his basement— just as a hobby, of course—to find the cause of the error. And he or someone else is going to find out what makes those coils work, or maybe a way to improve them!"

"And we have the patents . . ."

"Correct. They will be doing the research that will take them out of the massive-lift-propulsion business and into the field of pure spaceflight."

"And in doing so they will be making us rich—whenever the time comes to manufacture," the young man said cynically.

"We will all be rich, son," the older man said, patting him on the shoulder. "Believe me, you're not going to recognize this old world ten years from now."

# NOT ME,
# NOT AMOS
# CABOT!

The morning mail had arrived while Amos Cabot was out shopping and had been thrown onto the rickety table in the front hall. He poked through it even though he knew there would be nothing for him; this wasn't the right day. On the thirteenth his Social Security check came and on the twenty-fourth the union check. There never was anything else except for a diminishing number of cards every Christmas. Nothing, he knew it.

A large blue envelope was propped against the mirror but he couldn't make out the name. Damn that skinflint Mrs. Peavey and her two-watt bulbs. He bent over and blinked at it—then blinked again. By God, it was for him, and no mistake! Felt like a thick magazine or a catalog: he wondered what it could possibly be and who might have sent it to him. Clutching it to his chest with a knobby and liver-spotted hand, he began the long drag up the three flights of stairs to his room. He dropped his string bag with the two cans of beans and the loaf of day-old white bread onto the drainboard and sat down heavily in his chair by the window. Unsealing the envelope, he saw that it was a magazine, a thick glossy one with a black cover. He slid it out onto his lap and stared at it with horrified eyes.

**Hereafter**, the title read in black, prickly Gothic letters against a field of greenish gray. Underneath, it was subtitled *The Magazine of Preparedness*. The rest of the cover was black, solid midnight black, except for an inset photograph shaped like a tombstone that had a cheerful view of a cemetery filled with flower blossoms, ranked headstones, and brooding mausoleums. Was this all a very bad joke? It didn't seem so as Amos flipped through the pages, catching quick glimpses of caskets, coffins, cemetery plots, and urns of mortal ashes. With a grunt of disgust he threw the magazine onto the table, and as he did so a letter fell out and drifted to the floor. It was addressed to him, on the magazine's stationery, there was no mistake.

My Dearest Sir:

Welcome to the contented family of happy readers of *Hereafter—The Magazine of Preparedness* that smooths the road ahead. You, who are about to die, we salute you! A long, happy life lies behind you and ahead the Gates of Eternity are swinging open to welcome you, to return you to the bosom of your loved ones long since passed on. Now, at this friendly final hour, we stand behind you ready to help you on your way. Have you settled your will? Bet you've been remiss—but that's no problem now. Just turn to page 109 and read the inspirational article "Where There's a Will" and learn all there is to know. And then, on page 114, you'll find a full-sized, fold-out will that can be torn out along the handy perforations. Just fill in the few blanks, sign your name, and have your local notary public (he's usually in the stationery store!) witness the signature. Don't delay! And have you considered cremation? There is a wonderfully inspirational message from Dr. Philip Musgrove of The Little

Church Around the Corner from the Crematorium on
page . . .

Amos picked up the magazine with shaking hands and
threw it the length of the room, feeling slightly better when it
tore in two.

"What do you mean I'm going to die—what do you say that
for?" he shouted, then lowered his voice as Antonelli next
door hammered on the wall. "What's the idea of sending a
filthy thing like that to a person? What's the idea?"

What was the idea? He picked the two halves of the magazine up and smoothed them out on the table. It was all too
good-looking, too expensive to be a joke—these were real ads.
After some searching he found the contents page and worked
his way through the fine print, which he had hardly read, until
he came to the publisher's name: Saxon-Morris Publishers,
Inc. They must have money because they were in the Saxon-
Morris Building. He knew it, one of the new granite slabs on
Park Avenue.

They weren't getting away with it! A spark of anger blazed
bravely in Amos Cabot's thin bosom. He had made the Fifth
Avenue Coach Company send him a letter of apology about
the way that driver had talked to him on St. Patrick's Day.
The Triborough Automatic Drink Company had refunded
him fifty cents in stamps for coins their machines had consumed without giving refreshment in return. Now Saxon-
Morris was going to find out that they couldn't get away with
it either!

It had been warm out, but March was a changeable month:
he put on his heavy wool muffler. A couple of dollars should
more than cover the costs of the excursion, bus fares, and a
cup of tea in the Automat. He took two wrinkled bills from
behind the sugar can. Watch out, Saxon-Morris, you just
watch out.

It was very difficult to see anyone at Saxon-Morris without

an appointment. The girl with upswept red hair and layers of glazed makeup wasn't even sure that they had a magazine called *Hereafter*. There was a list of all the Saxon-Morris publications on the wall behind her red, kidney-shaped desk, but the gold letters on dark green marble were hard to read in the dim light. When he kept insisting, she searched through a booklet of names and telephone numbers and finally, reluctantly, agreed that it was one of their magazines.

"I want to see the editor."

"Which editor is it you want to see."

"Any editor, don't matter a damn." Her cold manner became even colder when the word touched her.

"Might I ask your business?"

"That's my business. Let me see the editor."

It was more than an hour before she found someone whom he could see, or perhaps she just grew tired of his sitting there and glowering at her. After a number of muffled conversations she hung up the phone.

"If you just go through that door there, first turn to the right then up one half flight, fourth door on the left, Mr. Mercer will see you Room seven eighty-two."

Amos was instantly lost in the maze of passages and gray doors. The second time he stumbled into a mail room one of the bored youths led him to 782. He pushed in without knocking.

"You Mercer, the editor of *Hereafter?*"

"Yes, I'm Mercer—but I'm not the editor." He was a chubby man with a round face and rounder glasses, squeezed behind a desk that filled the end of the tiny and windowless office. "This is circulation, not editorial. The girl at the front desk said you had a circulation problem."

"I got a problem all right—why you sending me your blasted magazine that I don't want?"

"Well—perhaps I can help you there, which publication are you referring to . . . ?"

*"Hereafter,* that's the one."

"Yes, that's one in my group." Mercer opened two files before he found the right folder; then he scratched through it and came up with a sheet of paper. "I'm afraid I can't be of any help to you, Mr. Cabot, you must be on the free subscription list and we can't cancel them. Sorry."

"What do you mean, *sorry!* I don't want the filthy thing and you better stop sending it!"

Mercer tried to be friendly and succeeded in conjuring up an artificial smile. "Let's be reasonable, Mr. Cabot, that's a high-quality magazine and you are receiving it for nothing; why, a subscription costs ten dollars a year! If you have been lucky enough to be chosen for a free sub you shouldn't complain . . ."

"Who chose me for a free subscription? I didn't send anything in."

"No, you wouldn't have to. Your name probably appeared on one of the lists that we purchase from insurance companies, veterans hospitals, and the like. *Hereafter* is one of our throwaway magazines; of course I don't mean that we throw them away, on the contrary they go to very selected subscribers. We don't make our costs back from subscriptions but from the advertisers' fees. In a sense they underwrite the costs of these fine magazines, so you can say it is sort of a public service. For new mothers, for instance, we buy lists from all the hospitals and send out six-month subs of *Your Baby,* with some really fine advice and articles, and of course the ads, which are educational in themselves . . ."

"Well, I'm no new mother. Why you sending me your rag?"

*"Hereafter* is a bit different from *Your Baby,* but is still a service publication. It's a matter of statistics, sir. Every day just so many people die, of certain ages and backgrounds and that kind of thing. The people in the insurance companies, actuaries I think they call them, keep track of all these facts and figures and draw up plenty of graphs and tables. Very

accurate, they assure me. They have life expectancy down to a fine art. They take a man, say, like yourself, of a certain age, background, physical fitness, environment, and so on, and pinpoint the date of death very exactly. Not the day and hour and that kind of thing—I suppose they could if they wanted to—but for our purposes a period of two years is satisfactory. This gives us a number of months and issues to acquaint the subscriber with our magazine and the services offered by our advertisers. By the time the subscriber dies the ad messages will have reached saturation."

"Are you telling me I'm going to die inside the next two years?" Amos shrieked hoarsely, flushing with anger.

"I'm not telling you, sir, no indeed!" Mercer drew away a bit and wiped some of the old man's spittle from his glasses with his handkerchief. "That is the actuaries' job. Their computer has come up with your name and sent it to me. They say you will die within two years. As a public service we send you *Hereafter*. A service—nothing more."

"I ain't going to die in two years, not me! Not Amos Cabot!"

"That is entirely up to you, sir. My position here is just a routine one. Your subscription has been entered and will be canceled only when a copy is returned with the imprint AD-DRESSEE DECEASED."

"I'm not going to die!"

"That might possibly happen, though I can't recall any cases offhand. But since it is a two-year subscription I imagine it will expire automatically at the end of the second year. If it is not canceled beforehand. Yes, that's what would happen."

It ruined Amos's day, and though the sun was shining warmly he never noticed it. He went home and thought so much about the whole thing that he couldn't sleep. The next day was no better, and he began to wonder if this was part of the message the dreadful magazine had conveyed. If death was close by—they were so sure of it!—why did he not relax and agree with them? Send in his will, order the plot, tomb, grave-stone, Last Message forms, and quietly expire.

"No! They'll not do it to me!"

At first he thought he would wait for next month's copy and write *addressee deceased* and send it back to them. That would stop the copies coming sure enough. Then he remembered fat little Mercer and could see his happy expression when the cancellation crossed his desk. Right again, dead on schedule as always. Old fool should've known you can't lick statistics. Old fool indeed! He would show them. The Cabots were a long-lived family no matter what the records said, and he was a hardheaded one, too. They weren't going to kill him off that easily.

After much wheedling he got in to see the doctor at his old union and talked him into making a complete and thorough physical checkup.

"Not bad, not bad at all for an old boy," the doctor told him while he was buttoning his shirt.

"I'm only eighty-two; that's not old."

"Of course it's not," the doctor said soothingly. "Just statistics, you know; a man of your age with your back-ground . . ."

"I know all about those damned statistics. I didn't come to you for that. What's the report say?"

"You can't complain about your physical shape, Amos," he said, scanning the sheet. "Blood pressure looks all right, but you're leaning toward anemia. Do you eat much liver and fresh greens?"

"Hate liver. Greens cost too much."

"That's your choice. But remember—you can't take it with you. Spend some more money on food. Give your heart a break—don't climb too many stairs."

"I live three flights up—so how do I avoid stairs?"

"That's your choice again. If you want to take care of the

old ticker move to the ground floor. And Vitamin D in the winter and . . ."

There was more, and after he had swallowed his first anger Amos made notes. There were food and vitamins and sleep and fresh air and a whole list of nonsense as long as your arm. But there was also the two-year subscription of *Hereafter:* he bent back over his notes.

Without his realizing why, the next months passed quickly. He was busy, finding a room on the ground floor, changing his eating habits, getting settled into his new place. At first he used to throw out *Hereafter* whenever its gloomy bulk shadowed his mail slot, but when a year had passed he grew bolder. There was an ad for mausoleums and one of the finest had a big tag on it labeled in red RESERVED FOR YOU. NOT FOR ME!!! he scrawled above it and tore it from the magazine and mounted it on the wall. He followed it with other pictures; friendly gravediggers beckoning toward raw openings in the earth, cut-to-order coffins with comfortable padding, and all the rest. When eighteen months had passed he enjoyed himself throwing darts at "A Photograph of the Founder of Incino-Top-Rate, the Urn for Eternity," and carefully checked off the passing days on the calendar.

Only in the final few months did he begin to worry. He felt fine and the union doctor congratulated him for being a great example, but this didn't matter. Were the actuaries right—had his time almost run out? He could have worried himself to death, but that was not the way Cabots died! He would face this out and win.

First there were weeks left, then only days. The last five days before the copy was due he locked himself in his room and had the delicatessen send up food. It was expensive but he wasn't going to risk any accidents in the street, not now. He had received his twenty-four copies and his subscription should have expired. The next morning would tell. He could not fall asleep at all that night, even though he knew that regular sleep was important. Just lay there until the sky brightened. He dozed for a bit then, but woke up as soon as he heard the postman's footsteps outside. This was the day, would the magazine be there? His heart was pounding and he made himself go slow as he got into the bathrobe. His room was the first on the ground floor, right next to the entrance, and all he had to do was step out into the hall and open the front door.

"Morning," he said to the postman.

"Yeah," the man answered, slinging his heavy bag around and digging into it. Amos closed the door first—then feverishly went through the mail.

It wasn't there.

He had won!

If this was not the happiest day in his life it was close to it. Besides this, his victories over the bus company and the coin-machine crooks were nothing. This was a war won, not a battle. He'd licked them, licked their statistics and actuaries, accountants, mechanical brains, card files, clerks, and editors. He had won! He went out and drank a beer, the first one in two years; then another. Laughed and talked with the gang at the bar. He had won! He fell into bed late and slept like a log until he was dragged awake by his landlady knocking on the door.

"Mail for you, Mr. Cabot. Mail."

Fear gripped him, then slowly ebbed away. It couldn't be. In two years *Hereafter* had never been late once, not one day. It must be some other mail—though this wasn't his check day. He slowly opened the door and took the large envelope, his grip so loose that it almost fell from his fingers.

Only when he had laid it on the bed did he breathe naturally again—it wasn't *Hereafter* in its vile blue envelope; this one was a gentle pink. It did contain a magazine, though, just about the size of *Hereafter,* a bulky magazine with lots of pages. Its title was *Senility*—and the black letters were drawn in such a way that they looked as though they were made of cracked and crumbling stone. Underneath the title it said *The*

*Magazine of Geri-ART-trics.* There was a picture of a feeble old man in a wheelchair with a blanket around his shoulders, sucking water through a curved glass tube. Inside was more. Ads for toilet chairs and hemorrhoid cushions, crutches and crank beds, articles on "Learn Braille When the Eyesight Goes," and "Happy Though Bedridden," and "Immobile for Twenty-five Years." A letter dropped out of the magazine and he half-read phrases here and there.

*Welcome to the family . . . the magazine of geri-ART-trics that teaches you the art of growing old . . . many long years ahead of you . . . empty years . . . what happiness to find a copy in your mailbox every month . . . speaking book edition for the blind . . . Braille for the blind and deaf . . . every month . . .*

There were tears in his eyes when he looked up. It was dark, a rainy and cold April morning with the wind rattling the window. Raindrops ran down the glass like great, cold tears.

# THE
# MOTHBALLED
# SPACESHIP

'll just swing in a bit closer," Meta said, touching the controls of the Pyrran spacer.

"I wouldn't if I were you," Jason said resignedly, knowing that a note of caution was close to a challenge to a Pyrran.

"Let us not be afraid this far away," Kerk said, as Jason had predicted. Kerk leaned close to look at the viewscreen. "It is big, I'll admit, three kilometers long at least, and probably the last space battleship existing. But it is over five thousand years old, and we are two hundred kilometers away from it . . ."

A tiny orange glow winked into brief existence on the distant battleship, and at the same instant the Pyrran ship lurched heavily. Red panic lights flared on the control panel.

"How old did you say it was?" Jason asked innocently, and received in return a sizzling look from the now-silent Kerk.

Meta sent the ship turning away in a wide curve and checked the warning circuitry. "Port fin severely damaged, hull units out in three areas. Repairs will have to be made in null-g before we make a planetfall again."

"Very good. I'm glad we were hit," Jason dinAlt said. "Perhaps now we will exercise enough caution to come out of this alive with the promised five hundred million credits. So set us

on a course to the fleet commander so we can find out all the grisly bits they forgot to tell us when we arranged this job by jump-space communication."


Admiral Djukich, the commander of the Earth forces, was a small man who appeared even smaller before the glowering strength of the Pyrran personality. Shrinking back when Kerk leaned over his desk toward him and spoke coldly. "We can leave now and the Rim Hordes will sweep through this system and that will be the end of you."

"No, it will not happen. We have the resources. We can build a fleet, buy ships, but it will be a long and tedious task. Far easier to use this Empire battleship."

"Easy?" Jason asked, raising one eyebrow. "How many have been killed attempting to enter it?"

"Well, easy is perhaps not the correct word. There are difficulties, certain problems . . . forty-seven people in all."

"Is that why you sent the message to Felicity?" Jason asked.

"Yes, assuredly. Our heavy-metals industry has been purchasing from your planet, that's how they heard of the Pyrrans. How less than a hundred of you conquered an entire world. We thought we would ask you to undertake this task of entering the ship."

"You were a little unclear as to who was aboard the ship and preventing anyone else from coming near."

"Yes, well, that is what you might call the heart of our little problem. There's no one aboard . . ." His smile had a definite artificial quality as the Pyrrans leaned close. "Please, let me explain. This planet was once one of the most important in the Empire. Although at least eleven other worlds claim themselves as the first home of mankind, we of Earth are much more certain that we are the original. This battleship seems proof enough. When the Fourth War of Galactic Expansion was over, it was mothballed here. Has remained so ever since, unneeded until this moment."

Kerk snorted with disbelief. "I will not believe that an unmanned, mothballed ship five millennia old has killed forty-seven people."

"I believe it most sincerely," Jason said. "And so will you as soon as you give it a little thought. Out there is three kilometers of almost indestructible fighting ship. It is propelled by the largest engines ever manufactured—which means the largest spaceship atomic generators as well. And of course the largest guns, the most advanced defensive and offensive weaponry ever conceived. Along with secondary batteries with parallel fail-safe circuitry, battle computers—ahh, you're smiling at last. A Pyrran dream of heaven—the most destructive single weapon ever conceived. What a pleasure to board a thing like this, to enter the control room, to be in control."

Kerk and Meta were grinning happily, eyes misty, nodding their heads in total agreement. Then the smiles faded as he went on. "But this ship has now been mothballed. Everything shut down and preserved for an emergency—everything, that is, except the power plant and the ship's armament. Part of the mothballing was obviously provision for the ship's computer to remain on the alert. To guard the ship against meteorites and any other chance encounters in space. In particular against anyone who felt he needed a spare battleship. We were warned off with a single shot. I don't doubt that it could have blasted us out of space just as easily. If this ship were manned and on the defensive, then nothing could be done about getting near it. Much less entering it. But this is not the case. We must outthink a computer, a machine. While it won't be easy, it should be possible." He turned and smiled at Admiral Djukich. "We'll take the job. The price has doubled. It will be one billion credits."

"Impossible! The sum is too great; the budget won't allow . . ."

"Rim Hordes, coming closer, bent on rapine and destruction. To stop them you order some spacers from the shipyard; schedules are late—they don't arrive on time. The Horde fleet descends. They break down this door and here, right in this office blood . . ."

"Stop!" the admiral gasped weakly, his face blanched white. A desk commander who had never seen action, as Jason had guessed.

"The contract is yours—but you have a deadline. Thirty days. One minute after that and you don't get a deci of a credit. Do you agree?"

Jason looked up at Kerk and Meta, who with instant warrior's decisions made their minds up, nodding at the same time.

"Done," Jason said. "But the billion is free and clear. We'll need supplies, aid from your space navy, material and perhaps men as well to back us up. You will supply what we need."

"It could be expensive," Admiral Djukich groaned, chewing at his lower lip. "Blood . . ." Jason whispered, and the admiral broke into a fine sweat as he reluctantly agreed.

"I'll have the papers drawn up. When can you begin?"

"We've begun. Shake hands on it and we'll sign later." He pumped the admiral's weak hand enthusiastically. "Now, I don't suppose you have anything like a manual that tells us how to get into the ship?"

"If we had that we wouldn't have called you here. We have gone to the archives and found nothing. All the facts we did discover are on record and available to you—for what they are worth."

"Not much if you killed forty-seven volunteers. Five thousand years is a long time, and even the most efficient bureaucracy loses things over that kind of distance. And of course the one thing you cannot mothball are instructions how to un-

mothball a ship. But we will find a way! Pyrrans never quit,
never. If you will have the records sent to our quarters, my
colleagues and I will now withdraw and make our plans for
the job. We shall beat your deadline."

"How?" Kerk asked as soon as the door of their apartment
had closed behind them.

"I haven't the slightest idea," Jason admitted, smiling happily at their cold scowls. "Now, let us pour some drinks and
put our thinking caps on. This is a job that may end up
needing brute force, but it will have to begin with man's intellectual superiority over the machines he has invented. I'll take
a large one with ice if you are pouring, darling."

"Serve yourself," Meta snapped. "If you had no idea how
we were to proceed, why did you accept?"

Glass rattled against glass and strong beverage gurgled.
Jason sighed. "I accepted because it is a chance for us to get
some ready cash, which the budget is badly in need of. If we
can't crack into the damn thing, then all we have lost is thirty
days of our time."

He drank and remembered the hard-learned lesson that
reasoned argument was usually a waste of time with Pyrrans
and that there were better ways to quickly resolve a situation.
"You people aren't scared of this ship, are you?"

He smiled angelically at their scowls of hatred, the sudden
tensing of hard muscles, the whine of the power holsters as
their guns slipped toward their hands, then slid back out of
sight.

"Let us get started," Kerk said. "We are wasting time and
every second counts. What do we do first?"

"Go through the records, find out everything we can about
a ship like this. Then find a way in."


"I fail to see what throwing rocks at that ship can do," Meta
said. "We know already that it destroys them before they get

close. It is a waste of time. And now you want to waste food as well, all those animal carcasses . . ."

"Meta, my sweet—shut up. There is method to the apparent madness. The navy command ship is out there with radar beeping happily, keeping a record of every shot fired, how close the target was before it was hit, what weapon fired the shot, and so forth. There are thirty spacers throwing spatial debris at the battleship in a steady stream. This is not the usual thing that happens to a mothballed vessel and it can only have interesting results. Now, in addition to the stone-throwing, we are going to launch these sides of beef at our target, each spacegoing load of steak to be wrapped with twenty kilos of armilon plastic. They are being launched on different trajectories with different speeds. If any one of them gets through to the ship, we will know that a man in a plastic space suit made of the same material will get through as well. Now, if all that isn't enough burden on the ship's computer, a good-sized planetoid is on its way now in an orbit aimed right at our mothballed friend out there. The computer will either have to blow it out of space—which will take a good deal of energy. Or if it is possible it may fire up the engines. Anything it does will give us information, and any information will give us a handle to grab the problem with."

"First side of beef on the way," Kerk announced from the controls where he was stationed. "I cut some steaks off while we were loading them; have them for lunch. We have a freezer-ful now. Prime cuts only—from every carcass, maybe a kilo each. Won't affect the experiment."

"You're turning into a crook in your old age," Jason said.

"I learned everything I know from you. There goes the first one." He pointed to a tiny blip of fire on the screen. "Flare powder on each, blows up when they hit. Another one. They're getting closer than the rocks—but they're not getting through."

Jason shrugged. "Back to the drawing board. Let's have the

steaks and a bottle of wine. We have about two hours before the planetoid is due. That is an event we want to watch."

The expected results were anticlimactic to say the least. Millions of tons of solid rock that had been put into collision orbit at great expense, as Admiral Djukich was fond of reminding them, soared majestically in from the black depths of space. The battleship's radar pinged busily. As soon as the computer had calculated the course, the main engines fired briefly. The planetoid flashed by the ship's stern and continued on into interstellar space.

"Very dramatic," Meta said in her coldest voice.

"We gained information!" Jason was on the defensive. "We know the engines are still in good shape and can be activated at a moment's notice."

"And of what possible use is that information?" Kerk asked.

"Well, you never know. Might come in handy . . ."

"Communication control to Pyrrus One. Can you read me?"

Jason was at the radio instantly, flicking it on. "This is Pyrrus One. What is your message?"

"We have received a signal from the battleship on the 183.4 wavelength. Message is as follows. 'Nederuebla al navigacio centro. Kroniku cî tio sângôn . . .' "

"I cannot understand it," Meta said.

"It's Esperanto, the old Empire language. The ship simply sent a change-of-course instruction to navigation control. And we know its name now, the *Indestructible*."

"Is this important?"

"Is it!" Jason yipped with joy as he set the new wavelength into the communication controls. "Once you get someone to talk to you, you have them half-sold. Ask any salesman. Now, absolute silence, if you please, while I practice my best and most military Esperanto." He drained his wineglass, cleared his throat, and turned the radio on.

"Hello, *Indestructible,* this is Fleet Headquarters. Explain unauthorized course change."

"Course change authorized by instructions 590-L to avoid destruction."

"Your new course is a navigational hazard. Return to old course."

Silent seconds went by as they watched the screen—then the purple glow of a thrust drive illuminated the battleship's bow.

"You did it!" Meta said happily, giving Jason a loving squeeze that half-crushed his rib cage. "It's taking orders from you. Now tell it to let us in."

"I don't think it is going to be that easy—so let me sneak up on the topic in a roundabout way."

He spoke Esperanto to the computer again. "Course change satisfactory. State reasons for recent heavy expenditure of energy."

"Meteor shower. All meteors on collision orbit were destroyed."

"It is reported that your secondary missile batteries were used. Is this report correct?"

"It is correct."

"Your reserves of ammunition will be low. Resupply will be sent."

"Resupply not needed. Reserves above resupply level."

"Argumentative for a computer, isn't it?" Jason said, his hand over the microphone. "But I shall pull rank and see if that works.

"Headquarters overrides your resupply decision. Resupply vessel will arrive your cargo port in seventeen hours. Confirm."

"Confirmed. Resupply vessel must supply override mothball signal before entering two-hundred-kilometer zone."

"Affirmative, signal will be sent. What is current signal?"

There was no instant answer—and Jason raised crossed fingers as the silence went on for almost two seconds.

"Negative. Information cannot be supplied."

"Prepare for memory check of override mothball signal. This is a radio signal only?"

"Affirmative."

"This is a spoken sentence."

"Negative."

"This is a coded signal."

"Affirmative."

"Pour me a drink," Jason said with the microphone off. "This playing twenty questions may take some time."

It did. But patient working around the subject supplied, bit by bit, more of the needed information. Jason turned off the radio and passed over the scribbled sheet.

"This is something at least. The code signal is a ten-digit number. If we send the correct number, all the mothballing activity stops instantly and the ship is under our control."

"And the money is ours," Meta said. "Can our computer be programmed to send a series of numbers until it hits on the right one?"

"It can—and just the same thought crossed my mind. The *Indestructible* thinks that we are running a communications check and tells me that it can accept up to seven hundred signals a second for repeat and verification. Our computer will read the returned signal and send an affirmative answer to each one. But of course all the signals will be going through the discrimination circuits, and if the correct signal is sent, the mothball defenses will be turned off."

"That seems like an obvious trick that would not fool a five-year-old," Kerk said.

"Never overestimate the intelligence of a computer. You forget that it is a machine with zero imagination. Now, let me see if this will do us any good." He punched keys rapidly, then muttered a curse and kicked the console. "No good. We will have to run nine to the tenth power numbers and, at seven hundred a second, it will take us about five months to do them all."

"And we have just three weeks left."

"I can still read a calendar, thank you, Meta. But we'll have to try in any case. Send alternate numbers from one up and counting from 9,999,999,999 back down. Then we'll get the navy code department to give us all their signals to send as well; one of them might fit. The odds are still about five to one against hitting the right combination, but that is better than no odds at all. And we'll keep working to see what else we can think of."

The navy sent over a small man named Shrenkly, who brought a large case of records. He was head of the code department, and a cipher and puzzle enthusiast as well. This was the greatest challenge of his long and undistinguished career. He hurled himself into the work with growing enthusiasm.

"Wonderful opportunity, wonderful. The ascending and descending series are going out steadily. In the meantime I am taping permutations and substitutions of signals which will—"

"That's fine, keep at it," Jason said, smiling enthusiastically and patting the man on the back. "I'll get a report from you later, but right now we have a meeting to attend. Kerk, Meta, time to go."

"What meeting?" Meta asked as he tried to get her through the door.

"The meeting I just made up to get away from that monomaniacal enthusiast," he said when he finally got her into the corridor. "Let him do his job while we see if we can find another way in."

"I think what he has to say is very interesting."

"Fine, you talk to him—but not while I am around. Let us now spur our brains into action and see what we can come up with."

What they came up with was a number of ideas of varying quality but uniform record of failure. There was the miniature-flying-robot fiasco, where smaller and smaller robots were sent and blasted out of existence, right down to the smallest, about the size of a small coin. Obsessed by miniaturization, they constructed a flying-eye apparatus no larger than the head of a pin. It dragged a threadlike control wire after it that also supplied current for the infinitesimal ion drive. This device sparked and sizzled its way to within fifteen kilometers of the *Indestructible* before the sensors detected it and neatly blasted it out of existence with a single shot.

There were other suggestions and brilliant plans, but none of them worked out in practice. The great ship floated serenely in space, reading seven hundred numbers a second and, in its spare time, blowing into fine dust any object that approached it. Each attempt took time; the days drifted by steadily. Jason was beginning to have a chronic headache and had difficulty sleeping. The problem seemed insoluble. He was feeding figures about destruction distances into the computer when Meta looked in on him.

"I'll be with Shrenkly if you need me," she said.

"Wonderful news."

"He taught me about frequency tables yesterday, and today he is going to start me on simple substitution ciphers."

"How thrilling."

"Well, it is to me. I've never done anything like this before. And it has some value: we are sending signals and one of them could be the correct one. It certainly is accomplishing more than you are with all your flying rocks. And there are only two days to go, too."

She stalked out and slammed the door. Jason slumped with fatigue, aware that failure was hovering close. He was pouring himself a huge glass of Old Fatigue Killer when Kerk came in.

"Two days to go," Kerk said.

"Thanks. I wouldn't have known if you hadn't told me. I

am well aware that a Pyrran never gives up, but I am getting the sneaking suspicion that we are licked."

"We are not beaten yet. We can fight."

"A very Pyrran answer—but it won't work this time. We just can't barge in there in battle armor and shoot the place up."

"Why not? Small-arms fire would just bounce off of us—as well as the low-powered rays. All we have to do is dodge the big stuff and bull through."

"That's all! Do you have any idea how we are going to arrange that?"

"No. But you will figure something out. And you better hurry."

"I know, two days. I suppose it's easier to die than admit failure. We suit up, fly at the battleship behind a fleet of rocks that are blasted by the heavy stuff. Then we tell the enemy discrimination circuits that we are not armored space suits at all, but just a couple of jettisoned plastic beer barrels that they can shoot up with the small caliber stuff. Which then bounces off us like hail and we land inside and get a billion credits and live happily ever after."

"That's the sort of thing. I'll go and get the suits ready."

"Before you do that, just consider one thing in this preposterous plan. How do we tell the discrimination circuitry . . ." Jason's voice ran down in mid sentence, and his eyes opened wide—then he clapped Kerk on the back. Heavily too, he was so excited, but the Pyrran seemed completely unaware of the blow.

"That's it, that's how we do it!" Jason chortled, rushing to the computer console. Kerk waited patiently while Jason fed in figures and muttered over the pages of information that poured from the printer. The answer was not long in coming.

"Here it is!" Jason held up a sheet. "The plan of attack—and it's going to work. It is just a matter of remembering that the computer on that battleship is just a big dumb answering machine that counts on its fingers. But it does it very fast. It always performs in the same manner because it is programmed to do so. So here is what happens. Because of the main drive tubes the area with the least concentration of fire power is dead astern. Only one hundred and fourteen gun turrets can be trained that way. Their slew time varies."

"Slew time?"

"The time it takes a turret to rotate one hundred and eighty degrees in azimuth. The small ones do it in less than a second. This is one factor. Other factors are which targets get that attention. Fastest-moving rocks get blasted first, even if they are farther away than a larger, slower-moving target. There are other factors like rate of fire, angle of depression of guns, and so forth. Our computer has chomped everything up and come up with this!"

"What does it reveal?"

"That we can make it. We will be in the center of a disk of flying rocks that will be aimed at the rear of the *Indestructible*. There will be a lot of rock, enough to keep all the guns busy that can bear on the spot. Our suits will be half the size of the smallest boulder. We will all be going at the same speed, in the same direction, so we should get the small-caliber stuff. Now, another cloud of rock, real heavy stuff, will converge on the stern of the ship from a ninety-degree angle, but it will not hit the two-hundred-kilometer limit until after the guns start blasting at us. The computer will track it and as soon as our wave is blasted will slew the big guns to get rid of the heavy stuff. As soon as these fire, we accelerate toward the stern tubes. We will then become prime targets, but, before the big guns can slew back, we should be inside the tubes."

"It sounds possible. What is the time gap between the instant we reach the tubes and the earliest the guns can fire?"

"We leave their cone of fire exactly six-tenths of a second before they can blast us."

"Plenty of time. Let us go."

Jason held up his hand. "Just one thing. I'm game if you are. We carry cutting equipment and weapons. Once inside the ship there should not be too many problems. But it is not going to be that easy. I say that the two of us go. If we don't tell Meta she will stay here."

"Three have a better chance than two to get through."

"And two have a better chance than one. I'm not going unless you agree."

"Agreed. Set the plan up."

Meta was busy with her newfound interest in codes and ciphers; it was a perfect time. The Earth navy ships were well trained in precision rock-throwing—as well as being completely bored by it. They let the computers do most of the work. While the preparations were being made, Kerk and Jason suited up in the combat suits: more tanks than suits, heavy with armor and slung about with weapons. Kerk attached the special equipment they would need while Jason short-circuited the airlock indicator so that Meta, in the control room, would not know they had left the ship. Silently they slipped out.

No matter how many times you do it, no matter how you prepare yourself mentally, the sensation of floating free in space is not an enjoyable one. It is easy to lose orientation, to have the sensation that all directions are up—or down. Jason was more than slightly glad of the accompanying bulk of the Pyrran.

"Operation has begun."

The voice crackled in their earphones; then they were too busy to be concerned about anything else. The computer informed them that the wall of giant boulders was sweeping toward them—they could see nothing themselves—and gave them instructions to pull aside. Then the things were suddenly there, floating ponderously by, already shrinking into the distance as the jets on the space suits fired. Again following instructions, they accelerated to the correct moving spot in

space and fitted themselves into the gap in the center of the
floating rock field. They had to juggle their jets until they had
the same velocity as the boulders. Then, power cut off, they
floated free.

"Do you remember the instructions?" Jason asked.

"Perfectly."

"Well, let me run through them again for the sake of my
morale, if you don't mind." The battleship was visible now far
ahead, a tiny splinter in space. "We do nothing at all to draw
attention as we come in. There will be plenty of activity
around us, but we don't use power except in an extreme emergency. And when we get hit by small-caliber fire—it will be the
best thing that can happen to us. Because it will mean the big
guns will be firing at something else. Meanwhile the other
attack of flying rocks will be coming in from our flank. We
won't see them—but our computer will. It is monitoring the
battleship as well. Then the instant the big guns are on the
second wave, it will send us the signal *go*. Then we go. Under
full power toward the main drive tube. When our suit radar
says we are eleven hundred meters from the ship, we put on
full reverse thrust because we will be out of reach of the guns.
See you at the bottom of the tube."

"What if the computer fires the tube to clear us out?"

"I have been trying not to think about that. We can only
hope that it is not programmed for such a complex action and
that its logic circuits will not come up with the answer . . ."

Space around them exploded with searing light. Their helmet visors darkened automatically, but the explosions could
still be clearly seen, they were so intense. And silent. A rock
the size of a small house fumed and vaporized soundlessly not
a hundred meters from Jason, and he cringed inside the suit.
The silent destruction continued—but the silence was suddenly shattered by deafening explosions. His suit vibrated with
the impacts.

He was being hit! Even though he had expected it, wanted

it, the jarring was intense and unbelievably loud. Then it stopped as suddenly as it had begun, and dimly, he heard a weak voice say *go*.

"Blast, Kerk, blast!" he shouted as he jammed on full power.

The suit kicked him hard, numbing him, slowing his fingers as they grappled for the intensity control on the helmet and turned it off. He winced against the glare of burning matter but could just make out the disk of the spaceship's stern before him, the main tube staring like a great black eye. It grew quickly until it filled space, and the sudden red glow of the present radar said he had passed the eleven-hundred-meter mark. The guns couldn't touch him here—but he could crash into the battleship and demolish himself. Then the full blast of the retrojets hit him, slamming him against the suit, stunning him again. Control was impossible. The dark opening blossomed before him, filling his vision, blacking out everything else.

He was inside it, the pressure lessening as the landing circuits took over and slowed his rate of descent. Had Kerk made it? He had stopped, floating free, when something plummeted from above, glanced off him, and crashed heavily into the end of the tube.

"Kerk!" Jason grabbed the limp figure as it rebounded after the tremendous impact, grappled it, and turned his lights on it. "Kerk!" No answer. Dead?

"Landed . . . faster than I intended."

"You did indeed. But we're here. Now let's get to work before the computer decides to burn us out."

Spurred by this danger, they unshipped the molecular unbinder torch, the only thing that would affect the tough tube liners, and worked a circular line on the wall just above the injectors. It took almost two minutes of painstaking work to slowly cut the opening, and every second of the time they waited for the tube to fire.

It did not. The circle was completed, and Kerk put his shoulder to it and fired his jets. The plug of metal and the Pyrran instantly vanished from sight. Jason dived in right behind him, into the immense, brightly lit engine room.

Made suddenly brighter by a flare of light behind him. Jason spun about just as the flames cut off. It had been a microsecond blast. "A smart computer," he said weakly. "Smart indeed."

Kerk had ignored the blast and dived into a control room to one side. Jason followed him, met him as he emerged with a large chart in a twisted metal frame.

"Diagram of the ship. Tore it from the wall. Central control this way. Go."

"All right, all right," Jason muttered, working to keep pace with the Pyrran's hustling form. This was what Pyrrans did best; it was an effort to keep up the pace.

"Repair robots," he said when they entered a long corridor, pointing to the tall, metal forms. "They won't bother us . . ."

Before he had finished speaking, the two robots had raised their welding torches and rushed to the attack. But the instant that they moved, Kerk's gun blasted twice, blowing them into instant junk.

"The ship's computer is too smart. It will turn anything against us. Stay alert and cover my back."

There was no more time for talking. They changed their course often, so it would not be obvious that they were heading toward cent control. Every machine along the way wanted to destroy them. Housekeeping robots rushed at them with brooms, TV screens exploded as they passed, airtight doors tried to close on them. The suddenly electrified floors arced and sputtered. It was a battle, but a one-sided one as long as they stayed alert. Their suits were invulnerable to small-scale attack and well insulated from electricity. In the end they came to a door marked CENTRA KONTROLO. Kerk offhandedly blasted it open and floated through. The lights were lit, the room and the controls were spotlessly clean.

"We've done it," Jason said, looking at the pressure gauge, then cracking his helmet and smelling the cool air. "One billion credits. We've licked this bucket of bolts . . ."

"THIS IS A FINAL WARNING," the voice boomed, and their guns nosed about for the source before they realized it was just a recording. "THIS BATTLESHIP HAS BEEN ENTERED BY ILLEGAL MEANS. YOU ARE ORDERED TO LEAVE WITHIN THE NEXT FIFTEEN SECONDS OR THE ENTIRE SHIP WILL BE DESTROYED. CHARGES HAVE BEEN SET TO ASSURE THIS BATTLESHIP DOES NOT FALL INTO ENEMY HANDS. FOURTEEN . . ."

"We can't get out in time!" Jason shouted.

"Shoot up the controls!"

"No! The destruction controls won't be here."

"TWELVE—"

"What can we do?"

"Nothing! Absolutely nothing at all . . . !"

"EIGHT—"

They looked at each other wordlessly. Jason put out his armored hand and Kerk touched it with his own.

"SEVEN—"

"Well, goodbye," Jason said, and tried to smile.

"FOUR . . . errrk. THR—"

There was silence; then the mechanical voice spoke again, a quieter voice. "De-mothballing activated. Defenses disarmed. Am awaiting instructions."

"What . . . happened?" Jason asked.

"De-mothballing signal received. Am awaiting instructions."

"Just in time," Jason said, swallowing with some difficulty. "Just in time." He fumbled with the unfamiliar controls until he finally turned on the communicator. Meta's face glared from the screen at him.

"Is that where you got to! You should not have gone without me and I shall never forgive you."

"I couldn't take you," Jason said. "I wouldn't have gone myself if you had insisted. You are worth more than a billion credits to me."

"That's the nicest thing you ever said to me." She smiled now and blew him a kiss. Kerk grunted and looked on with great disinterest.

"When you are through, would you tell us what happened?" he said. "Did the computer hit the right number?"

"Not at all. I did it." She smiled into the shocked silence. "I told you how interested I am now in codes and ciphers. Simply thrilling, with many military applications, too, of course. Shrenkly told me about substitution ciphers and I tried one, the most simple. Where the letter A is one, B is two and so forth. Next I put a word into this cipher but it came out 81122021, which was two numbers short. Then Shrenkly told me that there must be two digits for each letter or there would be transcription problems, like you have to use 01 for A instead of just the number. So I added a zero to the two one-digit numbers, and that made ten digits. Then I fed the number into the computer and it was sent and that was that."

"The jackpot with your first number—with your first try?" Jason asked hollowly. "Wasn't that pretty lucky?"

"Not really. You know military people don't have much imagination. You must have told me that a thousand times at least. So I took the simplest possible, looked it up in the Esperanto dictionary . . ."

"*Haltu?*"

"That's right. I encoded it and sent it. And that was that."

"And just what does that word mean?" Kerk asked.

"Stop," Jason said, "just plain stop."

"I would have done the same thing myself," Kerk said, nodding in agreement. "Let us collect the money and go home."

# COMMANDO
# RAID

Private Truscoe and the captain had left the truck, parked out of sight in the jungle, then had walked a good hundred yards farther down the road. They were crouched now in the dense shadows of the trees, with the silver light of the full moon picking out every rut and hollow of the dirt track before them.

"Be quiet!" the captain whispered, putting a restraining hand on the soldier's arm, listening. Truscoe held his breath and struggled to keep absolutely still. Captain Carter was a legendary jungle fighter, with the scars and medals to prove it. If he thought there was something dangerous, creeping closer in the darkness . . . Truscoe suppressed an involuntary shudder.

"It's all right," the captain said, this time in a normal speaking tone. "Something big out there, buffalo or deer. But it's downwind and it took off as soon as it caught our smell. You can smoke if you want to."

The soldier hesitated, not sure how to answer. Finally, he said, "Sir, aren't we supposed . . . I mean someone could see the flame?"

"We're not hiding, Private Truscoe. William—do they call you Billy?"

"Why, yes sir."

"We picked this spot, Billy, because none of the locals normally come this way at night. Light up. The smoke will let all the wildlife know that we're here and they'll keep their distance. They are a lot more afraid of us than you are of them. Not only that, but our informant can find us by the smell too. One whiff and he'll know that it's not the local leaf. That trail over here leads to the village and he'll probably come that way."

Billy looked but could see neither trail nor opening in the jungle wall where the officer pointed. But if the captain said so, it had to be true. He clutched his M16 rifle tightly and looked around at the buzzing, clattering darkness.

"It's not so much the critters out there, sir. I've done plenty of hunting in Alabama and I know this gun can stop anything around. Except maybe another gun. I mean, this geek, sir, the one that's coming. Isn't he kind of a traitor? You know, if he finks on his own people how can we know he won't do the same to us?"

Carter's voice was patient and gave no indication how much he loathed the word *geek*.

"The man's an informant, not a traitor, and he is more eager than we are for this deal to go through. He was originally a refugee from a village in the south, one that was wiped out by that earthquake some years back. You have to understand that these people are very provincial and he'll be a 'foreigner' in this village—as long as he lives. His wife is dead, he has nothing to stay here for. When we approached him for information he jumped at the chance. We'll pay him enough so that he won't ever have to work again. He'll retire to a village close to the one where he was raised. It's a good deal."

Billy was emboldened by the darkness and the presence of the solitary officer. "Still, seems sort of raw for the people he lived with. Selling them out."

"No one is being sold out." The captain was much more

positive now. "What we are doing for them is for their own good. They may not see it that way now, but it is. It is the long-term results that count."

The captain sounded a little peeved. Billy shifted uneasily and did not answer. He should have remembered you don't talk to officers like they were real people or something.

"Stand up, here he comes," Carter said.

Billy had the feeling that maybe the captain could have outhunted him even in his own stand of woods back in Alabama. He neither saw nor heard a thing. Only when the short, turbaned figure appeared at their sides did he know that the informant had arrived.

"Tuan?" the man whispered, and Carter spoke to him quietly in his own tongue. It was so much geek talk to Billy: they had had lectures on the language, but he had never bothered to listen. When they stepped out into the flood of moonlight he saw that the man was a typical geek, too. Scrawny and little and old. There was more cloth in the turban than in his loincloth. All of his possessions, the accumulation of a lifetime, were rolled in a straw mat that he carried in one hand. He sounded very frightened.

"Let's get back to the truck," Captain Carter ordered. "He won't talk here. Too afraid the villagers will find him."

He's got cause to worry, Billy thought, following the disproportionate pair back down the road. The captain was half bent over as he talked to the little man.

Once the truck had coughed to life and the driver was tooling her back to camp, the informant relaxed. He talked steadily in a high, birdlike voice, and the captain put a sheet of paper on his map case and sketched in the details of the village and the surrounding area. Billy nodded, bored, with his rifle between his legs, looking forward to some chow and hitting the sack. There was an all-night cook in the MP mess who would fry up steak and eggs for you if you were on late duty. The voice twittered on and the map grew.

* * *

"Don't want to drop government property, do you, Billy?" Carter asked, and Billy realized that he had dozed off and the M16 had fallen from his fingers. But the captain had caught it and held it safe for him. The sharp blue illumination of the mercury vapor lights of the camp poured into the open back of the truck. Billy opened his mouth, but did not know what to say. Then the officer was gone, with the tiny native scrambling after him, and Billy was alone. He jumped down, boots squelching in the mud, and stretched. Even though the captain had saved his neck rather than report him, he still wasn't sure whether he liked him or not.

Less than three hours after he had fallen asleep the light came on above him in the tent, and the recorded notes of reveille sawed out of the speaker mounted next to it. Billy blinked at his watch and saw that it was just after two.

"What the hell is all this about?" someone shouted "Another damn night maneuver?"

Billy knew, but before he could open his mouth the CO came on the speaker and told them first.

"We're going in, men. This is it. The first units jump off in two hours' time. H Hour will be at first light, at exactly 0515. Your unit commanders will give you complete and detailed instructions before we roll. Full field packs. This is what you have been training for—and this is the moment that you have been waiting for. Don't get rattled, do your job, and don't believe all the latrine rumors that you hear. I'm talking particularly to you new men. I know you have been chewed out a lot, and you have been called 'combat virgins' and a lot worse. Forget it. You're a team now—and after tomorrow you won't even be virgins."

The men laughed at that, but not Billy. He recognized the old bushwa when it was being fed to him. At home, at school,

it was the same old crap. Do or die for our dear old High.
Crap.

"Let's go, let's go," the sergeant shouted, throwing open the
flap of the tent. "We don't have all night and you guys are
creeping around like wrinklies in a geriatric sack race. Move
it!"

That was more like it. The sergeant didn't horse around.
With him you knew just where you stood, all the time.

"Roll the packs tighter, they look like they're stuffed full of
turds." The sergeant had never really taken the orders on use
of purified language to heart.

It was still hot, dark and hot and muggy, and Billy could feel
the sweat already soaking into his clean dungarees. They double-timed to chow, stuffed it down, and double-timed back.
Then, packs on backs, they lined up at the QM stores for field
issue. A tired and yellowish corporal signed in Billy's M16,
checked the serial number, then handed him a Mark-13 and a
sack of reloads. The cool metal slipped through Billy's hands
and he almost dropped it.

"Keep that flitgun out of the mud or you'll be signing
statements of charges for life," the corporal growled, by reflex,
and was already turning to the next man.

Billy gave him the finger—as soon as his back was turned—
and went out into the company street. Under a light he looked
at the riot gun, turning it over and over. It was new, right out
of the Cosmoline, smooth and shining, with a wide stock, a
thick barrel, and a thicker receiver. Heavy, too, eighteen
pounds. But he didn't mind.

"Fall in, fall in—snap shit!" The sergeant was still in good
voice.

They fell into ranks and waited at ease for a long time.
Hurry up and wait, it was always like this, and Billy slipped a
piece of gum into his mouth when all the noncoms had their
backs turned, then chewed it slowly. His squad was finally

called out and dogtrotted off to the copters, where Captain Carter was waiting.

"Just one thing before we board," the captain said. "You men here are in the shock squad and you have the dirty work to do. I want you to stay behind me at all times, in loose order, and watch on all sides and still watch me at the same time. We can expect trouble. But no matter what happens, do not and I repeat that—do not act upon your own initiative. Look to me for orders. We want this to be a model operation and we don't want any losses."

He unrolled a big, diagrammatic map, then pointed to the front rank. "You two men, hold this up so the others can see it. Look close now, all of you. This is the target we are going to hit. The village is on the river, with the rice fields between it and the houses. The hovercraft will come in right over the fields, so no one will get out that way. There is a single dirt road in through the jungle, and that will be plugged. There will be squads on every trail out of the place. The villagers can dive into the jungle if they want, but they won't get far. They'll have to cut their way through and we can follow them easily and bring them back. There are men assigned to all these duties and they will all be in position at H Hour. Then we hit. We come in low and fast so we can sit down in the center of the houses. Here, in this open spot, before anyone even knows that we are on the way. If we do it right the only resistance will be the dogs and chickens."

"Shoot the dogs and eat the chickens," someone shouted from the back, and everyone laughed. The captain smiled slightly to show that he appreciated the joke, but disapproved of chatter while they were fallen in. He tapped the map.

"As we touch down the other units will move in. The headman in the village, this is his house here, is an old rogue with military service and a bad temper. Everyone will be too shocked to provide much resistance unless he orders it. I'll take care of him. Now, are there any questions?" He looked around at the silent men. "All right then, let's load up."

The big, double-rotored copters squatted low, their wide doors close to the ground. As soon as the men were aboard, the starters whined and the long blades began to turn slowly. The operation had begun.

When they rose above the trees they could see the lightening of the eastern horizon. They stayed low, their wheels almost brushing the leaves, like a flock of ungainly birds of prey. It wasn't a long flight, but the sudden tropical dawn was on them almost before they realized it.

The ready light flashed on and the captain came down from the cockpit and gave them the thumbs-up signal. They went in.

It was a hard landing, almost a drop, and the doors banged open as they touched. The shock squad hit the ground and Captain Carter went first.

The pounded dirt compound was empty. The squad formed on the captain and watched the doorways of the rattan-walled buildings where people were beginning to appear. The surprise had been absolute. There was the grumble of truck engines from the direction of the road and a roar of sound from the river. Billy glanced that way and saw the hovercraft moving over the paddies in a cloud of spray. Then he jumped, raising the riot gun, as a shrill warbling ripped at his ears.

It was the captain. He had a voice gun with a built-in siren. The sound wailed, shriller and shriller, then died away as he flipped the switch. He raised it and spoke into the microphone, and his voice filled the village.

Billy couldn't understand the geek talk, but it sounded impressive. For the first time he realized that the captain was unarmed—and even wore a garrison cap instead of his helmet. That was taking a big chance. Billy raised the flitgun to the ready and glanced around at the people who were slowly emerging from the houses.

Then the captain pointed toward the road and his echoing

voice stopped. All of the watching heads, as though worked by a single string, turned to look where he indicated. A half-track appeared, engine bellowing, trailing a thick column of dust. It braked, sliding to a stop, and a corporal jumped from the back and ran the few paces to the town well. He had a bulky object in his arms, which he dropped into the well—then dived aside.

With a sharp explosion the well blew up. Dirt flew and mud and water spattered down. The walls collapsed. Where the well had once been there remained only a shallow, smoking pit. The captain's voice cut through the shocked silence that followed.

Yet, even as his first amplified words swept the compound, a hoarse shout interrupted them. A gray-haired man had emerged from the headman's house. He was shouting, pointing at the captain, who waited until the other had finished, then answered back. He was interrupted before he was done. The captain tried to argue, but the headman ran back inside the building.

He was fast. A moment later he came out with an archaic steel helmet on his head, waving a long-bladed sword over his head. There hadn't been a helmet made like that in forty years. And a sword. Billy almost laughed out loud until he realized that the headman was playing it for real. He ran at the captain, sword raised, ignoring the captain's voice completely. It was like watching a play, being in a play, with no one moving and only the captain and the old man playing their roles.

The headman wasn't listening. He attacked, screeching, and brought the sword down and around in a wicked, decapitating cut. The captain blocked the blow with the voice gun, which coughed and died. He was still trying to reason with the old man, but his voice sounded smaller and different now—and the headman wasn't listening.

Twice he struck, and a third time, and each time the captain backed away a bit and parried with the voice gun, which was rapidly being reduced to battered junk. As the sword came up again, the captain called back over his shoulder.

"Private Truscoe, take this man out. This has gone far enough."

Billy was well trained and knew what to do without even thinking about it. A step forward, the flitgun raised to his shoulder and aimed, the safety off, and when the man's head filled the sight he squeezed off the shot.

With a throat-clearing cough the cloud of compressed gas blasted out and struck the headman full in the face.

"Masks on," Captain Carter ordered, and once more the movement was automatic.

Small of the stock in his left hand, right hand free, grasp the handle (gas mask, actuating) under the brim of his helmet, and pull. The transparent plastic reeled down and he hooked it under his chin. All by the numbers.

But then something went wrong. The Mace-IV that the flitgun expelled was supposed to take anyone out. Down and out. But the headman was not going down. He was retching, his belly working in and out uncontrollably while the vomit ran down his chin and onto his bare chest. He still clutched the long sword and, with his free hand, he threw his helmet to the ground and pried open one streaming eye. He must have made out Billy's face through his tears, because he turned from the captain and came on, sword raised, staggering.

Billy brought the flitgun up, but it was in his left hand and he couldn't fire. He changed the grip, fumbling with it, but the man was still coming on. The sword glistened as the rising sun struck it.

Billy swung the gun around like a club and caught the headman across the temple with the thick barrel. The headman pitched face forward to the ground and was still.

Billy pointed the gun down at him and pulled the trigger, again and again, the gas streaming out and covering the sprawled figure . . .

Until the captain knocked the gun from his hand and pulled him about, almost throwing him to the ground.

"Medic!" the captain shouted; then, almost a whisper through his clenched teeth, "You fool, you fool."

Billy just stood, dazed, trying to understand what had happened, as the ambulance pulled up. There were injections, cream on the man's face, oxygen from a tank; then he was loaded onto a stretcher and the doctor came over.

"It's touch and go, Captain. Possible skull fracture, and he breathed in a lot of your junk. How did it happen?"

"It will be in my report," Captain Carter answered in a toneless voice.

The doctor started to speak, thought better of it, and turned and climbed into the ambulance. It pulled away, dodging around the big trucks that were coming into the village. The people were out of the houses now, huddled in knots, talking under their breaths. There would be no more resistance.

Billy was aware that the captain was looking at him, looking as if he wanted to kill. The gas mask was suddenly hot on Billy's face and he pulled it free.

"It wasn't my fault, sir," Billy explained. "He just came at me."

"He came at me too. I didn't fracture his skull. It was your fault."

"No, it's not. Not when some old geek swings a rusty damn pig-sticker at me."

"He is not a geek, Private, but a citizen of this country and a man of stature in this village. He was defending his home and was within his rights."

Billy was angry now. He knew it was all up with him and the Corps and his plans, and he didn't give a damn. He turned to the officer, fists clenched.

"He's a crummy geek from Geeksville, and if he got rights what are we doing here, just tell me that?"

The captain was coldly quiet now. "We were invited here by

the country's president and the Parliament, you know that as well as I do." His voice was drowned out as a truck passed close by and the exhaust blatted out at them. It stopped and men jumped down and began to unload lengths of plastic piping. Billy looked the captain square in the eye and told him off, what he had always wanted to say.

"In a pig's ass we were invited here. Some big shot these local geeks never heard of says okay and we drop down their throats and spend a couple billion dollars of the U.S. taxpayers' money to give some geeks the good life they don't know nothing about and don't need—so what the hell!" He shouted the last words. The captain was much quieter.

"I suppose it would be better if we helped them the way we helped in Vietnam? Came in and burned them and shot them and blasted them right back to the Stone Age?"

Another truck stopped and began unloading sinks, toilets, electric stoves.

"Well, why not? Why not! If they trouble Uncle Sam then knock them out. We don't need anything from these kind of broken-down raggedy people. Now Uncle Sam—Uncle Sap is taking care of the world and the taxpayers footing the bill . . ."

"Shut up and listen, Private." There was an edge to the captain's voice that Billy had never heard before, and he shut up. "I don't know how you got into the Aid Corps but I do know that you don't belong in it. This is one world and it gets smaller every year. The Eskimos in the Arctic have DDT poisoning from the farms in the Midwest. The strontium ninety from a French atom test in the Pacific gives bone cancer to a child in New York. This is spaceship Earth and we're all aboard it together, trying to stay alive on it.

"The richest countries had better help the poorest—or else. Because it's all the same spaceship. And it's already almost too late. In Vietnam we spent five million dollars a head to kill the citizens of that country, and our profit was the undying hatred of everyone there, both north and south, and the loathing of the civilized world. We've made our mistakes—so it's time now to learn how to profit from them.

"For far less than one thousandth of the cost of killing a man, and making his friends our enemies, we can save a life and make the man our friend. Two hundred bucks a head, that's what this operation costs. We've blown up the well here because it was a cesspit of infection, and we are drilling a new well to bring up pure water from the strata below. We are putting toilets into the houses, and sinks. We are killing the disease-breeding insects. We are running in power lines and bringing in a medical mission to save their lives. We are opening a birth-control clinic so they can have families like people, not breed like rats, pulling the world down with them. They are going to have scientific agriculture so they can eat better. Education as well so they can be more than working animals. We are going to bring them about five percent of the 'benefits' you enjoy in the sovereign state of Alabama and we are doing it from selfish motives. We want to stay alive. But at least we are doing it."

The captain looked at his clenched fist, then slowly opened it. "Sergeant," he called out as he turned away. "Put this man under arrest and see that he is sent back to the camp at once."

A crate of composting toilets thudded to the ground almost at Billy's feet and a thread of hot anger snapped inside of him. Who were these people to get waited on like this? He had grown up in a sharecropper's shack and had never seen a toilet like these until he was more than eight years old. Now he had to help give them away to . . .

"Niggers, that's what these people are! And we give them everything on a silver platter. It's bleeding hearts like you, Captain, crying your eyes out for these poor helpless people, that are causing the trouble!"

Captain Carter stopped, and slowly turned about. He

looked at the young man who stood before him and felt only a terrible feeling of depression.

"No, Private William Truscoe, I don't cry for these people. I don't cry. But if I ever could—I would cry for you."

After that he went away.

# THE
# REPAIRMAN

The Old Man had that look of intense glee on his face that meant someone was in for a very rough time. Since we were alone, it took no great feat of intelligence to figure it would be me. I talked first, bold attack being the best defense and so forth.

"I quit. Don't bother telling me what dirty job you have cooked up, because I have already quit and you do not want to reveal company secrets to me."

The grin was even wider now and he actually chortled as he thumbed a button on his console. A thick legal document slid out of the delivery slot onto his desk.

"This is your contract," he said. "It tells how and when you will work. A steel-and-vanadium-bound contract that you couldn't crack with a molecular disruptor."

I leaned out quickly, grabbed it and threw it into the air with a single motion. Before it could fall, I had my Solar out and, with a wide-angle shot, burned the contract to ashes.

The Old Man pressed the button again and another contract slid out on his desk. If possible, the smile was still wider now.

"I should have said a duplicate of your contract—like this one here." He made a quick note on his secretary plate. "I

have deducted thirteen credits from your salary for the cost of the duplicate—as well as a hundred-credit fine for firing a Solar inside a building."

I slumped, defeated, waiting for the blow to land. The Old Man fondled my contract.

"According to this document, you can't quit. Ever. I therefore have a little job I know you'll enjoy. Repair job. The Procyon beacon has shut down. It's a Mark Three beacon . . ."

"What kind of beacon?" I asked him. I have repaired hyperspace beacons from one arm of the galaxy to the other and was sure I had worked on every type or model made. But I had never heard of this kind.

"Mark Three," the Old Man repeated with sly humor. "I never heard of it either until Records dug up the specs. They found them buried in the back of their oldest warehouse. This was the earliest type of beacon ever built—by Earth, no less. Considering its location on one of the Procyon planets, it might very well be the first beacon ever made."

I looked at the blueprints he handed me and felt my eyes glaze with horror. "It's a monstrosity! It looks more like a distillery than a beacon—must be at least a few hundred meters high. I'm a repairman, not an archaeologist. This pile of junk is over two thousand years old. Just forget about it and build a new one."

The Old Man leaned over his desk, breathing into my face. "It would take a year to install a new beacon—besides being too expensive—and this relic is on one of the main routes. We have ships making fifteen-light-year detours now."

He leaned back, wiped his hands on his handkerchief, and gave me Lecture Forty-four on Company Duty and My Troubles.

"This department is officially called Maintenance and Repair, when it really should be called Troubleshooting. Hyperspace beacons are made to last forever—or damn close to it.

When one of them breaks down, it is never an accident, and repairing the thing is never a matter of just plugging in a new part."

He was telling me—the guy who did the job while he sat back on his fat paycheck in an air-conditioned office.

He rambled on. "How I wish that were all it took! I would have a fleet of parts ships and junior mechanics to install them. But it's not like that at all. I have a fleet of expensive ships that are equipped to do almost anything—all of them manned by a bunch of irresponsibles just like you."

I nodded moodily at his pointing finger.

"How I wish I could fire you all! Combination space jockeys, mechanics, engineers, soldiers, conmen, and anything else it takes to do the repairs. I have to browbeat, bribe, blackmail, and bulldoze you thugs into doing a simple job. If you think you're fed up, just think how I feel. But the ships must go through! The beacons must operate!"

I recognized this deathless line as the curtain speech and crawled to my feet. He threw the Mark III file at me and went back to scratching in his papers. Just as I reached the door, he looked up and impaled me on his finger again.

"And don't get any fancy ideas about jumping your contract. We can attach that bank account of yours on Algol Two long before you could draw the money out."

I smiled, a little weakly I'm afraid, as if I had never meant to keep that account a secret. His spies were getting more efficient every day. Walking down the hall, I tried to figure a way to transfer the money without his catching on—and at the same time I knew that he was busy figuring a way to outfigure me.

It was all very depressing, so I stopped for a drink, then went on to the spaceport.

By the time the ship was serviced, I had a course charted. The nearest beacon to the broken-down Procyon beacon was on one of the planets of Beta Circinus, and I headed there first, a short trip of only about nine days in hyperspace.

To understand the importance of the beacons, you have to understand hyperspace. Not that many people do, but it is easy enough to understand that in this nonspace the regular rules don't apply. Speed and measurements are a matter of relationship, not constant facts like the fixed universe.

The first ships to enter hyperspace had no place to go—and no way to even tell if they had moved. The beacons solved that problem and opened the entire universe. They're built on planets and generate tremendous amounts of power. This power is turned into radiation that is punched through into hyperspace. Every beacon has a code signal that is part of its radiation and represents a measurable point in hyperspace. Triangulation and quadrature of the beacons works for navigation—only it follows its own rules. The rules are complex and variable, but they are still rules that a navigator can follow.

For a hyperspace jump, you need at least four beacons for an accurate fix. For long jumps, navigators use as many as seven or eight. So every beacon is important and every one has to keep operating. That is where I and the other troubleshooters come in.

We travel in well-stocked ships that carry a little bit of everything; only one man to a ship, because that is all it takes to operate the overly efficient repair machinery. Due to the very nature of our job, we spend most of our time just rocketing through normal space. After all, when a beacon breaks down, how do you find it?

Not through hyperspace. All you can do is approach as close as you can by using other beacons, then finish the trip in normal space. This can take months, and often does.

This job didn't turn out to be quite that bad. I zeroed the Beta Circinus beacon and ran a complicated eight-point problem through the navigator, using every beacon I could get an accurate fix on. The computer gave me a course with an estimated point-of-arrival as well as a built-in safety factor I never could eliminate from the machine.

I would much rather take a chance of breaking through near some star than spend time just barreling through normal space, but apparently Tech knows this, too. They had a safety factor built into the computer so you couldn't end up inside a sun no matter how hard you tried. I'm sure there was no humaneness in this decision. They just didn't want to lose the ship.

It was a twenty-hour jump, ship's time, and I came through in the middle of nowhere. The robot analyzer chuckled to itself and scanned the brightest surrounding stars, comparing each to the spectrum of Procyon. It finally rang a bell and blinked a light. I peeped through the eyepiece.

A last reading with the photocell gave me the apparent magnitude, and a comparison with its absolute magnitude showed its distance. Not as bad as I had thought—a six-week run, give or take a few days. After feeding a course tape into the robot pilot, I strapped into the acceleration tank and went to sleep.

The time went fast. I rebuilt my camera for about the twentieth time and just about finished a correspondence course in nucleonics. Repairmen take these courses. They have a value in themselves, because you never know what bit of odd information will come in handy. Not only that, the company grades your pay by the number of specialties you can handle. All this, with some oil painting and free-fall workouts in the gym, passed the time. I was asleep when the alarm went off that announced planetary distance.

Planet Two, where the beacon was situated according to the old charts, was a mushy-looking, wet kind of globe. I worked hard to make sense out of the ancient directions and finally located the right area. Staying outside the atmosphere, I sent a Flying Eye down to look things over. In this business, you learn early when and where to risk your own skin. The Eye would be good enough for the preliminary survey.

The old boys had enough brains to choose a traceable site for the beacon, equidistant on a line between two of the most prominent mountain peaks. I located the peaks easily enough and started the Eye out from the first peak and kept on a course directly toward the second. There was a nose and tail radar in the Eye, and I fed their signals into a scope as an amplitude curve. When the two peaks coincided, I spun the Eye controls and dived the thing down.

I cut out the radar and cut in the nose TV pickup and sat back to watch the beacon appear on the screen.

The image blinked, focused—and a great damn pyramid swam into view. I cursed and wheeled the Eye in circles, scanning the surrounding country. It was flat, marshy bottomland without a bump. The only thing within a ten-mile circle was this pyramid—and that definitely wasn't my beacon.

Or was it?

I dived the Eye lower. The pyramid was a crude-looking thing of undressed stone, without carvings or decorations. There was a shimmer of light from the top and I took a closer look at it. On the peak of the pyramid was a hollow basin filled with water. When I saw that, something clicked in my mind.

Locking the Eye in a circular course, I dug through the Mark III plans—and there it was. The beacon had a precipitating field and a basin on top of it for water; this was used to cool the reactor that powered the monstrosity. If the water was still there, the beacon was still there—inside the pyramid. The natives, who, of course, weren't even mentioned by the idiots who constructed the thing, had built a nice heavy, thick stone pyramid under the beacon.

I took another look at the screen and realized that I had locked the Eye into a circular orbit about twenty feet above the pyramid. The summit of the stone pile was now covered with lizards of some type, apparently the local life-form. They had what looked like throwing stones and arbalests and were trying to shoot down the Eye, a cloud of rocks and arrows flying in every direction.

I pulled the Eye straight up and away and punched in the control circuit that would return it automatically to the ship.

Then I went to the galley for a long strong drink. My beacon was not only locked inside a mountain of handmade stone, but I managed to irritate the things who had built the pyramid. Everything was clearly designed to drive a stronger man than me to the bottle.

Normally, a repairman stays away from native cultures. They are poison. Anthropologists may not mind being dissected for their science, but a repairman wants to make no sacrifices of any kind for his job. For this reason, most beacons are built on uninhabited planets. If a beacon has to go on a planet with a culture, it is usually built in some inaccessible place.

Why this beacon had been built within reach of the local claws, I had yet to find out. But that would come in time. The first thing to do was to make contact. To make contact, you have to know the local language.

And for that, I had long before worked out a system that was foolproof.

I had a Pryeye of my own construction. It looked like a piece of rock about a foot long. Once on the ground, it would never be noticed, though it was a little disconcerting to see it float by. I located a lizard town about a thousand kilometers from the pyramid and dropped the Eye. It swished down and landed at night in the bank of the local mud wallow. This was a favorite spot that drew a good crowd during the day. In the morning, when the first wallowers arrived, I flipped on the recorder.

After about five of the local days, I had a stack of native conversation in the memory bank of my machine translator and had even tagged a few expressions. This is fairly easy to do when you have a machine memory to work with. One of the lizards gargled at another one and the second one turned around. I tagged the expression with the phrase "Hey, George!" and waited for my chance to use it. Later the same day, I caught one of them alone and shouted "Hey, George!" at him. It gurgled out through the speaker in the local tongue, and he turned around.

When you get enough reference phrases in the memory bank, the MT brain takes over and starts filling in the missing pieces. As soon as the MT could give a running translation of any conversation it heard, I figured it was time to make contact.

I found him easily enough. He was the Centaurian version of a goat-boy—he herded a particularly loathsome form of local life in the swamps outside the town. I had one of the working Eyes dig a cave in an outcropping of rock and wait for him.

When he passed next day, I whispered into the mike: "Welcome, O Goat-boy Grandson! This is your grandfather's spirit speaking from paradise." This fitted in with what I could make out of the local religion.

Goat-boy stopped as if he'd been shot. Before he could move, I pushed a switch and a handful of the local currency, wampum-type shells, rolled out of the cave and landed at his feet.

"Here is some money from paradise, because you have been a good boy." Not really from paradise—I had lifted it from the treasury the night before. "Come back tomorrow and we'll talk some more," I called after the fleeing figure. I was pleased to notice that he took the cash before taking off.

After that, Grandpa in paradise had many heart-to-heart talks with Grandson, who found the heavenly loot more than he could resist. Grandpa had been out of touch with things since his death and Goat-boy happily filled him in.

I learned all I needed to know of the history, past and recent, and it wasn't nice.

In addition to the pyramid being around the beacon, there was a nice little religious war going on around the pyramid.

It all began with the land bridge. Apparently the local lizards had been living in the distant swamps when the beacon had been built, but the builders hadn't thought much of them. They were a low type and confined to a distant continent. The idea that the race would develop and might reach this continent never occurred to the beacon mechanics. Which is, of course, what happened.

A little geological turnover, a swampy land bridge formed in the right spot, and the lizards began to wander up Beacon Valley. And found religion. A shiny metal temple out of which poured a constant stream of magic water—the reactor-cooling water pumped down from the atmosphere condenser on the roof. The radioactivity in the water didn't seem to hurt the natives. If anything it caused mutations that bred true.

A city was built around the temple and, through the centuries, the pyramid was put up around the beacon. A special branch of the priesthood served the temple. All went well until one of the priests violated the temple and destroyed the Holy Waters. There had been revolt, strife, murder, and destruction since then. But still the Holy Waters would not flow. Now armed mobs fought around the temple each day and a new band of priests guarded the sacred fount.

And I had to walk into the middle of that mess and repair the thing.

It would have been easy enough to do if we were allowed a little organized violence. I could have had a lizard fry, fixed the beacon, and taken off. I could not do this since all native life-forms were quite well protected. There were spy cells on my ship, all of which I hadn't found, that would cheerfully rat on me when I got back.

Diplomacy was called for. I sighed and dragged out the plastiflesh equipment.

Working from 3-D snaps of Grandson, I modeled a passable reptile head over my own features. It was a little short in the jaw, me not having one of their toothy mandibles, but that was all right. I didn't have to look exactly like them, just something close. To soothe the native mind. It's logical. If I were an ignorant aborigine of Earth and I ran into a Spican, who looks like a two-foot gob of dried shellac, I would immediately leave the scene. However, if the Spican was wearing a suit of plastiflesh that looked remotely humanoid, I would at least stay and talk to him. This was what I was aiming to do with the Centaurians.

When the head was done, I peeled it off and attached it to an attractive suit of green plastic, complete with tail. I was really glad they had tails. The lizards didn't wear clothes, and I wanted to take along a lot of electronic equipment. I built the tail over a metal frame that anchored around my waist. Then I filled the frame with all the equipment I would need and began to wire the suit.

When it was done, I tried it on in front of a full-length mirror. It was horrible but effective. The tail dragged me down in the rear and gave me a duck-waddle, but that only helped the resemblance.

That night I took the ship down, into the hills nearest the pyramid. An out-of-the-way dry spot where the amphibious natives would never go. A little before dawn the Eye hooked onto my shoulders and we sailed straight up. We hovered above the temple at about two thousand meters, until it was light, then dropped down. It must have been a grand sight. The Eye was camouflaged to look like a flying lizard, sort of a cardboard pterodactyl, and the slowly flapping wings obviously had nothing to do with our flight. But it was impressive enough for the natives. The first one that spotted me screamed and dropped over on its back. The others came running. They milled and mobbed and piled on top of one another, and by the time I had landed in the plaza fronting the temple the priesthood arrived.

I folded my arms in a regal stance. "Greetings, O noble servers of the Great God," I said. Of course I didn't say it out loud, just whispered softly enough for the throat mike to catch. This was radioed back to the MT, and the translation shot back to a speaker in my jaws.

The natives chomped and rattled, and the translation rolled out almost instantly. I had the volume turned up and the whole square echoed to my amplified machine voice.

Some of the more credulous natives prostrated themselves, and others fled screaming. One doubtful type raised a spear, but no one else tried that after the pterodactyl Eye picked him up and dropped him in the swamp. The priests were a hard-headed lot and weren't buying any lizards in a poke; they just stood and muttered. I had to take the offensive again.

"Begone, O faithful steed," I said to the Eye, and pressed the control in my palm at the same time.

It took off straight up a bit faster than I wanted; little pieces of wind-torn plastic rained down. While the crowd was ogling this ascent, I walked through the temple doors.

"I would talk with you, O noble priests," I said. Before they could think up a good answer, I was inside.

The temple was a small one built against the base of the pyramid. I hoped I wasn't breaking too many taboos by going in. Since I wasn't stopped I was all right so far. The temple was a single room with a murky-looking pool at one end. Sloshing in the pool was an ancient reptile who clearly was one of the leaders. I waddled toward him and he gave me a cold and fishy eye, then growled something.

The MT whispered into my ear, "Just what in the name of the thirteenth sin are you—and what are you doing here?"

I drew up my scaly figure in a noble gesture and pointed

toward the ceiling. "I come from your ancestors to help you. I am here to restore the Holy Waters."

This raised a buzz of conversation behind me, but got no useful response out of the chief. He sank slowly into the water until only his eyes were showing. I could almost hear the wheel turning behind that moss-covered forehead. Then he lunged up and pointed a dripping finger at me.

"You are a liar! You are no ancestor of ours! You will—"

"Stop!" I thundered before he got so far in that he couldn't back out. "I said your ancestors sent me as emissary—I am not one of your ancestors. Do not try to harm me or the wrath of those who have Passed On will turn against you."

When I said this, I turned to jab a claw at the other priests, using the motion to cover my flicking a coin grenade toward them. It blew a nice hole in the door with a great show of noise and smoke.

The First Lizard knew I was talking sense then and immediately called a meeting of the shamans. It, of course, took place in the public bathtub and I had to join them there. We jawed and gurgled for about an hour and settled all the major points. I found out that they were all new priests; the previous ones had all been boiled alive for letting the Holy Waters cease.

Cheered by this information, I explained that I was there only to help them restore the flow of the waters. They bought this, tentatively, and we all heaved out of the tub and trickled muddy paths across the floor. There was a bolted and guarded door that led into the pyramid proper. While it was being opened, the First Lizard turned to me.

"Undoubtedly you know of the rule," he said. "Because the old priests did pry and peer, it was ordered henceforth that only the blind could enter the Holy of Holies." I would swear he was smiling; if thirty teeth peeking out of what looked like a crack in an old suitcase can be called smiling.

He was also signaling over an underpriest who carried a brazier of charcoal, complete with red-hot irons. All I could

do was stand and watch as he stirred up the coals, pulled out
the ruddiest iron and turned toward me. He was just drawing
a bead on my right eyeball when my brain got back in gear.

"Of course," I said. "Blinding is only right. But in my case
you will have to blind me later, before I leave the Holy of
Holies, not now. I need my eyes to see and mend the Fount of
Holy Waters. Once the waters flow again, I will laugh as I hurl
myself on the burning iron."

He took a good thirty seconds to think it over and in the end
had to agree with me. The local torturer sniffled a bit and
threw a little more charcoal on the fire. The gate crashed open
and I stalked through; then it banged to behind me and I was
alone in the dark.

But not for long—there was a shuffling nearby and I took
a chance and turned on my flash. Three priests were groping
toward me, their eye sockets red pits of burned flesh. They
knew what I wanted and led the way without a word.

A crumbling and cracked stone stairway brought us up by
a solid metal doorway labeled in archaic script MARK III BEA-
CON—ENTRANCE TO AUTHORIZED PERSONNEL ONLY. The overly
trusting builders had counted on the sign to do the whole job,
for there wasn't a trace of a lock on the door. One lizard
merely turned the handle and we were inside the beacon.

I unzipped the front of my camouflage suit and pulled out
the blueprints. With the faithful priests stumbling after me I
approached the antique machinery. There was a residue of
charge in the emergency batteries, just enough to give a dim
light. The meters and indicators looked to be in good shape;
if anything, unexpectedly bright from constant polishing. I
checked the readings carefully and found just what I had
suspected. One of the eager lizards had managed to open a
circuit box and had polished the switches inside. While doing
this, he had thrown one of the switches and that had caused
the trouble.

Rather, that had started the trouble. It wasn't going to be

ended by just reversing the water-valve switch. This valve was supposed to be used only for repairs, and then only after the atomic pile had been damped. When the water was cut off with the pile in operation, it had started to overheat and the automatic safeties had dumped the whole works down into the pit.

I could start the water again easily enough, but there was no fuel left in the reactor.

But I wasn't going to play with the fuel problem at all. It would be far easier for me to install a new power plant. I had one in the ship that was about a tenth of the size of the ancient bucket of bolts. Before I sent for it, I checked over the rest of the beacon. In two thousand years there should be some signs of wear, tear, and fatigue.

The old boys had built well, I'll give them credit for that. Ninety percent of the machinery had no moving parts and had suffered no wear whatever. Other parts they beefed up figuring they would wear, but slowly. The water-feed pipe from the roof, for example. The pipe walls were at least three meters thick—and the pipe opening itself no bigger than my head. There were some things I could do, though, and I made a list of parts.

The parts, the new power plant, and a few other odds and ends were sorted into a neat pile on the ship. I checked all the parts by screen before they were loaded into a small metal crate. In the darkest hour before dawn, the heavy-duty Eye dropped the crate outside the temple and darted away without being seen.

I watched the priests through the Pryeye while they tried to open it. When they had given up, I boomed orders at them through a speaker in the crate. They spent most of the day sweating the heavy box up through the narrow temple stairs, and I enjoyed a good sleep. It was resting inside the beacon door when I woke up.

The repair didn't take long, though there was plenty of groaning from the blind lizards when they heard me ripping the wall open to get to the power leads. I even hooked a gadget to the water pipe so their Holy Waters would have the usual refreshing radioactivity when they started flowing again. The moment this was all finished, I did the job they waited for.

I threw the switch that started the water flowing again.

There were a few minutes while the water began to gurgle down through the dry pipe. Then a roar came from outside the pyramid that must have shaken its stone walls. Shaking my hands once over my head, I went down for the eye-burning ceremony.

The blind lizards were waiting for me by the door and looked even unhappier than usual. When I tried the door, I found out why—it was bolted and barred from the other side.

"It has been decided," a lizard said, "that you shall remain here forever and tend to the Holy Waters. We will stay with you and serve your every need."

A delightful prospect, eternity spent in a locked beacon with three blind lizards. In spite of their hospitality, I couldn't accept.

"What! You dare interfere with the messenger of your ancestors!" I had the speaker on full volume and the vibration almost shook my head off.

The lizards cringed, and I set my Solar for a narrow beam and ran it around the doorjamb. There was a great crunching and banging from the junk piled against it, and then the door swung free. I threw it open. Before they could protest, I had pushed the priests out through it.

The rest of their clan showed up at the foot of the stairs and made a great ruckus while I finished welding the door shut. Running through the crowd, I faced up to the First Lizard in his tub. He sank slowly beneath the surface.

"What lack of courtesy!" I shouted. He made little bubbles in the water. "The ancestors are annoyed and have decided to forbid entrance to the Inner Temple forever. Though, out of their eternal kindness, they will let the waters flow. Now I must return—so on with the eyeball ceremony!"

The torture-master was too frightened to move, so I grabbed his hot iron out of the coals. A touch on the side of my face dropped a steel plate over my eyes, under the plasti-skin. Then I jammed the iron hard into my phony eye sockets and the plastic gave off an authentic odor.

A cry went up from the crowd as I dropped the iron and staggered in blind circles. I must admit it went off pretty well.

But enough was enough. Before they could get any more bright ideas, I threw the switch and my plastic pterodactyl sailed in through the door.

I couldn't see it, of course, but I knew it had arrived when the grapples in the claws latched onto the steel plates on my shoulders. I had got turned around after the eye-burning and my flying beast hooked onto me backward. I had meant to sail out bravely, blind eyes facing into the sunset; instead, I faced the crowd as I soared away, so I made the most of a bad situation and threw them a snappy military salute. Then I was out in the fresh air and away.

When I lifted the plate and poked holes in the seared plastic, I could see the pyramid growing smaller behind me, water gushing out of the base and a happy crowd of reptiles sporting in its radioactive rush. I counted off on my talons to see if I had forgotten anything.

One: The beacon was repaired.

Two: The door was sealed, so there should be no more sabotage, accidental or deliberate.

Three: The priests should be satisfied. The water was running again, my eyes had been duly burned out, and they were back in business. Which added up to—

Four: The fact that they would probably let another repair-man in, under the same conditions, if the beacon conked out again. At least I had done nothing, like butchering a few of them, that would make them antagonistic toward future ancestral messengers.

I stripped off my tattered lizard suit back in the ship, very glad it would be some other repairman who would get the job.

# BRAVE
# NEWER
# WORLD

L ivermore liked the view from the little white balcony outside his office. Even though the air at this height, at this time of year, had a chill bite to it. He was standing there now, trying to suppress a shiver, looking out at the new spring green on the hillsides and the trees in the old town. Above and below him the white steps of the levels of New Town stretched away in smooth elegance. A great A in space with the base a half-mile wide, rising up almost to a point on top. Every level fringed with a balcony, every balcony with an unobstructed view. Well designed. Livermore shivered again and felt the loud beat of his heart; old valves cheered on by new drugs. His insides were as carefully propped up and as well designed as the New Town building. Though his outside left a lot to be desired. Brown spots, wrinkles, and white hair; he looked as weathered as the homes in Old Town. It was damned cold—and the sun went behind a cloud. He thumbed a button, and when the glass wall slid aside, went back gratefully into the purified and warmed air of the interior.

"Been waiting long?" he asked the old man who sat, scowling, in the chair on the far side of his desk.

"Well, you asked, Doctor. I was never one to complain, but . . ."

"Then don't start now. Stand up. Open your shirt. Let me have those records. Ahh, Grazer, I remember you. Planted a kidney seed, didn't they? How do you feel?"

"Poorly, that's the only word for it. Off my feed, can't sleep. When I do I wake up with the cold sweats. And the bowels! Let me tell you about the bowels. . . . *Hey!*"

Livermore slapped the cold pickup of the stethoscope against the bare skin of Grazer's chest. Patients liked Dr. Livermore but hated his stethoscope, swearing that he must keep it specially chilled for them. They were right. There was a thermoelectric cooling plate in the case. Livermore felt that it gave them something to think about. "Hmmrr . . ." he said, frowning, the earpieces in his ears, hearing nothing. He had plugged the stethoscope with wax a year earlier. The systolic, diastolic murmurs disturbed his concentration; he heard enough of that from his own chest. Everything was in the records in any case, since the analysis machines did a far better job than he could ever do. He flipped through the sheets and graphs.

"Button your shirt, sit down, take two of these right now. Just the thing for this condition."

He shook the large red sugar pills from the jar in his desk drawer and pointed to the plastic cup and water carafe. Grazer reached for them eagerly: this was real medicine. Livermore found the most recent X rays and snapped them into the viewer. Lovely. The new kidney was growing, as sweetly formed as a little bean. Still tiny now beside its elderly brother, but in a year's time they would be identical.

Science conquereth all, or at least almost all; he slammed the file on the table. It had been a difficult morning, and even this afternoon surgery was not as relaxing as it usually was. The old folks, the AKs, his peer group, they appreciated one another. Very early in his career he had taken his M.D.; that was all that they knew about him. A doctor, their age. He sometimes wondered if they connected him at all with the Dr.

Rex Livermore in charge of the ectogenetic program. That is, if they had ever heard of the program.

"I'm sure glad for the pills, Doc. I don't like those shots no more. But my bowels—"

"Goddamn and blast your bowels. They're as old as my bowels and in just as good shape. You're just bored, that's your trouble."

Grazer nodded approvingly at the insults—a touch of interest in an otherwise sterile existence. "Bored is the very word, Doc. The hours I spend on the pot—"

"What did you do before you retired?"

"That was a real long time ago."

"Not so long that you can't remember. And if you can't, why then you're just too old to waste food and space on. We'll just have to hook that old brain out of your skull and put it in a bottle with a label saying *senile brain* on it."

Grazer chuckled; he might have cried if someone younger had talked to him this way. "Said it was a long time ago, didn't say I forgot. Painter. Housepainter, not the artist kind, worked at it eighty years before the union threw me out and made me retire."

"Pretty good at it?"

"The best. They don't have my kind of painter around anymore."

"I can't believe that. I'm getting damn tired of the eggshell off-white superplastic eternal finish on the walls of this office. Think you could repaint it for me?"

"Paint won't stick to that stuff."

"If I find one that will?"

"I'm your man, Doc."

"It'll take time. Sure you won't mind missing all the basket-weaving, social teas, and television?"

Grazer snorted in answer, and he almost smiled.

"All right, I'll get in touch with you. Come back in a month in any case so I can look at that kidney. As for the rest, you're in perfect shape after your geriatric treatments. You're just bored with television and the damned baskets."

"You can say that again. Don't forget about that paint, hear?"

A distant silver bell chimed, and Livermore pointed to the door, picking up the phone as soon as the old man had gone. Leatha Crabb's tiny and distraught image looked up at him from the screen.

"Oh, Dr. Livermore, another bottle failure."

"I know. I was in the lab this morning. I'll be down there at fifteen hundred and we can talk about it then." He hung up and looked at his watch. Twenty minutes until the meeting— he still had time to see another patient or two. Geriatrics was not his field, and he really had very little interest in it. It was the people who interested him. He sometimes wondered if they knew how little they needed him, now that they were on constant monitoring and automated medical attention. Perhaps they just enjoyed seeing and talking to him as he did to them. No harm done in any case.

The next patient was a thin, white-haired woman who began complaining as she came through the door. Did not stop even as she put her crutches aside and sat carefully in the chair. Livermore nodded and made doodles on the pad before him and admired her flow of comment, criticism, and invective over a complaint she had covered so well and so often before. It was just a foot she was talking about, which might seem a limited area of discussion—toes, tendons, and not much else. But she had unusual symptoms, hot flushes and itching in addition to the usual pain, all of which was made even more interesting by the fact that the foot under discussion had been amputated over sixty years earlier. Phantom limbs with phantom symptoms were nothing new—there were even reported cases of completely paralyzed patients with phantom sexual impulses terminating in phantom orgasms—but the longevity of this case was certainly worth noting. He relaxed under the wave of detailed complaint, and when he finally gave her some of the sugar pills and ushered her out, they both felt a good deal better.

Catherine Ruffin and Sturtevant were already waiting in the boardroom when he came in. Sturtevant, impatient as always, was tapping green-stained fingers on the marble tabletop, one of his cancer-free tobacco-substitute cigarettes dangling from his lip. His round and thick glasses and sharp nose made him resemble an owl, but the thin line of his mouth was more like that of a turtle. It was a veritable bestiary of a face. His ears could be those of a moose, Livermore thought, then sniffed and rubbed his nose.

"Those so-called cigarettes of yours smell like burning garbage, Sturtevant, do you know that?"

"You have told him that before," Catherine Ruffin said in her slow, careful English. She had emigrated in her youth from South Africa, to marry the long-dead Mr. Ruffin, and still had the accents of her Boer youth. Full-bosomed and round in a very Dutch-housewife manner, she was nevertheless a senior administrator with a mind like a computer.

"Never mind my cigarettes." Sturtevant grubbed the butt out and instantly groped for a fresh one. "Can't you be on time just once for one of these meetings?"

Catherine Ruffin rapped with her knuckles on the table and switched on the recorder.

"Minutes of the meeting of the Genetic Guidance Council, Syracuse New Town, Tuesday, January 14, 2025. Present— Ruffin, Sturtevant, Livermore. Ruffin chairman."

"What's this I hear about more bottle failures?" Sturtevant asked.

Livermore dismissed the matter with a wave of his hand. "A few bottle failures are taken for granted. I'll look into these latest ones and have a full report for our next meeting. Just a mechanical foul-up and nothing to bother us here. What does bother me is our genetic priorities. I have a list."

He searched the pockets of his jacket, one after another, while Sturtevant frowned his snapping-turtle frown at him.

"You and your lists, Livermore. We've read enough of them. Priorities are a thing of the past. We now have a prepared program that we need only follow."

"Priorities are not outdated. And by saying that, you show a sociologist's typical ignorance of the realities of genetics."

"You're insulting!"

"It's the truth. Too bad if it hurts." He found a crumpled piece of paper in an inside pocket and smoothed it out on the table before him. "You're so used to your damn charts and graphs, demographic curves and projections that you think they are really a description of the real world—instead of being rough approximations well after the fact. I'm not going to trouble you with figures. They're so huge as to be meaningless. But I want you to consider for a moment the incredible complexity of our genetic pool. Mankind as we know it has been around about a half-million years, mutating, changing, and interbreeding. Every death in all those generations was a selection of some kind, as was every mating. Good and bad traits, pro- and anti-survival mutations, big brains and hemophilia, hairy armpits and agile fingers. Everything happened and all this was stirred up and spread through the human race. Now we say we are going to improve that race by gene selection. We have an endless reservoir of traits to draw from, ova from every woman, sperm from every man. We can analyze these for genetic composition, then feed the results to the computer to work out favorable combinations. After that we combine the sperm and ova and grow the fetus ectogenetically. If all goes well, nine months later we decant the infant of our selection and the human race has been improved by that small increment. But what is an improvement, what is a favorable combination? Dark skin is a survival trait in the tropics, but dark skin in the northern hemisphere cuts off too much ul-  .

traviolet so the body cannot manufacture vitamin D, and rickets follows. Everything is relative."

"We have been over this ground before," Catherine Ruffin said.

"But not often enough. If we don't constantly renew and review our goals, we are going to start down a one-way road. Once genetic traits have been discarded they are gone forever. In a way the team in San Diego New City have an easier job. They have a specific goal. They are out to build new breeds of men, specific types for different environments. Like the spacemen who can live without physical or mental breakdowns during the decade-long trips to the outer planets. Or the low-temperature- and low-pressure-resistant types for Mars settlers. They can discard genes ruthlessly and aim for a clear and well-established goal. We simply aim to improve—and what a vague ambition that is. But while we are making this new race of supermen what will we lose? Will new-man be pink, and if so, what has happened to the Oriental and the Negro—"

"For God's sake, Livermore, let us not start on that again," Sturtevant shouted. "We have fixed charts, rules, regulations, everything carefully mapped out for all the operations."

"I said you had no real knowledge of genetics and that proves it once again. You simply can't get it through your head that genetic selection does not work that way. With each selection the game starts completely over again. As they say in the historical 3V's, it's a brand-new ball game. The entire world is born anew with every child."

"I think you tend to overdramatize," Catherine Ruffin said stolidly.

"Not in the slightest. Genes are not bricks. We can't use them to build a desired structure to order. We just aim for optimum, then see what we have and try again. No directives can lay down the details of every choice or control every random combination. Every technician is a small god, making real decisions of life and death. And some of these decisions are questionable in the long run."

"Impossible," Sturtevant said, and Catherine Ruffin nodded agreement.

"No, it's just going to be very expensive. We must find a closer examination of every change made and get some predictions of where we are going."

"You are out of order, Dr. Livermore," Catherine Ruffin broke in. "Your proposal has been made in the past, a budget forecast was estimated, and the entire matter was then turned down because of cost. This was not our decision you will recall, but came down from Genguidecounchief. We accomplish nothing by raking over these well-raked coals yet another time. There is new business we must consider that I wish to place before this council."

Livermore had the beginnings of a headache, and he fumbled a pill from the carrier in his pocket. The other two were talking, and he paid them no attention at all.

When Leatha Crabb hung up the phone after talking with Dr. Livermore, she felt as though she wanted to cry. She had been working long hours for weeks and not getting enough sleep. Her eyes stung, and she was a little ashamed of this unaccustomed weakness: she was the sort of person who simply did not cry, woman or no. But seventeen bottle failures, seventeen deaths. Seventeen tiny lives snuffed out before they had barely begun to live. It hurt, almost as though they had been real children. . . .

"So small you can't hardly see it," Veazy said. The laboratory assistant held one of the disconnected bottles up to the light and gave it a shake to swish the liquid about inside it. "You sure it's dead?"

"Stop that!" Leatha snapped, then curbed her temper: she had always prided herself on the way that she treated those who worked beneath her. "Yes, they are all dead, I've checked that. Decant, freeze, and label them. I'll want to do examinations later."

Veazy nodded and took the bottle away. She wondered what had possessed her thinking of them as lives, children. She must be tired. They were groups of growing cells with no more personality than the cells grouped in the wart on the back of her hand. She rubbed at it, reminding herself again that she ought to have it taken care of. A handsome, well-formed girl in her early thirties, with hair the color of honey and tanned skin to match. But her hair was cropped short, close to her head, and she wore not the slightest trace of makeup, while the richness of her figure was lost in the heavy folds of her white laboratory smock. She was too young for it, but a line of worry was already beginning to form between her eyes. When she bent over her microscope, peering at the stained slide, the furrow deepened.

The bottle failures troubled her, deeply, more than she liked to admit. The program had gone so well the past few years that she was beginning to take it for granted, already looking ahead to the genetic possibilities of the second generation. It took a decided effort to forget all this and turn back to the simple mechanical problems of ectogenesis. . . .

Strong arms wrapped about her from behind; the hands pressed firmly against the roundness of her body below the waist; hard lips kissed the nape of her neck.

"Don't!" she said, surprised, pulling away. She look around. Her husband. Gust dropped his arms at once, stepping back from her.

"You don't have to get angry," he said. "We're married you know, and no one is watching."

"It's not your pawing me I don't like. But I'm working, can't you see that?"

Leatha turned to face him, angry at his physical touch despite her words. He stood dumbly before her, a solid black-haired and dark-complexioned man with slightly protruding lower lip that made him look, now, as though he were pouting.

"You needn't look so put out. It's work time, not play time."

"Damn little playtime anymore." He glanced quickly around to see if anyone was within earshot. "Not the way it was when we were first married. You were pretty affectionate then." He reached out a slow finger and pressed it to his midriff.

"Don't do that." She drew away, raising her hands to cover herself. "It's been absolute hell here today. A defective valve in one of the hormone feed lines, discovered too late. We lost seventeen bottles. In an early stage, luckily."

"So what's the loss? There must be a couple of billion sperm and ova in the freezers. They'll pair some more and put you back in business."

"Think of the work and labor in gene-matching, all wasted."

"That's what technicians are paid for. It will give them something to do. Look, can we forget work for a while, take off an evening? Go to Old Town. There's a place there I heard about, Sharm's. They have real cult cooking and entertainment."

"Can't we talk about it later? This really isn't the time. . . ."

"By Christ, it never is. I'll be back here at seventeen thirty. See if you can't possibly make your mind up by then."

He pushed angrily out of the door, but the automatic closing mechanism prevented him from slamming it behind him. Something had gone out of life, he wasn't sure just what. He loved Leatha and she loved him, he was sure of that, but something was missing. They both had their work to do, but it had never caused trouble before. They were used to it, even staying up all night sometimes, working in the same room in quiet companionship. Then coffee, perhaps as dawn was breaking, a drowsy pleasant fatigue, falling into bed, making love. It just wasn't that way anymore and he couldn't think why. At the elevators he entered the nearest and called out, "Fifty." The doors closed, and the car fell smoothly away. They would go out tonight: he was resolved that this evening would be different.

Only after he had emerged from the elevator did he realize that it had stopped at the wrong floor. Fifteen, not fifty; the number analyzer in the elevator computer always seemed to have trouble with those two. Before he could turn, the doors shut behind him, and he noticed the two old men frowning in his direction. He was on one of the eldster floors. Instead of waiting for another car, he turned away from their angry looks and hurried down the hall. There were other old people about, some shuffling along, others riding powered chairs, and he looked straight ahead so he wouldn't catch their eyes. They resented youngsters coming here.

Well, he resented them occupying his brand-new building. That wasn't a nice thought, and he was sorry at once for even thinking a thing like that. This wasn't his building; he was just one of the men on the design team who had stayed on for construction. The eldsters had as much right here as he did, more so, since this was their home. And a pleasant compromise it had been, too. This building, New Town, was designed for the future, but the future was rather slow coming, since you could accelerate almost everything in the world except fetal growth. Nine months from conception to birth, in either bottle or womb. Then the slow years of childhood, the quick years of puberty. It would be wasteful for the city to stay vacant all those years.

That was where the eldsters came in, the leftover debris of an overpopulated world. Geriatrics propped them up and kept them going. They were growing older together, the last survivors of the greedy generations. They were the parents who had fewer children and even fewer grandchildren as the realities of famine, disease, and the general unwholesomeness of life were driven home to them. Not that they had done this voluntarily. Left alone they would have responded as every other generation of mankind had done: selfishly. If the world is going to be overpopulated—it is going to be overpopulated with *my* kids. But the breakthrough in geriatric treatment and drugs came along at that moment and provided a far better carrot than had ever been held in front of the human donkey before. The fewer children you had the more treatment you received. The birthrate dived to zero almost overnight. The indifferent overpopulators had decided to overpopulate with themselves instead of their children. If life was being granted, they preferred to have it granted to them.

The result was that a child of the next generation might have, in addition to his mother and father, a half-dozen surviving relatives who were elders. A married couple might have ten or fifteen older relatives, all of them alone in the world, looking to their only younger kin. There could be no question of this aging horde moving in with the present generation, who had neither room for them nor money to support them. They were a government burden and would remain so. A decreasing burden that required less money every year as old machinery, despite the wonders of medicine, finally ran down. When the new cities were being designed for the future, scientifically planned generations, the wise decision had been made to move the eldsters into them. The best of food, care, and medicine could be provided with the minimum effort and expense. Life in the older cities would be happier, relieved of the weight of the solid block of aging citizenry. And since the geriatric drugs didn't seem to work too well past the middle of the second century, a timetable could be established for what was euphemistically called "phasing out." Dying was a word no one liked to use. So as the present inhabitants were phased out to the phasing place of their choice, the growing generations would move in. All neat. All tidy.

As long as you stayed away from the eldster floors.

Looking straight ahead, Gust went swiftly along the street-like corridor. Ignoring the steam rooms and bathing rooms, tropical gardens and sandy beaches that opened off to either side. And the people. The next bank of elevators was a welcome sight, and this time he very clearly enunciated "fif-tee" as the door closed.

When he reached the end of the unfinished corridor, the work shift was just going off duty. The flooring terminated here, and ahead was just the rough gray of raw cement still showing the mold marks where it had been cast in place; floodlights stood high on wiry legs.

"Been having trouble with the squatter, Mr. Crabb," the shift boss complained. These men had grown up in a world of smoothly operating machines and were hurt when they occasionally proved fallible.

"I'll take a look at it. Anything in the hopper?"

"Half full. Should I empty it out?"

"No, leave it. I'll try a run before I call maintenance."

As the motors on the machines were turned off one by one, an echoing silence fell on the immense and cavernlike area. The men went away, their footsteps loud, calling to each other, until Gust was alone. He climbed the ladder to the top of the hulking squatter and unlocked the computer controls. When he typed a quick condition query the readout revealed nothing wrong. These semi-intelligent machines could analyze most of their own troubles and deliver warnings, but there were still occasional failures beyond their capacity to handle or even recognize. Gust closed the computer and pressed the *power* button.

There was a far-off rumble and the great bulk of the machine shuddered as it came to life. Most of the indicator lights blinked on red, turning swiftly to green as the motors came to speed. When the operation-ready light also turned green, he squinted at the right-hand television screen, which showed the floor level buried under the squatter. The newly laid flooring ended abruptly where the machine had stopped. He backed it a few feet so the sensors could come into operation, then started it forward again at the crawling pace of working speed. As soon as the edge was reached the laying began again. The machine guided itself and controlled the mix and pouring. About all the operator had to do was turn the entire apparatus on and off. Gust watched the hypnotically smooth flow of new floor appear and could see nothing wrong. It was pleasant here, doing a simple yet important job like this.

A warning buzzer sounded and a light began flashing red on the controls. He blinked and had a quick glimpse of something black on the screen before it moved swiftly out of sight. He stopped the forward motion and put the squatter into reverse again, backing the huge mass a good ten feet before killing all the power and climbing back down. The newly laid plastic flooring was still hot under his feet and he trod gingerly almost up to the forward edge. There was a cavity in the flooring here, like a bowl or a bubble a foot wide. As though the machine had burped while spewing out its flow. Perhaps it had. The technicians would set it right. He spoke a note to call them in his pocket phone, killed all except the standby lights, then went back to the elevators. Calling out his floor number very carefully.

Dr. Livermore and Leatha were bent over a worktable in the lab, heads lowered as though at a wake. As perhaps they were. Gust came in quietly, listening, not wanting to interrupt.

"There were some of the most promising new strains here," Leatha said. "The Reilly-Stone in particular. I don't know how much computer time was used in the preliminary selection, but the technicians must have put in a hundred hours on this fertilized ovum alone."

"Isn't that a little unusual?" Livermore asked.

"I imagine so, but it was the first application of the Bershock multiple-division cross-trait selection, and you know how those things go."

"I do indeed. It will be easier the next time. Send the records back, noting the failures. Get them started on replacements. Hello, Gust, I didn't hear you come in."

"I didn't want to bother you."

"No bother. We are finished in any case. Had some bottle failures today."

"So I heard. Do you know why?"

"If I knew everything, I would be God, wouldn't I?"

Leatha looked at the old man, shocked. "But Doctor, we do know why the embryos were killed. The valve failed on the input—"

"But why did the valve fail? There are reasons beyond reasons in everything."

"We're going to Old Town, Doctor," Gust said, uncomfortable with this kind of abstract conversation and eager to change the subject.

"Don't let me stop you. Don't bring back any infections, hear?"

Livermore turned to leave, but the door opened before he reached it. A man stood there, looking at them without speaking. He entered, and the silence and the severe set of his features struck them silent as well. When the door had closed behind him he called their names in a deep voice, looking at each of them in turn as he spoke.

"Dr. Livermore, Leatha Crabb, Gust Crabb. I am here to see you. My name is Blalock."

It was clear that Livermore did not enjoy being addressed in this manner. "Call my secretary for an appointment. I'm busy now." He started to leave, but Blalock raised his hand, at the same time taking a thin wallet from his pocket.

"I would like to see you now, Doctor. This is my identification."

Livermore could not have left without pushing the man aside. He stopped and blinked at the golden badge.

"FBI. What on earth are you after here?"

"A killer." A stunned silence followed. "I can tell you now, though I would appreciate your not telling anyone else, that one of the technicians working here is an agent from the bureau. He makes regular reports to Washington about conditions on the project."

"Meddling and spying!" Livermore was angry.

"Not at all. The government has a large investment here and believes in protecting it—and in guarding the taxpayers' money. You have had a number of bottle failures here in the first weeks after implanting."

"Accidents, just accidents," Leatha said, then flushed and was silent when Blalock turned his cold, unsmiling gaze on her.

"Are they? We don't think so. There are four other New Towns in the United States, all of them with projects working along the same lines as yours. They have had bottle failures as well, but not in the numbers you have here."

"A few more in one place or another means nothing," Livermore said. "The law of averages covers minor differences."

"I'm sure it does. Minor differences, Doctor. But the rate of failure here is ten times higher than that of the other laboratories. For every bottle failure they have, you have ten. For their ten, you have a hundred. I am not here by accident. Since you are in charge of this project, I would like a letter from you giving me permission to go anywhere on the premises and to speak with anyone."

"My secretary will have gone by now. In the morning—"

"I have the letter here, typed on your stationery. It just needs your signature."

Livermore's anger was more forced than real. "I won't have this. Stealing my office supplies. I won't have it."

"Don't be rude, Doctor. Your stationery is printed by the Government Printing Office. They supplied it to me to make my job easier. Don't *you* make it harder."

There was a coldness in that *you* that stopped Livermore and sent him fumbling with his pen to sign the letter. Gust and Leatha looked on, not knowing what to do. Blalock folded the letter and put it back into his pocket.

"I'll want to talk to you all later," he said, and left. Livermore waited until he was gone, then went out as well, without a word.

"What an awful man," Leatha said.

"It doesn't matter how awful he is if what he said was right. Bottle sabotage—can that be?"

"Easily enough done."

"But why should it be done?" Gust asked. "That's the real question. It's so meaningless, so wanton. There's simply no reason."

"That's Blalock's worry, what he's getting paid for. Right now I've had a long day, and I'm hungry and more concerned with my dinner. You go ahead to the apartment and defrost something. I won't be a minute finishing up these tests."

He was angry. "The first blush is off our marriage, isn't it? You've completely forgotten that I asked you out to dinner in Old Town."

"It's not that . . ." Leatha said, then stopped, because it really was. Gust wasn't completely right; the work was so distracting, and then this Blalock person. She tidied up quickly without finishing the tests and took off her smock. Her dress was dark gray and no less severe. It was thin, too, designed for wear in the constant temperature of New Town.

"If it's cold outside, I should get a coat."

"Of course it's cold out. It's still March. I checked out a car earlier and put your heavy coat in it. Mine as well."

They went in silence to the elevator and down to the parking level. The bubble-dome car was at the ready ramp; the top swung up when he turned the handle. They put on their coats before they climbed in, and Gust turned on the heat as he started the car. The battery-powered electric engine hummed strongly as they headed for the exit, the doors opened automatically for them as the car approached. There was a brief wait in the lock while the inner door closed before the outer one opened; then they emerged on the sloping ramp that led up to Old Town.

It had been a long time since their last visit outside the New Town walls, and the difference was striking. The streets were patched and had an unkempt appearance, with dead grass and weeds protruding from the cracks. There were pieces of paper caught against the curbs, and when they passed an empty lot a cloud of dust swirled around them. Leatha sank deeper into her seat and shivered even though the heater was going full on. The buildings had a weathered and even a decayed look about them, the wooden buildings most of all, and the limbs of the gray trees were bare as skeletons in the fading daylight. Gust tried to read the street signs and lost his way once, but finally found a garish spotlit sign that read SHARM's. Either they were early or business wasn't booming, because they could park right in front of the door. Leatha didn't wait but ran the few feet through the chill wind while Gust locked up the car. Inside, Sharm himself was waiting to greet them.

"Welcome, welcome," he said with bored professional exuberance. A tall, wide Negro, very black, wearing a brilliant kaftan and red fez. "I've got just the table for you, right at the ringside."

"That will be nice," Gust said.

Sharm's hospitality was easily understood; there was only one other couple in the restaurant. A heavy smell of cooking hung in the air, some of it not too fresh, and the tablecloth was a cartography of ancient stains only partially removed.

"Like a drink?" Sharm asked.

"I guess so. Any suggestions?"

"Bet your life. Bloody Mary with tequila, the house special. I'll fetch a jug."

They must have been premixed, because he was back a

moment later with the tray and two menus tucked under his arm. He poured their drinks and then one for himself and pulled up a chair to join them. The atmosphere of Sharm's was nothing if not relaxed.

"Salud," he said, and they drank. Leatha puckered her lips and put her glass down quickly, but Gust liked the sharp bite of the drink.

"Great. Never tasted one before. How about the menu—any house specials there?"

"Everything's special. My wife is great at any kind of cult-food. Black-eyed peas and corn dodgers, kosher hot dogs and Boston baked beans, we got them all. Just take your pick. Music's starting now, and Aikane will be in to dance in about a half an hour. Drink up, folks, these are on the house."

"Very kind," Gust said, sipping his.

"Not at all. I want to pump your brain, Mr. Crabb, and I pay in advance. I saw you on 3V last week talking about New Town. Pretty fancy if I say so myself. What's the chances of opening a restaurant in your place?" He drained his glass and poured himself another one, topping up their glasses at the same time.

"That's not easy to say."

"What's easy? Living on the dole and maybe blowing your brains out from boredom, that's easy. Me, I got bigger plans. Everyone likes cultfood. Eldsters, reminds them of the old days; kids think it's real pit-blasting. But people here in Old Town don't eat out much, not that much loose pesos around. Got to go to where the change is. New Town. What're the odds?"

"I can find out. But you have to realize, Mr. Sharm . . ."

"Just plain Sharm. A first name."

"You have to realize that the eldsters have special diets, special sanitary regulations on their food."

"This beanery isn't bug-finky. We got plenty of sanitary examinations."

"That's not what I meant, I'm sorry, don't misunderstand me. It's special diets really, to go with the medication. Really special if you understand, practically worked out and cooked in the labs."

A loud drumming interrupted him as a sad-looking American Indian did a quick Indian war beat on the bass drum. He switched on the audio with his toe, then worked rhythm on the traps as the recording played an Israeli folk song. It was all very unimpressive—but loud.

"What about the younger people then?" Sharm shouted to be heard. "Like you folks. You come this far to eat cultfood, why not have it closer to home?"

"There's not enough of us, not yet. Just technicians and construction teams. No more than ten percent of the children who will occupy the city have even been born yet, so I don't know if you even have a big enough group to draw from. Later, perhaps."

"Yeah, later. Big deal. Wait twenty years." Sharm sank down, wrapped in gloom, moving only to empty the jug into his glass. He rose reluctantly when another customer entered, ending the embarrassing interlude.

They both ordered mixed plates of all the specialties and a bottle of wine, since Leatha was not that enthusiastic about the Bloody Marys. While they ate, a slightly dark-skinned girl, of possibly Hawaiian descent, emerged from the rear and did an indifferent hula. Gust looked on with some pleasure, since she wore only a low-slung grass skirt with many tufts missing and was enough overweight to produce a great deal of jiggling that added a certain something to the dance.

"Vulgar," Leatha said, wiping her eyes with her napkin after taking too much horseradish on her gefilte fish.

"I don't think so." He put his hand on her leg under the table, and she pushed it away without changing expression.

"Don't do that in public."

"Or in private either! Damn it, Lea, what's happening to

our marriage? We both work, A-OK, that's fine, but what about our life together? What about our raising a newborn?"

"We've talked about this before. . . ."

"You've said no before, that's what has happened. Look, Lea honey, I'm not trying to push you back to the Middle Ages with one in the hand, one on the hip, and one in the belly. Women have been relieved at last of all the trouble and danger of childbirth, but by God they are still women. Not men with different builds. A lot of couples don't want kids, fine, and I agree that crèche-raised babies have all the advantages. But other couples are raising babies, and women can even nurse them after the right injections."

"You don't think I'd do *that?*"

"I'm not asking you to do *that*—as you so sweetly put it—though it's nowhere near as shocking as your tone of voice indicates. I would just like you to consider raising a child, a son. He would be with us evenings and weekends. It would be fun."

"Not exactly my idea of fun."

The answer that was on his lips was sharp, bitter, and nasty and would have surely started an even worse fight, but before he could speak she grabbed him by the arm.

"Gust, there in the corner at that back table—isn't that the horrible person who was at the lab?"

"Blalock? Yes, it looks like him. Though it's hard to tell in this over-romantic light. What difference does it make?"

"Don't you realize that if he is here, he followed us and is watching us? He thinks *we* may have been responsible for the bottle failures."

"You're imagining too much. Maybe he just likes cultfood. He looks the type who might even live on it."

Yet why was he at the restaurant? If he was there to worry them, he succeeded. Leatha pushed her plate away and Gust had little appetite as well. He called for the check and, depressed in spirits, they shrugged into their coats and went out into the cold night, past the silent and accusing eyes of Sharm, who knew he was not going to live the new life in New Town no matter how much he wanted to.

Many years before, Catherine Ruffin had developed a simple plan to enable her to get her work done, a plan that was not part of her work routine. She had discovered, early in her career, that she had an orderly mind and a highly retentive memory that were great assets in her work. But she had to study facts slowly and deliberately without interruptions, something that was impossible during the routine of a busy office day. Staying after work was not the answer; the phone still rang, and she was often too fatigued to make the most of the opportunity. Nor was it always possible to bring work back to her apartment. Since she had always been an early riser, she found that her colleagues were all slugabeds and would rather do anything than come to work five minutes early. She went to her office now at seven every morning and had the solid core of her work done before anyone else appeared. It was a practical and satisfactory solution to the problem and one that appealed to her. However, she was so used to being alone at these early hours that she looked upon anyone else's presence as an interruption and an annoyance.

She found the note on her desk when she came in; it certainly had not been there when she left the previous evening. It was typed and quite clear:

Please see me now in bottlelab. Urgent. R. Livermore.

She was annoyed at the tone and the interruption and, perhaps, the idea that someone had actually come to work before her. Been here all night, more likely; the scientific staff tended to do that unless specifically forbidden. Still it looked urgent, so she had better comply. There would be time for recriminations later if Livermore had overstepped himself. She put her massive purse in the bottom drawer of her desk and went to the elevator.

There was no one in sight on the laboratory floor, nor in the office when she went in. A motion caught her eye, and she turned to look at the door that led into the bottle rooms; it was closed now—yet she had the feeling that it had moved a moment before. Perhaps Livermore had gone through and was waiting for her. As she started forward there was the sharp sound of breaking glass from behind the door, again and again. At the same instant an alarm bell began ringing loudly in the distance. She gasped and stood frozen an instant at the suddenness of it. Someone was in there, breaking the apparatus. The bottles! Running heavily, she threw the door open and rushed inside.

Glass littered the floor; fluids still dripped from the shattered bottles. There was no one there. She looked about her, stunned by the destruction and the suddenness, shocked by the abrupt termination of these carefully plotted lives. The almost invisible masses of cells that were to be the next generation were dying, even while she stood there gaping. And there was nothing she could do about it. It was horrifying, and she could not move. Shards of glass were at her feet and in the midst of the glass and the widening pool of liquid was a hammer. The killer's weapon? She bent down and picked the hammer up and when she stood upright again someone spoke behind her.

"Turn about slowly. Don't do anything you'll regret."

Catherine Ruffin was out of her depth, floundering. Everything was happening too fast, and she could not grasp the reality of it.

"What?" she said. "What?" Turning to look at the stranger in the doorway behind her, who held what appeared to be a revolver.

"Put that hammer down slowly," he said.

"Who are you?" The hammer clattered on the floor.

"I'll ask the same thing of you. I am Blalock, FBI. My identification is here." He held out his badge.

"Catherine Ruffin. I was sent for. By Dr. Livermore. What does this mean?"

"Can you prove that?"

"Of course. This note, read it for yourself."

He pinched it between the tips of his fingers and looked at it briefly before dropping it into an envelope and putting it into his pocket. His gun had vanished.

"Anyone could have typed that," he said. "You could have typed it yourself."

"I don't know what you're talking about. It was on my desk when I came to work a short while ago. I read it, came here, heard the sound of glass being broken, entered. Saw this hammer and picked it up. Nothing else."

Blalock looked at her closely for a long instant, then nodded and waved her after him to the outer office. "Perhaps. We will check that out later. For the moment you will sit here quietly while I make some calls."

He had a list of numbers, and the first one he dialed rang a long time before it was answered. Leatha Crabb's sleep-puffed face finally appeared on the screen.

"What do you want?" she asked, her eyes widening when she saw who the caller was.

"Your husband. I wish to talk to him."

"He's—he's asleep." She looked about uneasily, and Blalock did not miss the hesitation in her voice.

"Is he? Then wake him and bring him to the phone."

"Why? Just tell me why?"

"Then I will be there at once. Would that embarrass you, Mrs. Crabb? Will you either wake your husband—or tell me the truth?"

She lowered her eyes and spoke in a small voice.

"He's not here. He hasn't been here all night."

"Do you know where he is?"

"No. And I don't care. We had a difference of opinion, and he stamped out. And that is all I wish to tell you." The screen went dark. Blalock instantly dialed another number. This time there was no answer. He turned to Catherine Ruffin, who sat, still dazed by the rapid passage of events.

"I want you to take me to Dr. Livermore's office."

Still not sure what had happened, she did exactly as he asked. The door was unlocked. Blalock pushed by her and looked in. The pale early sunlight streamed in through the glass walls. The office was empty. Blalock sniffed at the air, as though searching out a clue, then pointed to the door in the right-hand wall.

"Where does this lead?"

"I'm sure I don't know."

"Stay here."

Catherine Ruffin disliked his tone, but before she could tell him so, he was across the room and standing to one side as he carefully opened the door. Livermore lay asleep on the couch inside, with a thin blanket pulled over him and clutched to his neck by one hand. Blalock went in silently and took him by the wrist, his forefinger inside below the base of the thumb. Livermore opened his eyes at the touch, blinked, and pulled his hand away.

"What the devil are you doing here?"

"Taking your pulse. You don't mind, do you?"

"I certainly do." He sat up and threw the blanket aside. "I'm the doctor here, and I do the pulse-taking. I asked you what you meant by breaking in like this?"

"There has been more sabotage in the bottle room. I had alarms rigged. I found this woman there with a hammer."

"Catherine! Why would you do a foolish thing like that?"

"How dare you! You sent a note, I received it, asking me to go there, to trap me—perhaps *you* broke those bottles!"

Livermore yawned and rubbed at his eyes, then bent and groped under the couch for his shoes.

"That's what Dick Tracy here thinks." He grunted as he pulled a shoe on. "Finds me sleeping here, doesn't believe that, tries to take my pulse and see if I've been running around with that hammer, faster pulse than a sleeping pulse. Idiot!" He snapped the last word and rose to his feet.

"I am in charge of this project, it's *my* project. Before you accuse me of sabotaging it, you had better find a better reason than baseless suspicion. Find out who typed that fool note, and maybe you will have a lead."

"I fully intend to," Blalock said, and the phone rang.

"For you," Livermore said, and passed it to the FBI man, who listened silently, then issued a sharp command.

"Bring him here."

Before she left, Catherine Ruffin made a sworn statement, and it was recorded on Livermore's office machine. Then Livermore did the same thing. Yes, he had not been in his apartment. He had worked late in his office, and as he did many times, he had slept on the couch in the adjoining room. He had gone to sleep around 0300 hours and had neither seen nor heard anything since that time, not until Blalock had wakened him. Yes, it was possible to get from the bottle room by way of the rear door, and through the business office to this office, but he had not done that. He was just finishing the statement when a stranger, with the same dour expression and conservative cut of clothes as Blalock, brought Gust Crabb in. Blalock dismissed the man and turned the full power of his attention on Gust.

"You were not in your apartment all night. Where were you?"

"Go to hell."

"Your attitude is not appreciated. Your whereabouts are unknown—up to a few minutes ago when you arrived at your office. During the time in question someone broke into the bottle room and sabotaged this project with a hammer. I ask you again. Where were you?"

Gust, who was a simple man in all except his work, now enacted a pantomime of worry, guilt, and unhappiness complete with averted eyes and a fine beading of sweat on his forehead. Livermore felt sorry for him and turned away and harrumphed and found his tie and busied himself knotting it.

"Talk," Blalock said loudly, using all the pressure he could to increase the other's discomfort.

"It's not what you think," Gust said in a hollow voice.

"Give me a complete statement or I'll arrest you now for willful sabotage of a government project."

The silence lengthened uncomfortably. It was Livermore who broke it.

"For God's sake, Gust, tell him. You couldn't have done a thing like this. What is it—a girl?" He snorted through his nose at the sudden flushing of Gust's face. "It is. Spill it out, it won't go beyond this room. The government doesn't care about your sex life, and I'm well past the age where these things have much importance."

"No one's business," Gust muttered.

"Crime is the government's business—" Blalock said but was cut off by Livermore.

"But love affairs aren't, so will you shut up? Tell him the truth, Gust, tell him or you'll be in trouble. It was a girl?"

"Yes," Gust said most reluctantly, staring down at the floor.

"Good. You stayed the night with her. A few details would be appreciated, and then you will no longer be a suspect."

Under painful prodding Gust managed to mumble these details. The girl was a secretary with the engineering commission; he had known her a long time. She liked him, but he stayed away from her until last night, a fight with Leatha, he had stamped out, found himself at Georgette's door—you won't tell anyone?—and she took him in, one thing led to another. There it was.

"There it is," Livermore said. "Do your work, Blalock,

Gust will be here with me if you want him. Find the girl, get her story, then leave us alone. Investigate the mysterious note, take fingerprints from the hammer, and do whatever you do in this kind of thing. But leave us be. Unless you have some evidence and want to arrest me, get out of my office."

When they were alone, Livermore made some coffee in his anteroom and brought a cup to Gust. Who stood looking out at the hillside now shaded by clouds and curtained with rain.

"You think I'm a fool," Gust said.

"Not at all. I think there's trouble between you and Leatha and that you're making it worse instead of better."

"But what can I do!"

Livermore ignored the note of pleading in the man's voice and stirred his coffee to cool it. "You know what to do without bothering me. It's your problem. You're an adult. Solve it. With your wife or family counseling or whatever. Right now I have something slightly more important to think about with this sabotage and the FBI and the rest of it."

Gust sat up straighter and almost smiled. "You're right. My problem isn't that world-shaking and I'll take care of it. Do you realize that you and I and Leatha seem to be the FBI's prime suspects? He must have called the apartment if he knew I wasn't there. And he followed us to the restaurant last night. Why us?"

"Propinquity, I imagine. We and the technicians are the only ones who go in and out of the bottle rooms at will. And one of the technicians is a plant, he told us that, so they are being watched from their own ranks. Which leaves us."

"I don't understand it at all. Why *should* anyone want to sabotage the bottles?"

Livermore nodded slowly.

"That's the question that Blalock should be asking. Until he finds out the why of this business he's never going to find who is doing it."

*  *  *

Leatha came silently into the office and said nothing as she
closed the door behind her. Gust looked up from the papers
on his desk, surprised; she had never been in his office before.

"Why did you do it, why?" she said in a hoarse voice, her
face drawn, ugly with the strain of her emotions. He was
stunned into silence.

"Don't think I don't know—that Blalock came to see me
and told me everything. Where you were last night, about *her,*
so don't try to deny it. He wasn't lying, I could tell."

Gust was tired and not up to playing a role in a bitter
exchange. "Why would he tell you these things?" he asked.

"Why? That's fairly obvious. He doesn't care about you or
me, just his job. He suspects me, I could tell that, thinks I
could sabotage the bottles. He wanted me to lose my temper,
and I did, not that it did any good. Now answer me—*pig*—
why did you do it? That's all I want to know, why?"

Gust looked at his fists clenched on the desk before him. "I
wanted to, I suppose."

"You wanted to!" Leatha shrieked the words. "That's the
kind of man you are, you wanted to, so you just went there.
I suppose I don't have to bother asking you what happened—
my imagination is good enough for that."

"Lea, this isn't the time or place to talk about this—"

"Oh, isn't it? It doesn't take any special place for me to tell
you what I think of you, you . . . traitor!"

His fixed and silent face only angered her more, beyond
words. On the table close by was a cutaway model of New
Town, prepared when it was still in the design stage. She seized
it in both hands, raised it over her head, and hurled it at him.
But it was too light, and it spun end over end in the air,
striking him harmlessly on the arm and falling to the floor
where it broke, shedding small chunks of plastic.

"You shouldn't have done that," Gust said, bending to

retrieve the model. "Here you've broken it and it costs money. I'm responsible for it." The only response was a slam, and he looked up to see that Leatha was gone.

Anger filled her, stronger than anything she had ever experienced before in her life. Her chest hurt and she had trouble breathing. How could he have done this to her? She walked fast, until she had to gasp for breath, through the corridors of New Town. Aimlessly, she thought, until she looked at the entrance to the nearby offices and realized that she had had a goal all the time. CENTENGCOM, the sign read, an unattractive acronym for the Central Engineering Commission. Could she enter here, and if she did, what could she say? A man came out and held the door for her; she couldn't begin to explain why she was standing there so she went in. There was a floor plan on the facing wall, and she pressed the button labeled SECRE-TARIAL POOL, then turned in the indicated direction.

It really proved quite easy to do. A number of girls worked in the large room surrounded by the hum of office machines and typers. People were going in and out, and she stood for a minute until a young man carrying a sheaf of papers emerged. He stopped when she spoke to him.

"Could you help me? I'm looking for a . . . Miss Georgette Booker. I understand she works here."

"Georgy, sure. Over there at that desk against the far wall, wearing the white shirt or whatever you call it. Want me to tell her you're here?"

"No, that's fine, thank you very much. I'll talk to her my-self."

Leatha waited until he had gone, then looked over the bent heads to the desk against the far wall and gasped. Yes, it had to be that girl, white blouse and dark hair, rich chocolate-colored skin. Leatha pushed on into the office and took a roundabout path through the aisles between the desks that would enable her to pass by the girl, slowing as she came close.

She was pretty, no denying that, she was pretty. A nicely sculptured face, thin-bridged nose, but too heavily made up with the purple lipstick that was in now. And tiny silver stars dusted across one cheek and onto her chest. There was enough of that, and most of it showing too in the new peekie-look thin fabric, almost completely transparent. The large breasts rose halfway out of the blouse, and through it the black circles of her nipples could be seen. Feeling the eyes on her, Georgette looked up and smiled warmly at Leatha, who turned away and walked past her, faster and faster.

By the middle of the afternoon Dr. Livermore was very tired. He had had little sleep the previous night, and the FBI man's visit had disturbed him. Then he had to put the technicians to work clearing up the mess in the bottle room, and while they could be trusted to do a good job, he nevertheless wanted to check it out for himself when they were done. He would do that and then perhaps take a nap. He pushed the elaborate scrawled codes of the gene charts away from him and rose stiffly. He was beginning to feel his years. Perhaps it was time to consider joining his patients in the warm comfort of the geriatric levels. He smiled at the thought and started for the labs.

There was little formality among his staff, and he never thought to knock on the door of Leatha's private office when he found it closed. His thoughts were on the bottles. He pushed the door open and found her bent over the desk, her face in her hands, crying.

"What is wrong?" he called out before he realized that it might have been wiser to leave quietly. He had a sudden insight as to what the trouble might be.

She raised a tear-dampened and reddened face, and he closed the door behind him.

"I'm sorry to walk in like this. I should have knocked."

"No, Dr. Livermore, that's all right." She dabbed at her eyes with a tissue. "I'm sorry you have to see me like this."

"Perfectly normal. I think I understand."

"No, it has nothing to do with bottles."

"I know. It's that girl, isn't it? I had hoped you wouldn't find out."

Leatha was too distraught to ask him how he knew but began sobbing again at this reminder. Livermore wanted to leave but could think of no way to do it gracefully. At the present moment he just could not be interested in this domestic tragedy.

"I saw her," Leatha said. "I went there, God knows why, driven, I suppose. To see just what he preferred to me was so humiliating. A blowsy thing, vulgar, the obvious kind of thing a man might like. And she's *colored.* How could he have done this. . . ."

The sobbing began again and Livermore stopped, his hand on the knob. He had wanted to leave before he became involved himself. Now he was involved.

"I remember your talking to me about it once," he said. "Where you come from. Somewhere in the South, isn't it?"

The complete irrelevancy of the question stopped Leatha, even slowed her tears. "Yes, Mississippi. A little fishing town near Biloxi."

"I thought so. And you grew up with a good jolt of racial bias. The worst thing you have against this girl is the fact that she is black."

"I never said that. But there are things . . ."

"No, there are *not* things, if you mean races or colors or religions or anything like that. I am shocked to hear you, a geneticist, even suggest an idea like that. Deeply shocked. Though, unhappily, I'm not surprised."

"I don't care about her. It's him, Gust, what he did to me."

"He did nothing at all. My God, woman, you want equality

and equal pay and freedom from childbearing—and you have all these things. So you can't very well complain if you throw a man out of your bed, and he goes to someone else."

"What do you mean?" she gasped, shocked.

"I'm sorry. It's not my place to talk like this. I became angry. You're an adult; you'll have to make your own decisions about your marriage."

"No. You can't leave it like that. You said something, and you're going to tell me exactly what you meant."

Livermore was still angry. He dropped into a chair and ordered his thoughts before he spoke again.

"I'm an old-fashioned M.D., so perhaps I had better talk from a doctor's point of view. You're a young woman in good health in the prime of your life. If you came to me for marriage counseling I would tell you that your marriage appears to be in trouble and you are probably the cause, the original cause, that is. Though it has gone far enough now so that you both have a good deal to be responsible for. It appears that in your involvement in your work, your major interests outside your marriage, you have lost your sexuality. You have no time for it. And I am not talking about sex now but all the things that make a woman feminine. The way you dress, apply makeup, carry yourself, think about yourself. Your work has come to occupy the central portion of your life, and your husband has to take second best. You must realize that some of the freedom women gained deprived the men of certain things. A married man now has no children or a mother for his children. He has no one who is primarily interested in him and his needs. I don't insist that all marriages must exist on a master-and-slave relationship, but there should be a deal more give and take in a marriage than yours appears to offer. Just ask yourself—what *does* your husband get out of this marriage other than sexual frustration? If it's just a sometime companion, he would be far better off with a male roommate, an engineer he could talk shop with."

The silence lengthened, and Livermore finally coughed and cleared his throat and stood.

"If I have interfered unreasonably, I'm sorry."

He went out and saw Blalock stamping determinedly down the hall. After scowling at the man's receding back for a moment he entered the laboratory to check the bottle installations.

The FBI man let himself into Catherine Ruffin's office without knocking. She looked up at him, her face cold, then back at her work.

"I'm busy now, and I don't wish to talk to you."

"I've come to you for some help."

"Me?" Her laugh had no humor in it. "You accused me of breaking those bottles, so how can you ask for aid?"

"You are the only one who can supply the information I need. If you are as innocent as you insist, you should be pleased to help."

It was an argument that appealed to her ordered mind. She had no good reason—other than the fact that she disliked him—for refusing the man. And he was the agent officially sent here to investigate the sabotage.

"What can I do?" she asked.

"Help me to uncover a motive for the crimes."

"I have no suspicions, no information that you don't have."

"Yes, you do. You have access to all the records and to the computer—and you know how to program it. I want you to get all the data you can on the contents of those bottles. I have been looking at the records of losses, and there seems to be a pattern, but not one that is necessarily obvious. The fact that certain bottles were broken, three out of five, or that all the bottles in a certain rank on a certain day had their contents destroyed. There must be a key to this information in the records."

"This will not be a small job."

"I can get you all the authorization you need."

"Then I will do it. I can make the comparisons and checks and program the computer to look for relevant information. But I cannot promise you that there will be the answer you seek. The destruction could be random, and if it is, this will be of no help."

"I have my own reasons for thinking that it is not random. Do this and call me as soon as you have the results."

It took two days of concentrated effort. Catherine Ruffin was very satisfied with the job that she had done. Not with the results themselves; she could see no clues to any form of organization in any of the figures. But the federal agent might. She put in a call to him, then went through the results again until he arrived.

"I can see nothing indicative," she said, passing over the computer readouts.

"That's for me to decide. Can you explain these to me?"

"This is a list of the destroyed or damaged bottles." She handed him the top sheet. "Code number in the first column, then identification by name."

"What does that mean?"

"Surname of the donors, an easy way to remember and identify certain strains. Here, for instance, Wilson-Smith; sperm Wilson, ovum Smith. The remaining columns are details about the selections, which traits were selected and information of that kind. Instead of the index numbers, I have used the names of the strains for identification in the processing. These are the remaining sheets which are the results of various attempts to extract meaningful relationships. I could find none. The names themselves convey more."

He looked up from the figures. "What do you mean?"

"Nothing at all. A foolish habit of my own. I am by birth a Boer, and I grew up on one of the white reservations in South Africa after the revolution. Until we emigrated here, when I was eleven, I spoke only Afrikaans. So I have an emotional tie to the people—the ethnic group, you would call it—in which I was born. It was a small group, and it is very rare to meet a Boer in this country. So I look at lists of names, an old habit, to see if I recognize any Boers among them. I have met a few people that way in my lifetime. For some talk about the old days behind barbed wire. That is what I meant."

"How does that apply to these lists?"

"There are no Boers among them."

Blalock shrugged and turned his attention back to the paper. Catherine Ruffin, born Katerina Bekink, held the list of names before her and pursed her lips over it.

"No Afrikaaners at all. All of them Anglo-Irish names, if anything."

Blalock looked up sharply. "Please repeat that," he said.

She was correct. He went through the list of names twice and found only sternly Anglo-Saxon or Irish surnames. It appeared to make no sense, nor did the fact, uncovered by Catherine Ruffin with the name relationship as a clue, that there were no Negroes either.

"It makes no sense, no sense at all," Blalock said, shaking the papers angrily. "What possible reason could there be for this kind of deliberate action?"

"Perhaps you ask the wrong question. Instead of asking why certain names appear to be eliminated, perhaps you should ask why others do not appear on the list. Afrikaaners, for instance."

"Are there Afrikaans names on any of the bottle lists?"

"Of course. Italian names, German names, that kind of thing."

"Yes, let us ask that question," Blalock said, bending over the lists again.

It was the right question to ask.

* * *

The emergency meeting of the Genetic Guidance Council was called for 2300 hours. As always, Livermore was late. An extra chair had been placed at the foot of the big marble table, and Blalock was sitting there with the computer printouts arranged neatly before him. Catherine Ruffin switched on the recorder and called the meeting to order when Livermore arrived. Sturtevant coughed, then grubbed out his vegetable cigarette and immediately lit another one.

"Those burning compost heaps will kill you yet," Livermore said.

Catherine Ruffin interrupted the traditional disagreement before it could get under way.

"This meeting has been called at the request of Mr. Blalock, of the Federal Bureau of Investigation, who is here investigating the bottle failures and apparent sabotage. He is now ready to make a report."

"About time," Livermore said. "Find out yet who is the saboteur?"

"Yes," Blalock said tonelessly. "You are, Dr. Livermore."

"Well, well, big talk from little man. But you'll have to come up with some evidence before you wring a confession out of me."

"I think I can do that. Since the sabotage began and even before it was recognized as sabotage, one out of every ten bottles was a failure. This percentage is known as a tithe, which is indicative of a certain attitude or state of mind. It is also ten times the average failure ratio at other laboratories, which is normally about one percent. As further evidence the bottles sabotaged all had Irish or English surnamed donors."

Livermore sniffed loudly. "Pretty flimsy evidence. And what does it have to do with me?"

"I have here a number of transcripts of meetings of this council where you have gone on record against what you call discrimination in selection. You seem to have set yourself up as a protector of minorities, claiming at different times that Negroes, Jews, Italians, Indians, and other groups have been discriminated against. The records reveal that no bottles bearing names of donors belonging to any of these groups have ever been lost by apparent accident or deliberate sabotage. The connection with you seems obvious, as well as the fact that you are one of the few people with access to the bottles as well as the specific knowledge that would enable you to commit the sabotage."

"Sounds more like circumstantial evidence, not facts, to me. Are you planning to bring these figures out in a public hearing or trial or whatever you call it?"

"I am."

"Then your figures will also show the unconscious and conscious discrimination that is being practiced by the genetic-selection techniques now being used. Because it will reveal just how many of these minority groups are *not* being represented in the selection."

"I know nothing about that."

"Well I do. With these facts in mind I then admit to all the acts you have accused me of. I did it all."

A shocked silence followed his words. Catherine Ruffin shook her head, trying to understand.

"Why? I don't understand why you did it," she said.

"You still don't know, Catherine? I thought you were more intelligent than that. I did everything within my power to change the errant policies of this board and all the other boards throughout the country. I got exactly nowhere. With natural childbirth almost completely a thing of the past, the future citizens of this country will *all* come from the gene pool represented by the stored sperm and ova. With the selection techniques existing now, minority after minority will be eliminated. With their elimination countless genes that we simply cannot lose will be lost forever. Perhaps a world of fair-skinned, blue-eyed, blond, and muscular Anglo-Saxon Protestants is your idea of an ideal society. It is not mine—nor is it very attractive to the tinted-skin people with the funny foreign ways, odd names, and strangely shaped noses. They deserve to survive just as much as we do—and to survive right here in their country. Which is the United States of America. So don't tell me about Italian and Israeli gene pools in their native lands. The only real Americans here with an original claim to that name are the American Indians, and they are being dropped out of the gene pool as well. A crime is being committed. I was aware of it and could convince no one else of its existence. Until I chose this highly dramatic way of pointing out the situation. During my coming trial these facts will be publicized, and after that the policy will have to be reexamined and changed."

"You foolish old man," Catherine Ruffin said, but the warmth in her voice belied the harshness of her words. "You've ruined yourself. You will be fined, you may go to jail, at the least you will be relieved of your position, forced into retirement. You will never work again."

"Catherine my dear, I did what I had to do. Retirement at my age holds no fears. In fact I have been considering it and rather looking forward to it. Leave genetics and practice medicine as a hobby with my old fossils. I doubt the courts will be too hard on me. Compulsory retirement, I imagine, no more. Well worth it to get the facts out before the public."

"In that you have failed," Blalock said coldly, putting the papers together and dropping them into his case. "There will be no public trial, simply a dismissal, better for all concerned that way. Since you have admitted guilt, your superiors can make a decision in camera as to what to do."

"That's not fair!" Sturtevant said. "He only did these things to publicize what was happening. You can't take that away from him. It's not fair. . . ."

"Fair has nothing to do with it, Mr. Sturtevant. The genetic program will continue unchanged." Blalock seemed almost ready to smile at the thought. Livermore looked at him with distaste.

"You would like that, wouldn't you? Don't rock the boat. Get rid of disloyal employees—and at the same time rid this country of dissident minorities."

"You said it, Doctor, I didn't. And since you have admitted guilt, there is nothing you can do about it."

Livermore rose slowly and started from the room, turning before he reached the door.

"Quite the contrary, Blalock, because I shall insist upon a full public hearing. You have accused me of a crime before my associates, and I wish my name cleared, since I am innocent of all charges."

"It won't wash." Blalock was smiling now. "Your statement of guilt is on tape, recorded in the minutes of this meeting."

"I don't think it is. I did one final bit of sabotage earlier today. On that recorder. The tape is blank."

"That will do you no good. There are witnesses to your words."

"Are there? My two associates on the council are two committed human beings, no matter what our differences. If what I have said is true I think they will want the facts to come out. Am I right, Catherine?"

"I never heard you admit guilt, Dr. Livermore."

"Nor I," Sturtevant said. "I shall insist on a full departmental hearing to clear your name."

"See you in court, Blalock," Livermore said, and went out.

"I thought you would be at work. I didn't expect to see you here," Gust said to Leatha, who was sitting, looking out of the window of their living room. "I just came back to pack a bag, take my things out."

"Don't do that."

"I'm sorry what happened the other night, I just . . ."

"We'll talk about that some other time."

There was almost an embarrassed silence then, and he noticed her clothes for the first time. She was wearing a dress he had never seen before, a colorful print, sheer and low-cut. And her hair was different somehow, and her lipstick, more than she usually wore, he thought. She looked very nice, and he wondered if he should tell her that.

"Why don't we go out to that restaurant in Old Town," Leatha said. "I think that might be fun."

"It will be fun, I know it will," he answered suddenly, unreasonably, happier than he had ever been before.


Georgette Booker looked up at the clock and saw that it was almost time to quit. Good. Dave was taking her out again tonight, which meant that he would propose again. He was so sweet. She might even marry him, but not now. Life was too relaxed, too much fun, and she enjoyed people. Marriage was always there when you wanted it, but right now she just didn't want it.

She smiled. She was quite happy.


Sharm smiled and ate another piece of the ring-shaped roll.

"Top-pit," he said. "Really good. What is it called?"

"A bagel," his wife said. "You're supposed to eat them with smoked salmon and white cheese. I found it in this old cult-food book. I think they're nice."

"I think they're a lot better than nice. We're going to bake a whole lot of them, and I'm going to sell them in New Town because they got bread tastes like wet paper there. People will love them. They *have* to love them. Because you and I are going to move to New Town. They are going to love these bagels or something else we are going to sell them. Because you and I, we are going to live in that new place."

"You tell them, Sharm."

"I'm telling them. Old Sharm is going to get his cut of that good life, too."

# THE
# SECRET OF
# STONEHENGE

ow clouds rushed by overhead in the dusk and there
was a spattering of sleet in the air. When Dr. Lanning
opened the cab door of the truck the wind pounced on
him. Fresh from the Arctic, hurtling unimpeded across
Salisbury Plain. He buried his chin in his collar and climbed
down; Barker followed him out and tapped on the door of the
office nearby. There was no answer.

"Not so good," Lanning said, opening the rear door of the
truck and gently sliding the bulky wooden box down to the
ground. "We don't leave our national monuments unguarded
in the States."

"Really," Barker said, turning and striding to the gate in the
wire fence. "Then I presume those initials carved in the base
of the Washington Monument are neolithic graffiti. As you see
I brought the key."

He unlocked the gate and threw it open with a squeal of
unoiled hinges, then went to help Lanning with the case.

In the evening, under a lowering sky, that is the only way to
see Stonehenge. Without the ice cream wrappers and clamber-
ing children. The Plain settles flat upon the earth, pressed
outward to a distant horizon, and only the gray pillars of the
sarsen stones have the strength to push up skyward.

Lanning led the way, bending into the wind, up the broad path of the Avenue.

"They're always bigger than you expect them to be," he said, and Barker did not answer him, perhaps because it was true. They stopped next to the Altar Stone and lowered the case. "We'll know soon enough," Lanning said, throwing open the latches.

"Another theory?" Barker asked, interested in spite of himself. "Our megaliths seem to hold a certain fascination for you and your fellow Americans."

"We tackle our problems wherever we find them," Lanning answered, opening the cover and disclosing a chunky and complicated piece of apparatus mounted on an aluminum tripod. "I have no theories at all about these things. I'm here just to find out the truth—why this thing was built."

"Admirable," Barker said, and the coolness of his comment was lost in the colder wind. "Might I ask just what this device is?"

"Chronostasis temporal-recorder." He opened the legs and stood the machine next to the Altar Stone. "My team at MIT worked it up. We found that temporal movement other than our usual twenty-four hours into the future every day— is instant death for anything living. At least we killed off roaches, rats, and chickens; there were no human volunteers. But inanimate objects can be moved without damage."

"Time travel?" Barker said in what he hoped was a diffident voice.

"Not really, time stasis would be a better description. The machine stands still and lets everything else move by it. We've penetrated a good ten thousand years into the past this way."

"If the machine stands still that means that time is running backwards?"

"Perhaps it is—would you be able to tell the difference? Here, I think we're ready to go now."

Lanning adjusted the controls on the side of the machine,

pressed a stud, then stepped back. A rapid whirring came from the depths of the device: Barker raised one quizzical eyebrow.

"A timer," Lanning explained. "It's not safe to be close to the thing when it's operating."

The whirring ceased and was followed by a sharp click, immediately after which the entire apparatus vanished.

"This won't take long," Lanning said, and the machine reappeared even as he spoke. A glossy photograph dropped from a slot into his hand when he touched the back. He showed it to Barker.

"Just a trial run. I sent it back twenty minutes." Although the camera had been pointing at them, the two men were not in the picture. Instead, in darkish pastels due to the failing light, the photograph showed a view down the Avenue, with their parked truck just a tiny square in the distance. From the rear doors of the vehicle the two men could be seen removing the yellow box.

"That's very . . . impressive," Barker said, shocked into admission of the truth. "How far back can you send it?"

"Seems to be no limit, just depends on the power source. This model has nicad batteries and is good back to about ten thousand B.C."

"And the future?"

"A closed book, I'm afraid. But we may lick that problem yet." He extracted a small notebook from his hip pocket and consulted it, then set the dials once again.

"These are the optimum dates, about the time we figure Stonehenge was built. I'm making this a multiple-shot. This lever records the setting, so now I can feed in another one."

There were over twenty settings to be made, which necessitated a great deal of dial spinning. When it was finally done, Lanning actuated the timer and went to join Barker.

This time the departure of the chronostasis temporal-recorder was much more dramatic. It vanished readily enough, but left a glowing replica of itself behind, a shimmering golden outline easily visible in the growing darkness.

"Is that normal?" Barker asked.

"Yes, but only on the big time jumps. No one is really sure just what it is, but we call it a temporal echo. The current theory that it is sort of a resonance in time caused by the sudden departure of the machine. It fades away in a couple of minutes."

Before the golden glow was completely gone the device itself returned, appearing solidly in place of its spectral echo. Lanning rubbed his hands together, then pressed the print button. The machine clattered in response and extruded a long strip of connected prints.

"Not as good as I expected," Lanning said. "We hit the daytime all right, but there is nothing much going on."

There was enough going on to almost stop Barker's archeologist heart. Picture after picture of the megalith standing strong and complete, the menhirs upright and the lintels in place upon all the sarsen stones.

"Lots of rock," Lanning said, "but no sign of the people who built the thing. Looks like the dating theories are wrong. Do you have any idea when it was put up?"

"Sir J. Norman Lockyer believed that it was erected on June 24th, 1680 B.C.," he said abstractedly, still petrified by the photographs.

"Sounds good to me."

The dials were spun and the machine vanished once again. The picture this time was far more dramatic. A group of men in rough homespun genuflected, arms outstretched, facing toward the camera.

"We've got it now," Lanning chortled, and spun the machine about in a half circle so it faced in the opposite direction. "Whatever they're worshiping is behind the camera. I'll take a shot of it and we'll have a good idea why they built this thing."

The second picture was almost identical to the first, as were two more taken at right angles to the first ones.

"This is crazy," Lanning said, "they're all facing into the camera and bowing. Why, the machine must be sitting on top of whatever they are looking at."

"No, the angle proves that the tripod is on the same level that they are." Sudden realization hit Barker and his jaw sagged. "Is it possible that your temporal echo could be visible in the past as well?"

"Well . . . I don't see why not. Do you mean . . . ?"

"Correct. The golden glow of the machine caused by all those stops must have been visible on and off for years. It gave me a jolt when I first saw it and it must have been much more impressive to the people then."

"It fits," Lanning said, smiling happily and beginning to repack the machine. "They built Stonehenge around the image of the device sent back to see why they built Stonehenge. That's one problem solved."

"Solved! The problem has just begun. It's a paradox. Which of them, the machine or the monument, came first?"

Slowly, the smile faded from Dr. Lanning's face.

# RESCUE
# OPERATION

Pull! Pull steadily . . . !" Dragomir shouted, clutching at
the tarry cords of the net. Beside him in the hot darkness Pribislav Polasek grunted as he heaved on the wet
strands. The net was invisible in the black water, but
the blue light trapped in it rose closer and closer to the surface.

"It's slipping . . ." Pribislav groaned and clutched the rough
gunwale of the little boat. For a single instant he could see the
blue light on the helmet, a faceplate and the suited body that
faded into blackness—then it slipped free of the net. He had
just a glimpse of a dark shape before it was gone. "Did you see
it?" he asked. "Just before he fell he waved his hand."

"How can I know—the hand moved, it could have been the
net, or he might still be alive?" Dragomir had his face bent
almost to the glassy surface of the water, but there was nothing more to be seen. "He might be alive."

The two fishermen sat back in the boat and stared at each
other in the harsh light of the hissing acetylene lamp in the
bow. They were very different men, yet greatly alike in their
stained, baggy trousers and faded cotton shirts. Their hands
were deeply wrinkled and callused from a lifetime of hard
labor, their thoughts slowed by the rhythm of work and years.

"We cannot get him up with the net," Dragomir finally said, speaking first as always.

"Then we will need help," Pribislav added. "We have anchored the buoy here, we can find the spot again."

"Yes, we need help." Dragomir opened and closed his large hands, then leaned over to bring the rest of the net into the boat. "The diver, the one who stays with the widow Korenc, he will know what to do. His name is Kukovic and Petar said that he is a doctor of science from the university in Ljubljana."

They bent to their oars and sent the heavy boat steadily over the glasslike water of the Adriatic. Before they had reached shore, the sky was light and when they tied to the sea wall in Brbinj the sun was above the horizon.


Joze Kukovic looked at the rising ball of the sun, already hot on his skin, yawned, and stretched. The widow shuffled out with his coffee, mumbled good morning, and put it on the stone rail of the porch. He pushed the tray aside and sat down next to it, then emptied the coffee from the small, long-handled pot into his cup. The thick Turkish coffee would wake him up, in spite of the impossible hour. From the rail he had a view down the unpaved and dusty street to the port, already stirring to life. Two women, with the morning's water in brass pots balanced on their heads, stopped to talk. The peasants were bringing in their produce for the morning market, baskets of cabbages and potatoes and trays of tomatoes, strapped onto tiny donkeys. One of them brayed, a harsh noise that sawed through the stillness of the morning, bouncing echoes from the yellowed buildings. It was hot already. Brbinj was a town at the edge of nowhere, located between empty ocean and barren hills, asleep for centuries and dying by degrees. There were no attractions here—if you did not count the sea. But under the flat, blue calm of the water was another world that Joze loved.

Cool shadows, deep valleys, more alive than all the sun-blasted shores that surrounded it. Excitement, too: just the day before, too late in the afternoon to really explore it, he had found a Roman galley half-buried in the sand. He would get into it today, the first human in two thousand years, and Heaven alone knew what he would find there. In the sand about it had been shards of broken amphorae; there might be whole ones inside the hull.

Sipping happily at his coffee, he watched the small boat tying up in the harbor, and wondered why the two fishermen were in such a hurry. They were almost running, and no one ran here in the summer. Stopping below his porch, the biggest one called up to him.

"Doctor, may we come up? There is something urgent."

"Yes, of course." He was surprised and wondered if they took him for a physician.

Dragomir shuffled forward and did not know where to begin. He pointed out over the ocean.

"It fell, out there last night, we saw it, a sputnik without a doubt?"

"A traveler?" Joze Kukovic wrinkled his forehead, not quite sure that he heard right. When the locals were excited it was hard to follow their dialect. For such a small country Yugoslavia was cursed with a multitude of tongues.

"No, it was not a *putnik,* but a sputnik, one of the Russian spaceships."

"Or an American one." Pribislav spoke for the first time, but he was ignored.

Joze smiled and sipped his coffee. "Are you sure it wasn't a meteorite you saw? There is always a heavy meteor shower this time of the year."

"A sputnik," Dragomir insisted stolidly. "The ship fell far out in the Jadransko More and vanished, we saw that. But the space pilot came down almost on top of us, into the water. . . ."

"The WHAT?" Joze gasped, jumping to his feet and knocking the coffee tray to the floor. The brass tray clanged and rattled in circles unnoticed. "There was a man in this thing—and he got clear?"

Both fishermen nodded at the same time and Dragomir continued. "We saw this light fall from the sputnik when it went overhead and drop into the water. We couldn't see what it was, just a light, and we rowed there as fast as we could. It was still sinking and we dropped a net and managed to catch him. . . ."

"You have the pilot?"

"No, but once we pulled him close enough to the surface to see that he was in a heavy suit, with a window like a diving suit, and there was something on the back that might have been like your tanks there."

"He waved his hand," Pribislav insisted.

"He might have waved a hand, we could not be sure. We came back for help."

The silence lengthened and Joze realized that he was the help that they needed, and that they had turned the responsibility over to him. What should he do first? The astronaut might have his own oxygen tanks, Joze had no real idea what provisions were made for water landings, but if there was oxygen the man might still be alive.

Joze paced the floor while he thought, a short, square figure in khaki shorts and sandals. He was not handsome, his nose was too big and his teeth were too obvious for that, but he generated a certainty of power. He stopped and pointed to Pribislav.

"We're going to have to get him out. You can find the spot again?"

"A buoy."

"Good. And we may need a doctor. You have none here, but is there one in Osor?"

"Dr. Bratos, but he is very old. . . ."

"As long as he is still alive, we'll have to get him. Can anyone in this town drive an automobile?"

The fishermen looked toward the roof and concentrated, while Joze controlled his impatience.

"Yes, I think so," Dragomir finally said. "Petar was a partisan."

"That's right." The other fisherman finished the thought. "He has told many times how they stole German trucks and how he drove . . ."

"Well, then one of you get this Petar and give him the keys to my car, it's a German car so he should be able to manage. Tell him to bring the doctor back at once."

Dragomir took the keys, but handed them to Pribislav, who ran out.

"Now let's see if we can get the man up," Joze said, grabbing his scuba gear and leading the way toward the boat.

They rowed, side by side though Dragomir's powerful stroke did most of the work.

"How deep is the water out here?" Joze asked. He was already dripping with sweat as the sun burned on him.

"The Kvarneric is deeper up by Rab, but we were fishing off Trstenilc and the bottom is only about four fathoms there. We're coming to the buoy."

"Seven meters, it shouldn't be too hard to find him." Joze kneeled in the bottom of the boat and slipped into the straps of the scuba. He buckled it tight, checked the valves, then turned to the fisherman before he bit into the mouthpiece. "Keep the boat near this buoy and I'll use it for a guide while I search. If I need a line or any help, I'll surface over the astronaut, then you can bring the boat to me."

He turned on the oxygen and dipped over the side, the cool water rising up his body as he sank below the surface. With a powerful kick he started toward the bottom, following the dropping line of the buoy rope. Almost at once he saw the man, spread-eagled on white sand below.

Joze swam down, making himself stroke smoothly in spite of his growing excitement. Details were clearer as he dropped lower. There were no identifying marks on the pressure suit; it might be either American or Russian. It was a hard suit, metal or reinforced plastic, and painted green, with a single, flat faceplate in the helmet.

Because distance and size are so deceptive underwater, Joze was on the sand next to the figure before he realized that it was less than four feet long. He gasped and almost lost his mouthpiece.

Then he looked at the faceplate and saw that the creature inside was not human.

Joze coughed a bit and blew out a stream of bubbles: he had been holding his breath without realizing it. He just floated there, paddling slowly with his hands to stay in a position, looking at the face within the helmet.

It was still as a waxen cast, green wax with roughened surface, slit nostrils, slit mouth, and large eyeballs unseen but prominent as they pushed up against the closed lids. The arrangement of features was roughly human, but no human being had skin this color or had a pulpy crest, partially visible through the faceplate, growing up from above the closed eyes. Joze stared down at the suit made up of some unknown material, and at the compact atmosphere-regeneration apparatus on the alien's back. What kind of atmosphere? He looked back at the creature and saw that the eyes were open and the thing was watching him.

Fear was his first reaction; he shot back in the water like a startled fish, then, angry at himself, came forward again. The alien slowly raised one arm, then dropped it limply. Joze looked through the faceplate and saw that the eyes were closed again. The alien was alive, but unable to move; perhaps it was injured and in pain. The wreck of the creature's ship showed that something had been wrong with the landing. Reaching under as gently as he could, he cradled the tiny body in his arms, trying to ignore a feeling of revulsion when the cold fabric of the thing's suit touched his bare arms. It was only metal or plastic, he had to be a scientist about this. When he lifted it up, the eyes still did not open, and he bore the limp and almost weightless form to the surface.

"You great stupid clumsy clod of peasant, help me," he shouted, spitting out his mouthpiece and treading water on the surface, but Dragomir only shook his head in horror and retreated to the point of the bow when he saw what the physicist had borne up from below.

"It is a creature from another world and cannot harm you!" Joze insisted, but the fisherman would not approach.

Joze cursed aloud and only managed with great difficulty to get the alien into the boat, then climbed in after him. Though he was twice Joze's size, threats of violence drove Dragomir to the oars. But he used the farthest set of tholepins, even though it made rowing much more difficult. Joze dropped his scuba gear into the bottom of the boat and looked more closely at the drying fabric of the alien space suit. His fear of the unknown was forgiven in his growing enthusiasm. He was a nuclear physicist but he remembered enough of his chemistry and mechanics to know that this material was completely impossible—by Earth's standards.

Light green, it was as hard as steel over the creature's limbs and torso, yet was soft and bent easily at the joints as he proved by lifting and dropping the limp arm. His eyes went down the alien's tiny figure: there was a thick harness about the middle, roughly where a human waist would be, and hanging from this was a bulky container, like an oversize sporran. The suiting continued without an apparent seam—but the right leg! It was squeezed in and crushed as though it had been grabbed by a giant pliers. Perhaps this explained the creature's lack of motion. Could it be hurt? In pain?

Its eyes were open again and Joze realized in sudden horror that the helmet was filled with water. It must have leaked in, the thing was drowning. He grabbed at the helmet, seeing if it would screw off, tugging at it in panic.

Then he forced himself to think, and shakingly let go. The alien was still quiet, eyes open, no bubbles apparently coming from lips or nose. Did it breathe? Had the water leaked in—or was it possible it had always been there? Was it water? Who knew what alien atmosphere it might breathe; methane, chlorine, sulfur dioxide—why not water? The liquid was inside, surely enough, the suit wasn't leaking and the creature seemed unchanged.

Joze looked up and saw that Dragomir's panicked strokes had brought them into the harbor. A crowd was waiting on the shore.

The boat almost overturned as Dragomir leaped up onto the harbor wall, kicking backward in his panic. They drifted away and Joze picked the mooring line up from the floorboards and coiled it in his hands. "Here," he shouted, "catch this. Tie it onto the ring there."

No one heard him, or if they heard, did not want to admit it. They stared down at the green-cased figure lying in the stern sheets, and a rustle of whispering blew across them like wind among pine boughs. The women clutched their hands to their breasts, crossing themselves.

"Catch this!" Joze said through clenched teeth, forcing himself to keep his temper.

He hurled the rope onto the stones and they shied away from it. Then a youth grabbed it and slowly threaded it through the rusty ring, hands shaking and head tilted to one side, his mouth dropped in a permanent gape. He was feebleminded, too simple to understand what was going on: he simply obeyed the shouted order.

"Help me get this thing ashore," Joze called out, and even before the words were out of his mouth he realized the futility of the request.

The peasants shuffled backward, a blank-faced mob sharing

the same fear of the unknown, the women like giant, staring dolls in their knee-length flaring skirts, black stockings, and high felt shoes. He would have to do it himself. Balancing in the rocking boat, he cradled the alien in his arms and lifted it carefully up onto the rough stone of the harbor wall. The circle of watchers pushed back even farther, some of the women choking off screams and running back to their houses, while the men muttered louder: Joze ignored them.

These people were going to be no help to him—and they might cause trouble. His own room would be safest: he doubted if they would bother him there. He had just picked up the alien when a newcomer pushed through the watchers.

"There—what is that? A *vrag!*" The old priest pointed in horror at the alien in Joze's arms and backed away, fumbling for his crucifix.

"Enough of your superstition!" Joze snapped. "This is no devil but a sentient creature, a traveler. Now get out of my way."

He pushed forward and they fled before him. Joze moved as quickly as he could without appearing to hurry, leaving the crowd behind. There was a slapping of quick footsteps and he looked over his shoulder; it was the priest, Father Perc. His stained cassock flapped and his breath whistled in his throat with the unaccustomed exertion.

"Tell me, what are you doing . . . Dr. Kukovic? What is that . . . thing? Tell me. . . ."

"I told you. A traveler. Two of the local fishermen saw something come from the sky and crash. This . . . alien came from it." Joze spoke as calmly as possible. There might be trouble with the people, but not if the priest were on his side. "It is a creature from another world, a water-breathing animal, and it's hurt. We must help it."

Father Perc scrambled along sideways as he looked with obvious distaste at the motionless alien. "It is wrong," he mumbled, "this is something unclean, *zao duh. . . .*"

"Neither demon nor devil, can't you get that through your mind? The Church recognizes the possibility of creatures from other planets—the Jesuits even argue about it—so why can't you? Even the Pope believes there is life on other worlds."

"Does he? Does he?" the old man asked, blinking with red-rimmed eyes.

Joze brushed by him and up the steps to the widow Korenc's house. She was nowhere in sight as he went into his room and gently lowered the still-unconscious form of the alien onto his bed. The priest stopped in the doorway, quivering fingers on his rosary, uncertain. Joze stood over the bed, opening and closing his hands, just as unsure. What could he do? The creature was wounded, perhaps dying, something must be done. But what?

The distant droning whine of a car's engine pushed into the hot room and he almost sighed with relief. It was his car, he recognized the sound, and it would be bringing the doctor. The car stopped outside and the doors slammed, but no one appeared.

Joze waited tensely, realizing that the townspeople must be talking to the doctor, telling him what had happened. A slow minute passed and Joze started from the room, but stopped before he passed the priest, still standing just inside the door. What was keeping them? His window faced on an alleyway and he could not see the street in front of the building. Then the outside door opened and he could hear the widow's whispered voice, "In there, straight through."

There were two men, both dusty from the road. One was obviously the doctor, a short and dumpy man clutching a worn black bag, his bald head beaded with sweat. Next to him was a man, tanned and windburned, dressed like the other fisherman: this must be Petar the ex-partisan.

It was Petar who went to the bed first; the doctor just stood clutching his bag and blinking about the room.

"What is this thing?" Petar asked, then bent over, hands on

his knees, to stare in through the faceplate. "Whatever it is, it sure is ugly."

"I don't know. It's from another planet, that's the only thing I know. Now move aside so the doctor can look." Joze waved and the doctor moved reluctantly forward. "You must be Dr. Bratos. I'm Kukovic, professor of nuclear physics at the university in Ljubljana."

Perhaps waving around a little prestige might get this man's reluctant cooperation.

"Yes, how do you do. Very pleased to meet you, Professor, an honor I assure you. But what it is you wish me to do, I do not understand?" He shook ever so lightly as he spoke and Joze realized that the man was very old, well into his eighties or more. He would have to be patient.

"This alien . . . whatever it is . . . is injured and unconscious. We must do what we can to save its life."

"But what can we do? The thing is sealed in a metal garment—look it is filled with water—I am a doctor, a medical man, but not for animals, creatures like that."

"Neither am I, Doctor. No one on Earth is. But we must do our best. We must get the suit off the alien and then discover what we can do to help."

"It is impossible! The fluid inside of it, it will run out."

"Obviously, so we will have to take precautions. We will have to determine what the liquid is, then get more of it and fill the bathtub in the next room. I have been looking at the suit and the helmet seems to be a separate piece, clamped into position. If we loosen the clamps we should be able to get a sample."

For precious seconds Dr. Bratos stood there, nibbling at his lip, before he spoke. "Yes I suppose we could, but what could we catch the sample in? This is most difficult and irregular."

"It doesn't make any difference what we catch the sample in," Joze snapped, frustration pushing at his carefully held control. He turned to Petar, who was standing silently by, smoking a cigarette in his cupped hand. "Will you help? Get a soup plate, anything from the kitchen."

Petar simply nodded and left. There were muffled complaints from the widow, but he was back quickly with her best pot.

"That's good," Joze said, lifting the alien's head, "now slide it under here." With the pot in position he twisted one of the clamps; it snapped open but nothing else happened. A hairline opening was visible at the junction, but it stayed dry. But when Joze opened the second clamp there was a sudden gush of clear liquid under pressure, and before he fumbled the clamp shut again the pot was half full. He lifted the alien again and, without being told, Petar pulled the pot free and put it on the table by the window. "It's hot," he said.

Joze touched the outside of the container. "Warm not hot, about one hundred twenty degrees I would guess. A hot ocean on a hot planet."

"But . . . is it water?" Dr. Bratos asked haltingly.

"I suppose it is—but aren't you the one to find out? Is it fresh water or seawater?"

"I'm no chemist. . . . How can I tell? . . . It is very complicated."

Petar laughed and took Joze's water glass from the nightstand. "That's not so hard to find out," he said, and dipped it into the pot. He raised the half-filled glass, sniffed at it, then took a sip and puckered his lips. "Tastes like ordinary seawater to me, but there's another taste, sort of bitter."

Joze took the glass from him. "This could be dangerous," the doctor protested, but they ignored him. Yes, salt water, hot salt water with a sharpness to it.

"It tastes like more than a trace of iodine. Can you test for the presence of iodine, Doctor?"

"Here . . . no, it is quite complicated. In the laboratory with the correct equipment—" His voice trailed off as he opened his bag on the table and groped through it. He brought his hand out empty. "In the laboratory."

"We have no laboratory or any other assistance, Doctor. We will have to be satisfied with what we have here, ordinary seawater will have to do."

"I'll get a bucket and fill the tub," Petar said.

"Good. But don't fill the bathtub yet. Bring the water into the kitchen and we'll heat it, then pour it in."

"Right." Petar brushed past the silent and staring priest and was gone. Joze looked at Father Perc and thought of the people of the village.

"Stay here, Doctor," he said. "This alien is your patient and I don't think anyone other than you should come near. Just sit by him."

"Yes, of course, that is correct," Dr. Bratos said relieved, pulling the chair over and sitting down.

The breakfast fire was still burning in the big stove and flamed up when Joze slid in more sticks. On the wall hung the big copper washtub and he dropped it onto the stove with a clang. Behind him the widow's bedroom door opened, but slammed shut again when he turned. Petar came in with a bucket of water and poured it into the tub.

"What are the people doing?" Joze asked.

"Just milling about and bothering each other. They won't be any trouble. If you're worried about them, I can drive back to Osor and bring the police. Or telephone someone."

"No, I should have thought of that earlier. Right now I need you here. You're the only one who isn't either senile or ignorant."

Petar smiled. "I'll get some more water."

The bathtub was small and the washtub big. When the heated water was dumped in it filled it more than halfway, enough to cover the small alien. There was a drain from the bathtub but no faucets: it was usually filled with a hose from the sink. Joze picked up the alien, cradling it like a child in his arms, and carried it into the bath. The eyes were open again, following his every movement, but making no protest. He lowered the creature gently into the water, then straightened a moment and took a deep breath. "Helmet first, then we'll try to figure out how the suit opens." He bent and slowly twisted the clamps.

With all four clamps open the helmet moved freely. He opened it a wide crack, ready to close it quickly if there were any signs of trouble. The ocean water would be flowing in now, mixing with the alien water, yet the creature made no complaint. After a minute Joze slowly pulled the helmet off, cradling the alien's head with one hand so that it would not bump to the bottom of the tub.

Once the helmet was clear the pulpy crest above the eyes sprang up like a coxcomb, reaching up over the top of the green head. A wire ran from the helmet to a shiny bit of metal on one side of the creature's skull. There was an indentation there and Joze slowly pulled a metal plug out, perhaps an earphone of some kind. The alien was opening and closing its mouth, giving a glimpse of bony yellow ridges inside, and a very low humming could be heard.

Petar pressed his ear against the outside of the metal tube. "The thing is talking or something, I can hear it."

"Let me have your stethoscope, Doctor," Joze said, but when the doctor did not move he dug it from the bag himself. Yes—when he pressed it to the metal he could hear a rising and falling whine, speech of a kind.

"We can't possibly understand him—not yet," he said, handing the stethoscope back to the doctor, who took it automatically. "We had better try to get the suit off."

There were no seams or fastenings visible, nor could Joze find anything when he ran his fingers over the smooth surface. The alien must have understood what they were doing because it jerkingly raised one hand and fumbled at the metal sealing ring about the collar. With a liquid motion the suit split open down the front; the opening bifurcated and ran down each leg. There was a sudden welling of blue liquid from the injured leg. Joze had a quick glimpse of green flesh, strange organs, then he spun about. "Quick, Doctor—your bag. The creature is hurt, that fluid might be blood, we have to help it."

"What can I do?" Dr. Bratos said, unmoving. "Drugs, antiseptics—I might kill it—we know nothing of its body chemistry."

"Then don't use any of those. This is a traumatic injury, you can bind it up, stop the bleeding, can't you?"

"Of course, of course," the old man said, and at last his hands had familiar things to do, extracting bandages and sterile gauze from his bag, tape and scissors.

Joze reached into the warm and now murky water and forced himself to reach under the green leg and grasp the hot, green flesh. It was strange—but not terrible. He lifted the limb free of the water and they saw a crushed gap oozing a thick blue fluid. Petar turned away, but the doctor put on a pad of gauze and tightened the bandages about it. The alien was fumbling at the discarded suit beside it in the tub, twisting its leg in Joze's grip. He looked down and saw it take something from the sporran container. Its mouth was moving again, he could hear the dim buzz of its voice.

"What is it? What do you want?" Joze asked.

It was holding the object across its chest now with both hands: it appeared to be a book of some kind. It might be a book, it might be anything.

Yet it was covered in a shiny substance with dark markings on it, and at the edge seemed to be made of many sheets bound together. It could be a book. The leg was twisting now in Joze's grasp and the alien's mouth was open wider, as if it were shouting.

"The bandage will get wet if we put it back into the water," the doctor said.

"Can't you wrap adhesive tape over it, seal it in?"

"In my bag—I'll need some more."

While they talked the alien began to rock back and forth, splashing water from the tub, pulling its leg from Joze's grasp. It still held the book in one thin, multi-fingered hand, but with the other one it began to tear at the bandages on its leg.

"It's hurting itself, stop it. This is terrible," the doctor said, recoiling from the tub.

Joze snatched a piece of wrapping paper from the floor.

"You fool! You incredible fool!" he shouted. "These compresses you used—they're impregnated with sulfanilamide."

"I always use them, they're the best, American, they prevent wound infection."

Joze pushed him aside and plunged his arms into the tub to tear the bandages free, but the alien reared up out of his grasp sitting up above the water, its mouth gaping wide. Its eyes were open and daring and Joze recoiled as a stream of water shot from its mouth. There was a gargling sound as the water died to a trickle, and then, as the first air touched the vocal cords, a rising howling scream of pain. It echoed from the plaster ceiling, an inhuman agony as the creature threw its arms wide, then fell face forward into the water. It did not move again and, without examining it, Joze knew it was dead.

One arm was twisted back, out of the tub, still grasping the book. Slowly the fingers loosened, and while Joze looked on numbly, unable to move, the book thudded to the floor.

"Help me," Petar said, and Joze turned to see that the doctor had fallen and Petar was kneeling over him. "He fainted, or a heart attack. What can we do?"

His anger was forgotten as Joze kneeled. The doctor seemed to be breathing regularly and his face wasn't flushed, so perhaps it was only a fainting spell. The eyelids fluttered. The priest brushed by and looked down over Joze's shoulder.

Dr. Bratos opened his eyes, looking back and forth at the faces bent over him. "I'm sorry," he said thickly; then the eyes closed again as if to escape the sight of them.

Joze stood and found that he was trembling. The priest was gone. Was it all over? Perhaps they might never have saved the alien, but they should have done better than this. Then he saw the wet spot on the floor and realized the book was gone.

"Father Perc!" he shouted, crying it out like an insult. The man had taken the book, the priceless book!

Joze ran out into the hall and saw the priest coming from the kitchen. His hands were empty. With sudden fear Joze knew what the old man had done and brushed past him into the kitchen and ran to the stove, hurling open the door.

There, among the burning wood, lay the book. It was steaming, almost smoking as it dried, lying open. It was obviously a book; there were marks on the pages of some kind. He turned to grab up the shovel and behind him the fire exploded, sending a white flame across the room. It had almost caught him in the face, but he did not think of that. Pieces of burning wood lay on the floor, and inside the stove there was only the remains of the original fire. Whatever substance the book had been made of was highly inflammable once it had dried out.

"It was evil," the priest said from the doorway. "A *zao duh,* an abomination with a book of evil. We have been warned, such things have happened before on Earth, and always the faithful must fight back—"

Petar pushed in roughly past him and helped Joze to a chair, brushing the hot embers from his bare skin. Joze had not felt their burn; all he was aware of was an immense weariness.

"Why here?" he asked. "Of all places in the world why here? A few more degrees to the west and the creature would have come down near Trieste with surgeons, hospitals, modern facilities. Or, if it had just stayed on its course a little longer, it could have seen the lights, and would have landed at Rijeka. Something could have been done. But why here?" He surged to his feet, shaking his fist at nothing—and at everything.

"Here, in this superstition-ridden, simpleminded backwater of the world! What kind of world do we live in where there is a five-million-volt electron accelerator not a hundred miles from primitive stupidity? That this creature should come so far, come so close . . . why, why?"

Why?

He slumped back into the chair again, feeling older than he had ever felt before and tired beyond measure. What could they have learned from this book?

He sighed, and the sigh came from so deep within him that his whole body trembled as though shaken by awful fever.

# PORTRAIT
# OF THE
# ARTIST

**11** A.M.!!! the note blared at him, pinned to the upper right corner of his drawing board. **MARTIN'S OFFICE!!** He had lettered it himself with a number 7 brush. Funereal India ink on harsh yellow paper, big letters, big words.

Big end to everything. Pachs tried to make himself believe that this was just another one of Martin's royal commands: a lecture, a chewing-out, a complaint. That's what he had thought when he had knocked out this reminder for himself, before Miss Fink's large watery eyes had blinked at him as she had whispered hoarsely.

"It's on order, Mr. Pachs, coming today. I saw the receipt on his desk. A Mark Nine." She had blinked moistly again, rolled her eyes toward the closed door of Martin's office, then scurried away.

A Mark IX. He knew that it would have to come someday, knew without wanting to admit it. He had only been kidding himself when he said that they couldn't do without him. His hands spread out on the board before him, old hands, networked wrinkles and dark liver spots. Always stained a bit with ink and marked with a permanent callus on the inside of his index finger. How many years had he held a pencil, or a

brush there? He closed his hands into fists when he saw that they were shaking.

There was almost an hour left before he had to see Martin, plenty of time to finish up the story he was working on. He pulled the sheet of illustration board from the top of the pile and found the script. Page three of a piece of crap called "Prairie Love." For the July issue of *Real Rangeland Romances.* Love books with their heavy copy were always a snap. By the time Miss Fink had typed in the endless captions and dialogue on her big flatbed varityper at least half of every panel was full. He picked up the script, read panel one:

> In house, Judy C/U cries and Robert in BG very angry.

A size-three head for Judy in the foreground—he quickly drew the right size oval in blue pencil—then a stick figure for Robert in the background. Hand raised, fist closed, to show anger. The Mark VIII Robot Comic Artist would do all the rest. Pachs slipped the sheet of illustration board into the machine's holder—then quickly pulled it out again. He had forgotten the balloons. Sloppy, sloppy. He quickly blue-penciled their outlines and Vs for tails.

When he thumbed the switch, the machine hummed to life, the operating lights came on, there was a *dee*-buzzing from inside its dark case. He punched the control button for the heads, first the girl—GIRL HEAD, FULL FRONT, SIZE THREE, SAD HEROINE. Girls, of course, all had the same face in comic books; the HEROINE was just a note to the machine not to touch the hair. For a VILLAINESS it would be inked in black since all villainesses have black hair. Just as all villains have mustaches as well as the black hair, to distinguish them from the hero. The machine buzzed and clattered to itself while it sorted through the stock cuts, then clicked and banged down a rubber stamp of the correct head over the blue circle he had

drawn. MAN HEAD, FULL FRONT, SIZE SIX, SAD, HERO brought a
smaller stamp banging down on the other circle that topped
the stick figure. Of course the script said angry, but that was
what the raised fist was for. Since there are only sad and happy
faces in comics.

Life isn't that simple, he thought to himself, a very unorigi-
nal idea that he usually brought out at least once a day while
sitting at the machine. MAN FIGURE, BUSINESS SUIT, he set on the
dial, then hit the DRAW button. The pen-tipped arm dropped
instantly and began to quickly ink in a suited man's figure over
the blue direction lines he had put down. He blinked and
watched it industriously knocking in a wrinkle pattern that
hadn't varied a stroke in fifty years, then a collar and tie and
two swift neck lines to connect the neatly inked torso to the
rubber-stamped head. The pen leaped out to the cuff end of
the just-drawn sleeve and quivered there. A relay buzzed and
a dusty red panel flashed INSTRUCTIONS PLEASE at him. With a
savage jab he pushed the button labeled FIST. The light went
out and the flashing pen drew a neat fist at the end of the arm.

Pachs looked at the neatly drawn panel and sighed. The girl
wasn't unhappy enough; he dipped his crow quill into the
inkpot and knocked in two tears, one in the corner of each eye.
Better. But the background was still pretty empty in spite of
the small dictionary in each balloon. BALLOONS, he punched
automatically while he thought, and the machine pen darted
down and inked the outlines of the balloons that held the
lettering, ending each tail the correct distance from the
speaker's mouth.

A little background, it needed a touch. He pressed code 473,
which he knew from long experience stood for HOME WINDOW
WITH LACE CURTAINS. It appeared on the paper quickly, automatically scaled by the machine to be in perspective with the
man's figure before it. Pachs picked up the script and read
panel two:

Judy falls on couch Robert tries to console her mother rushes in angrily wearing apron.

There was a four-line caption in this panel and, after the three balloons had been lettered as well, the total space remaining was just about big enough for a single close-up, a small one. Pachs didn't labor this panel, as he might have, but took the standard way out. He was feeling tired today, very tired.

HOUSE, SMALL FAMILY produced a tiny cottage from which emerged the tails of the three balloons. Let the damn reader figure out who was talking.

The story was finished just before eleven. He stacked the pages neatly, put the script into the file, and cleaned the ink out of the pen in the Mark VIII; it always clogged if he left it to dry.

Then it was eleven and time to see Martin. Pachs fussed a bit, rolling down his sleeves and hanging his green eyeshade from the arm of his dazor lamp; yet the moment could not be avoided. Pulling his shoulders back a bit he went out past Miss Fink, hammering away industriously on the varityper, and walked in through the open door to Martin's voice.

"Come ON, Louis," Martin wheedled into the phone in his most syrupy voice. "If it's a matter of taking the word of some two-bit shoestring salesman in Kansas City, or of taking my word, who you gonna doubt? That's right . . . okay . . . right Louis. I'll call you back in the morning . . . right, you too . . . my best to Helen." He banged the phone back onto the desk and glared up at Pachs with his hard beebee eyes.

"What do you want?"

"You told me you wanted to see me, Mr. Martin."

"Yeah, yeah," Martin mumbled half to himself. He scratched flakes of dandruff loose from the back of his head with the chewed end of a pencil, rocked from side to side in his chair.

"Business is business, Pachs, you know that, and expenses go up all the time. Paper—you know how much it costs a ton? So we gotta cut corners. . . ."

"If you're thinking of cutting my salary again, Mr. Martin, I don't think I could . . . well, maybe not much . . ."

"I'm gonna have to let you go, Pachs. I've bought a Mark Nine to cut expenses and I already hired some kid to run it."

"You don't have to do that, Mr. Martin," Pachs said hurriedly, aware that his words were tumbling one over the other and that he was pleading, but not caring. "I could run the machine I'm sure, just give me a few days to catch on. . . ."

"Outta the question. In the first place I'm paying the kid beans because she's just a kid and that's the starting salary, and in the other place she's been to school about this thing and can really grind the stuff out. You know I'm no bastard, Pachs, but business is business. And I'll tell you what, this is only Tuesday, still I'm gonna pay you for the rest of the week. How's that? And you can take off right now."

"Very generous, particularly after eight years," Pachs said, forcing his voice to be calm.

"That's all right, it's the least I could do." Martin was congenitally immune to sarcasm.

The lost feeling hit Pachs then, a dropping away of his stomach, a sensation that everything was over. Martin was back on the phone again and there was really nothing that Pachs could say. He walked out of the office, walking very straight, and behind him he heard the banging of Miss Fink's machine halt for an instant. He did not want to see her, to face those tender and damp eyes, not now. Instead of turning to go back to the studio, where he would have to pass her desk, he opened the hall door and stepped out. He closed it slowly behind him and stood with his back to it for an instant, until he realized it was frosted glass and she could see his figure from the inside: he moved hurriedly away.

There was a cheap bar around the corner where he had a

beer every payday, and he went there now. "Good morning and top of the morning to you . . . Mr. Pachs," the robot bartender greeted him with recorded Celtic charm, hesitating slightly between the stock phrase and the search of the customer-tapes for his name. "And will you be having the usual?"

"No I will not be having the usual, you plastic-and-gas-pipe imitation of a cheap stage Irishman. I'll be having a double whiskey."

"Sure and you are the card, sir." The electronically affable bartender nodded, horsehair spit curl bobbing, as it produced a glass and bottle and poured a carefully measured drink.

Pachs drank it in a gulp and the unaccustomed warmth burned through the core of cold indifference that he had been holding on to. Christ, it was all over, all over. They would get him now with their Senior Citizens' Home and all the rest, he was good as dead.

There are some things that don't bear thinking about. This was one of them. Another double whiskey followed the first; the money for this was no longer important because he would be earning no more after this week. The unusual dose of alcohol blurred some of the pain. Now, before he started thinking about it too much, he had to get back to the office. Clean his personal junk out of the taboret and pick up his paycheck from Miss Fink. It would be ready, he knew that; when Martin was through with you he liked to get you out of the way, quickly.

"Floor please?" the voice questioned from the top of the elevator.

"Go straight to hell!" he blurted out. He had never before realized how many robots there were around. Oh how he hated them today.

"I'm sorry, that firm is not in this building, have you consulted the registry?"

"Twenty-three," he said and his voice quavered, and he was glad he was alone in the elevator. The doors closed.

There was a hall entrance to the studio and this door was standing open; he was halfway through before he realized why—then it was too late to turn back. The Mark VIII that he had nursed along and used for so many years lay on its side in the corner, uprooted and very dusty on the side that had stood against the wall.

Good, he thought to himself, and at the same time knew it was stupid to hate a machine, but still relished the thought that it was being discarded too. In its place stood a columnar apparatus in a gray crackle cabinet. It reached almost to the ceiling and appeared as ponderous as a safe.

"It's all hooked up now, Mr. Martin, ready to go with a hundred-percent lifetime guarantee as you know. But I'll just sort of preflight it for you and give you an idea just how versatile this machine is."

The speaker, dressed in gray coveralls of the exact same color as the machine's finish, was pointing at it with a gleaming screwdriver. Martin watched, frowning, and Miss Fink fluttered in the background. There was someone else there, a thin young girl in a pink sweater who bovinely chewed at a cud of gum.

"Let's give Mark Nine here a real assignment, Mr. Martin. A cover for one of your magazines, something I bet you never thought a machine could tackle before, and normal machines can't. . . ."

"Fink!" Martin barked and she rambled over with a sheet of illustration board and a small color sketch.

"We got just one cover in the house to finish, Mr. Martin," she said weakly. "You okayed it for Mr. Pachs to do. . . ."

"The hell with all that," Martin growled, pulling it from her hand and looking at it closely. "This is for our best book, do you understand that, and we can't have no hack horsing around with rubber stamps. Not on the cover of *Fighting Real War Battle Aces.*"

"You need not have the slightest worry, I assure you," the

man in the overalls said, gently lifting the sketch from Martin's fingers. "I'm going to show you the versatility of the Mark Nine, something that you might find it impossible to believe until you see it in action. A trained operator can cut a Mark Nine tape from a sketch or a description, and the results are always dramatic to say the least." He seated himself at a console with typewriter keys that projected from the side of the machine, and while he typed, a ribbon of punched tape collected in the basket at one side.

"Your new operator knows the machine code and breaks down any art concept into standard symbols, cut on tape. The tape can be examined or corrected, stored or modified and used over again if need be. There—I've recorded the essence of your sketch and now I have one more question to ask you. In what style would you like it to be drawn?"

Martin made a porcine interrogative sound.

"Startled aren't you, sir—well I thought you would be. The Mark Nine contains style tapes of all the great masters of the Golden Age. You can have Kubert or Caniff, Giunta or Barry. For figure work—you can use Raymond, for your romances, capture the spirit of Drake."

"How's about Pachs?"

"I'm sorry, I'm afraid I don't know of . . ."

"A joke. Let's get going. Caniff, that's what I want to see."

Pachs felt himself go warm all over, then suddenly cold. Miss Fink looked over and caught his eye, and looked down, away. He clenched his fists and shifted his feet to leave, but listened instead.

He could not leave, not yet.

". . . and the tape is fed into the machine, the illustration board centered on the impression table, and the cycle button depressed. So simple, once a tape has been cut, that a child of three could operate it. A press on the button and just stand back. Within this genius of a machine the orders are being analyzed and a picture built up. Inside the memory circuits are bits and pieces of every object that man has ever imagined or seen and drawn for his own edification. These are assembled in the correct manner in the correct proportions and assembled on the collator's screen. When the final picture is complete the all-clear light flashes—there it goes—and we can examine the completed picture on the screen here." Martin bent over and looked in through the hooded opening.

"Just perfect, isn't it? But if for any reason the operator is dissatisfied the image can be changed now in any manner desired by manipulation of the editorial controls. And when satisfied the print button is depressed, the image is printed in a single stroke onto the paper below."

A pneumatic groan echoed theatrically from the bowels of the machine as a rectangular box crept down on a shining plunger and pressed against the paper. It hissed and a trickle of vapor oozed out. The machine rose back to position and the man in the coveralls held up the paper, smiling.

"Now isn't that a fine piece of art?"

Martin grunted.

Pachs looked at it and couldn't take his eyes away: he was afraid he was going to be sick. The cover was not only good, it was good Caniff, just as the master might have drawn it himself. Yet the most horrible part was that it was Pachs's own cover, his own layout. Improved. He had never been what might be called a tremendous artist, but he wasn't a bad artist. He did all right in comics, and during the good years he was on top of the pack. But the field kept shrinking, and when the machines came in everything went bust and there was almost no spot for an artist, just a job here and there as sort of layout boy and machine minder. He had taken that—how many years now?—because old and dated as his work was, he was still better than any machine that drew heads with a rubber stamp.

Not any more. He could not even pretend to himself any more that he was needed, or even useful.

The machine was better.

He realized then that he had been clenching his fists so tight that his nails had sunk into the flesh of his palms. He opened and rubbed them together and they were shaking badly. The Mark IX was turned off and they were all gone: he could hear Miss Fink's machine takking away in the outer office. The young girl was telling Martin about the special supplies she would need to buy to operate the machine. When Pachs closed the connecting door he cut off the grumbling reply about extra expenses not being mentioned. Pachs warmed his fingers in his armpits until the worst of the tremors stopped. Then he carefully pinned a sheet of paper onto his drawing board and adjusted the light so it would not be in his eyes. With measured strokes he ruled out a standard comic page and separated it into six panels, making the sixth panel a big one, stretching the width of the page. He worked steadily at the penciling, stopping only once to stretch his back and walk over to the window and look out. Then he went back to the board and as the afternoon light faded he finished the inking. Very carefully he washed off his battered but still favorite Windsor & Newton brush and slipped it back into the spring holder.

There was a bustle in the outer office and it sounded like Miss Fink getting ready to leave, or maybe it was the new girl coming back with the supplies. In any case it was late, and he had to go now.

Quickly, before he could change his mind, he ran full tilt at the window, his weight bursting through the glass, hurtled the twenty-three stories to the street below. Miss Fink heard the breaking glass and screamed, then screamed louder when she came into the room. Martin, complaining about the noise, followed her, but shut up when he saw what had happened. A bit of glass crunched under his shoes when he looked out of the window. The doll-like figure of Pachs was visible in the center of the gathering crowd, sprawled from sidewalk to street and bent at an awful angle as it followed the step of the curb.

"Oh God, Mr. Martin, oh God look at this. . . ." Miss Fink wailed.

Martin went and stood next to her in front of the drawing board and looked at the page still pinned there. It was neatly done, well drawn and carefully inked.

In the first panel was a self-portrait of Pachs working on a page, bent over this same drawing board. In the second panel he was sitting back and washing out his brush, in the third standing. In the fourth panel the artist stood before the window, nicely rendered in chiaroscuro with backlighting. Five was a forced perspective shot from above, down the vertical face of the building with the figure hurtling through the air toward the pavement below.

In the last panel, in clear and horrible detail, the old man was bent broken and bloody over the wrecked fender of the car that was parked there: the spectators looked on, horrified.

"Look at that, will you," Martin said disgustedly, tapping the drawing with his thumb. "When he went out the window he missed the car by a good two yards. Didn't I always tell you he was never any good at getting the details right?"

# SURVIVAL
# PLANET

B ut this war was finished years before I was born! How can one robot torpedo—fired that long ago—still be of any interest?"

Dall the Younger was overly persistent—it was extremely lucky for him that Ship-Commander Lian Stane, both by temperament and experience, had a tremendous reserve of patience.

"It has been fifty years since the Greater Slavocracy was defeated—but that doesn't mean eliminated," Commander Stane said. He looked through the viewport of the ship, seeing ghostlike against the stars the pattern of the empire they had fought so long to destroy. "The Slavocracy expanded unchecked for over a thousand years. Its military defeat didn't finish it, just made the separate worlds accessible to us. We are still in the middle of that reconstruction, guiding them away from a slave economy."

"That I know all about," Dall the Younger broke in with a weary sigh. "I've been working on the planets since I came into the force. But what has that got to do with the Mosaic torpedo that we're tracking? There must have been a billion of them made and fired during the war. How can a single one be of interest this much later?"

"If you had read the tech reports," Stane said, pointing to the thumb-thick folder on the chart table, "you would know all about it." This advice was the closest the commander had ever come to censure. Dall the Younger had the good grace to flush slightly and listen with applied attention.

"The Mosaic torpedo is a weapon of space war, in reality a robot-controlled spaceship. Once directed it seeks out its target, defends itself if necessary, then destroys itself and the ship it has been launched against by starting the uncontrollable cycle of binding-energy breakdown."

"I never realized that they were robot-operated," Dall said. "I thought robots had an ingrained resistance to killing people?"

"In-built rather than ingrained would be more accurate," Stane said judiciously. "Robotic brains are just highly developed machines with no inherent moral sense. That is added afterward. It has been a long time since we built man-shaped robots with human-type brains. This is the age of the specialist, and robots can specialize far better than men ever could. The Mosaic torpedo brains have no moral sense—if anything they are psychotic, overwhelmed by a death wish. Though there are, of course, controls on how much they can kill. All the torpedoes ever used by either side had mass detectors to defuse them when they approached an object with planetary mass, since the reaction started by a torpedo could just as easily destroy a world as a ship. You can understand our interest when in the last months of the war, we picked up a torpedo fused only to detonate a planet.

"All the data from its brain was filed and recently interpreted. The torpedo was aimed at the fourth planet of the star we are approaching now."

"Anything on the record about this planet?" Dall asked.

"Nothing; it is an unexplored system at least as far as our records are concerned. But the Greater Slavocracy knew enough about this planet to want to destroy it. We are here to find out why."

Dall the Younger furrowed his brow, chewing at the idea. "Is that the only reason?" he finally asked. "Since we stopped them from wiping out this planet, that would be the end of it, I should think."

"It's thinking like that that shows why you are the low ranker on this ship," Gunner Arnild snapped as he came in. Arnild had managed to grow old in a very short-lived service, losing in the process his patience for everything except his computers and guns. "Shall I suggest some of the possibilities that have occurred even to me? Firstly—any enemy of the Slavocracy could be a friend of ours. Or conversely, there may be an enemy here that threatens the entire human race, and we may need to set off a Mosaic ourselves to finish the job the Slavers started. Then again, the Slavers may have had something here—like a research center that they would rather have destroyed than let us see. Wouldn't you say that any one of these would make the planet worth investigating?"

"We shall be in the atmosphere within twenty hours," Dall said as he vanished through the lower hatch. "I have to check the lubrication on the drive gears."

"You're too easy on the kid," Gunner Arnild said, staring moodily at the approaching star, already dimmed by the forward filters.

"And you're too hard," Stane told him. "So I guess it evens out. You forget he never fought the Slavers."

Skimming the outer edges of the atmosphere of the fourth planet, the scout ship hurled itself through the measured length of a helical orbit, then fled back into the safety of space while the ship's robot brain digested and made copies of the camera and detector instrument recordings. The duplicates were stored in a message torp, and only when the torp had started back to base did Commander Stane bother personally to examine the results of their survey.

"We're dispensable now," he said, relaxing. "So the best thing we can do is to drop down and see what we can stir up." Arnild grunted agreement, his index fingers unconsciously pressing invisible triggers. They leaned over the graphs and photographs spread out on the table. Dall peered between their shoulders and flipped through the photographs they tossed aside. He was first to speak.

"Nothing much there, really. Plenty of water, a big island continent—and not much else."

"Nothing else is detectable," Stane added, ticking off the graphs one by one. "No detectable radiation, no large masses of metal either above or below ground, no stored energy. No reason for us to be here."

"But we are," Arnild growled testily. "So let's touch down and find out more firsthand. Here's a good spot!" He tapped a photograph, then pushed it into the enlarger.

"Could be a primitive hut city, people walking around, smoke."

"Those could be sheep in the fields," Dall broke in eagerly. "And boats pulled up on the shore. We'll find out something here."

"I'm sure we will," Commander Stane said. "Strap in for landing."

Lightly and soundlessly the ship fell out of the sky, curving in a gentle arc that terminated at the edge of a grove of tall trees, on a hill above the city. The motors whined to a stop and the ship was silent.

"Report positive on the atmosphere," Dall said, checking off the analyzer dials.

"Stay at the guns, Arnild," Commander Stane said. "Keep us covered, but don't shoot unless I tell you to."

"Or unless you're dead," Arnild said with complete lack of emotion.

"Or unless I'm dead," Stane answered him, in the same toneless voice. "In which case you will assume command."

He and Dall buckled on planet kits, cycled through the lock, and sealed it behind them. The air was dry and pleasantly warm, filled with the freshness of growing plants.

"Really smells good after that canned stuff," Dall said.

"You have a great capacity for stating the obvious." Arnild's voice rasped even more than usual when heard through the bone conductor phones. "Can you see what's going on in the village?"

Dall fumbled his binoculars out. Commander Stane had been using his since they left the ship. "Nothing moving," Stane said. "Send an Eye down there."

The Eye whooshed away from the ship and they could follow its slow swing through the village below. There were about a hundred huts, simple pole-and-thatch affairs, and the Eye carefully investigated every one.

"No one there," Arnild said, as he watched the monitor screen. "The animals are gone too, the ones from the aerial pic."

"The people can't have vanished," Dall said. "There are empty fields in every direction, completely without cover. And I can see smoke from their fires."

"The smoke's there, the people aren't," Arnild said testily. "Walk down and look for yourself."

The Eye lifted up from the village and drifted back toward the ship. It swung around the trees and came to a sudden stop in midair.

"Hold it!" Arnild's voice snapped in their ears. "The huts are empty. But there's someone in the tree you're standing next to. About ten meters over your heads!"

Both men controlled a natural reaction to look up. They moved out a bit, where they would be safe from anything dropped from above.

"Far enough," Arnild said. "I'm shifting the Eye for a better look." They could hear the faint drone of the Eye's motors as it changed position.

"It's a girl. Wearing some kind of fur outfit. No weapons that I can see, but some kind of a pouch hanging from her waist. She's just clutching onto the tree with her eyes closed. Looks like she's afraid of falling."

The men on the ground could see her dimly now, a huddled shape against the straight trunk.

"Don't bring the Eye any closer," Commander Stane said. "But turn the speaker on. Hook my phone into the circuit."

"You're plugged in."

"We are friends. . . . Come down. . . . We will not hurt you." The words boomed down from the floating speaker above their heads.

"She heard it, but maybe she can't understand Esperanto," Arnild said. "She just hugged the tree harder while you were talking."

Commander Stane had had a good command of Slaver during the war; he groped in his memory for the words, doing a quick translation. He repeated the same phrase, only this time in the tongue of their defeated enemies.

"That did something, Commander," Arnild reported. "She jumped so hard she almost fell off. Then scooted up a couple of branches higher before she grabbed on again."

"Let me get her down, sir," Dall asked. "I'll take some rope and climb up after her. It's the only way. Like getting a cat out of a tree."

Stane pushed the thought around. "It looks like the best answer," he finally said. "Get the lightweight two-hundred-meter line and the climbing irons out of the ship. Don't take too long. It'll be getting dark soon."

The irons chunked into the wood and Dall climbed carefully up to the lower limbs. Above him the girl stirred and he had a quick glimpse of the white patch of her face as she looked down at him. He started climbing again until Arnild's voice snapped at him.

"Hold it! She's climbing higher. Staying above you."

"What'll I do, Commander?" Dall asked, settling himself in the fork of one of the big branches. He felt exhilarated by the climb, his skin tingling slightly with sweat. He snapped open his collar and breathed deeply.

"Keep going. She can't climb any higher than the top of the tree."

The climbing was easier now, the branches smaller and closer together. He went slowly so as not to frighten the girl into a misstep. The ground was out of sight, far below. They were alone in their own world of leaves and swaying boughs. The silver tube of the hovering Eye the only reminder of the watchers from the ship. Dall stopped to tie a loop in the end of the rope, doing it carefully so the knot would hold. For the first time since they had started on this mission he felt as if he was doing a full part. The two old warhorses weren't bad shipmates, but they oppressed him with the years of their experience. But this was something he could do best and whistled softly through his teeth with the thought.

It would have been possible for the girl to have climbed higher; the branches could have held her weight. But for some reason she had retreated out along a branch. There was another close to it, with good handholds, and he shuffled slowly after her.

"No reason to be afraid," he said cheerfully, and smiled. "Just want to get you down safely and back to your friends. Why don't you grab onto this rope?"

The girl just shuddered and backed away. She was young and good to look at, dressed only in a short fur kilt. Her hair was long, but had been combed and caught at the back of her head with a thong. The only thing that appeared alien about her was her fear. As he came closer he could see she was drenched with it. Her legs and hands shook with a steady vibration. Her teeth were clamped into her whitened lips and a thin trickle of blood reached to her chin. He hadn't thought it possible that human eyes could have stared so widely, have been so filled with desperation.

"You don't have to be afraid," he repeated, stopping just out of reach. The branch was thin and springy. If he tried to grab her they might both be bounced off it. He didn't want any accidents to happen now. Slowly pulling the rope from the coil, Dall tied it about his waist, then made a loop around the next branch. Out of the corner of his eye he saw the girl stir and look around wildly.

"Friends!" he said, trying to calm her. He translated into Slaver; she had seemed to understand that before.

*"Noi'r venn!"*

Her mouth opened wide and her legs contracted. The scream was terrible and more like a tortured animal's than a human voice. It confused him and he made a desperate grab. It was too late.

She didn't fall. With all her strength she hurled herself from the limb, jumping toward the certain death she preferred to his touch. For a heartbeat she seemed to hang, contorted and fear-crazed, at the apex of her leap, before gravity clutched hold and pulled her crashing down through the leaves. Then Dall was falling too, grabbing for nonexistent handholds.

The safety line he had tied held fast. In a half daze he worked his way back to the trunk and fumbled loose the knots. With quivering precision he made his way back to the ground. It took a long time, and a blanket was drawn over the deformed thing in the grass before he reached it. He didn't have to ask if she was dead.

"I tried to stop her. I did my best." There was a slight touch of shrillness to Dall's voice.

"Of course," Commander Stane told him, as he spread out the contents of the girl's waist pouch. "We were watching with the Eye. There was no way to stop her when she decided to jump."

"No need to talk Slaver to her either," Arnild said, coming

out of the ship. He was going to add something, but he caught
Commander Stane's direct look and shut his mouth. Dall saw
too.

"I forgot!" the young man said, looking back and forth at
their expressionless faces. "I just remembered she had understood Slaver. I didn't think it would frighten her. It was a
mistake maybe, but anyone can make a mistake! I didn't want
her to die. . . ."

He clamped his trembling jaws shut with an effort, and
turned away.

"You better get some food started," Commander Stane told
him. As soon as the port had closed he pointed to the girl's
body. "Bury her under the trees. I'll help you."

It was a brief meal; none of them were very hungry. Stane
sat at the chart table afterward, pushing the hard green fruit
around with his forefinger. "This is what she was doing in the
tree, why she couldn't pull the vanishing act like the others.
Picking fruit. She had nothing else in the pouch. Our landing
next to the tree and trapping her was pure accident." He
glanced at Dall's face, then turned quickly away.

"It's too dark to see now. Do we wait for morning?" Arnild
asked. He had a handgun disassembled on the table, adjusting
and oiling the parts.

Commander Stane nodded. "It can't do any harm—and it's
better than stumbling around in the dark. Leave an Eye with
an infrared projector and pickup over the village and make a
recording. Maybe we can find out where they all went."

"I'll stay at the Eye controls," Dall said suddenly. "I'm
not . . . sleepy. I might find something out."

The commander hesitated for a moment, then agreed.

"Wake me if you see anything. Otherwise, get us up at
dawn."

The night was quiet and nothing moved in the silent village
of huts. Dall watched, tired but not sleepy, dozed a little until
the alarm woke them all. At first light he and Commander

Stane walked down the hill, an Eye floating ahead to cover them. Arnild stayed behind in the locked ship, at the controls.

"Over this way, sir," Dall said. "Something I found during the night when I was making sweeps with the Eye."

The pit edges had been softened and rounded by the weather; large trees grew on the slopes. At the bottom, projecting from a pool of water, were the remains of rusted machinery.

"I think they're excavation machines," Dall said. "Though it's hard to tell, they've been down there so long."

The Eye dropped down to the bottom of the pit and nosed close to the wreckage. It sank below the surface and emerged after a minute, dripping with water.

"Digging machines, all right," Arnild reported. "Some of them turned over and half buried. Like they fell in, maybe thrown into the hole. All of them Slaver-built."

Commander Stane looked up intently. "Are you sure?" he asked.

"Sure as I can be when I read a label."

"Let's get on to the village," the commander said, chewing thoughtfully at the inside of his cheek.

Dall the Younger discovered where the villagers had gone. It was really no secret; they found out in the first hut they entered. The floor was made of pounded dirt, with a circle of rocks for a fireplace. All the other contents were of the simplest and crudest. Heavy, unfired clay pots, untanned furs, some eating utensils chipped out of hardwood. Dall was poking through a heap of woven mats behind the fireplace when he found the hole.

"Over here, sir!" he called.

The opening was almost a meter in diameter and sank into the ground at an easy angle. The floor of the tunnel was beaten as hard as the floor of the hut.

"They must be hiding out in there," Commander Stane said.

"Flash a light down and see how deep it is."

There was no way to tell. The hole was really a smooth-walled tunnel that turned at a sharp angle five meters inside the entrance. The Eye swooped down and hung, humming above the opening.

"I took a look in some of the other huts," Arnild said from the ship. "The Eye found a hole like this in every one of them. Want me to take a look inside?"

"Yes, but take it slowly," Commander Stane told him.

"If there are people hiding down there we don't want to frighten them any more. Drift down and pull back if you find anything."

The humming died as the Eye floated down the tunnel and out of sight.

"Joined another tunnel," Arnild reported. "And now another junction. Getting confused . . . don't know if I can get it back the way I sent it in."

"The Eye is expendable," the commander told him. "Keep going."

"Must be dense rock around . . . signal is getting weaker and I have a job holding control. A bigger cavern of some sort . . . hold it! There's someone! Caught a look at a man going into one of the side tunnels."

"Follow him," Stane said.

"Not easy," Arnild said after a moment's silence.

"Looks like a dead end. A rock of some kind blocking the tunnel. It must have rolled it back and blocked the passage after went by. I'll back out . . . blast!"

"What's wrong?"

"Another rock behind the Eye—they've got it trapped in that blocked-off piece of tunnel. Now the screen's dead. All I can get is an out-of-operation signal!" Arnild sounded exasperated and angry.

"Very neat," Commander Stane said. "They lured it in, trapped it—then probably collapsed the roof of the tunnel.

These people are very suspicious of strangers and seem to have a certain efficiency at getting rid of them."

"But why?" Dall asked. He looked around at the crude construction of the hut. "What could these people possibly have that the Slavers could have wanted so badly? Those machines we found, it's obvious that the Slavers put a lot of time and effort into trying to dig down there. But did they ever find what they were looking for? Did they try to destroy this planet because they had found it—or because they hadn't found it?"

"I wish I knew," Commander Stane said glumly. "It would make my job a lot easier. I'm getting a complete report off to HQ—maybe they will have some ideas."

On the way back to the ship they noticed the fresh dirt in the grove of trees. There was a raw empty hole where the girl had been buried. The ground had been torn apart and hurled in every direction. There were slash marks on the trunks of the trees, made by sharp blades . . . or giant claws. Something or somebody had come for the girl, dug up her body and vented a burning rage on the ground and the trees. A crushed trail led to an opening between the roots of one of the trees. It slanted back and down. Its dark mouth was as enigmatic and mysterious as the other tunnels.

Before they retired that night, Commander Stane made a double check that the ports were locked and all the alarm circuits activated. He went to bed but did not sleep. The answer to the problem seemed tantalizingly obvious, hovering just outside his reach. There should be enough facts here to draw a conclusion from. But what conclusion? He drifted into a fitful doze without finding the answer.

When he awoke the cabin was still dark, and he had the feeling something was terribly wrong. What had awakened him? He groped in his sleep-filled memories. A sigh. A rush of air. It could have been the cycling of the air lock. Fighting down the sudden fear, he snapped on the lights and pulled his gun from the bedside rack. Arnild appeared, yawning and blinking in the doorway.

"What's going on?" he asked.

"Get Dall! I think someone came into the ship."

"Gone out is more like it," Arnild snuffed. "Dall's not in his bunk."

"What!"

He ran to the control room. The alarm circuit had been turned off. There was a piece of paper on the control console. The commander grabbed it up and read the single word written on it. He gaped as comprehension struck him, then crushed the paper in his convulsive fist.

"The fool!" he shouted. "The damned young fool! Break out an Eye. No, fire up two of them! I'll work the duplicate control!"

"But what happened?" Arnild gaped. "What's young Dall done?"

"Gone underground. Into the tunnels. We have to stop him!"

Dall was nowhere in sight, but there were footprints, fresh crumbled dirt on the lip of the tunnel under the trees.

"I'll take an Eye down there," Commander Stane said.

"You take another one down the next nearest entrance. Use the speakers. Tell them that we are friends. Tell them that in Slaver."

"But you saw what reaction the girl had when Dall told her that." Arnild was puzzled, confused.

"I know what happened," Stane snapped. "But what other choice do we have? Now get on with it!"

Arnild started to ask another question, but the concentrated intensity of the commander at the controls changed his mind. He sent his own Eye rocketing toward the village.

If the people hiding in the maze of tunnels heard the message, they certainly didn't believe it. One Eye was caught in a dead-end tunnel when the opening behind it suddenly filled with soft soil. Commander Stane tried nosing the machine through the dirt, but it was firmly trapped and held. He could hear thumpings and digging as more soil was piled on top.

Arnild's Eye found a large underground chamber, filled with huddled and frightened sheep. There were none of the natives there. On the way out of this cavern the Eye was trapped under a fall of rocks.

In the end, Commander Stane admitted defeat. "It's up to them now. We can't affect the way this ends. Not one way or another."

"Something moving in the grove of trees, Commander," Arnild said sharply. "Caught it on the detector. It's gone now."

They went out hesitantly with their guns pointed, under a reddened dawn sky. They went, half-knowing what they would find, but fearful to admit it aloud while they could still hope.

Of course there was no hope. Dall the Younger's body lay near the tunnel mouth, out of which it had been pushed. The red dawn glinted from red blood. He had died terribly.

"They're fiends! Animals!" Arnild shouted. "To do that to a man who only wanted to help them. Broke his arms and legs, scratched away most of his skin. His face—nothing left . . ." The aging gunner choked out a sound that was half gasp, half sob. "They ought to be bombed out, blown up! Like the Slavers started . . ." He met the commander's burning stare and fell silent.

"That's probably just how the Slavers felt," Stane said. "Don't you understand what happened here?"

Arnild shook his head dumbly.

"Dall had a glimpse of the truth. His mistake was that he thought it was possible to change things. But at least he knew what the danger was. He went because he felt guilt for the girl's death. That was why he left the note with the word 'slave' on it. In case he didn't come back."

"What do you mean—?"

"It's really quite simple," Arnild said wearily, leaning back against a tree. "Only we were looking for something more complex and technical. When it wasn't really a physical problem, but a social one we were facing. This was a slave planet, set up and organized by the Slavers to fit their special needs."

"What?" Arnild asked, still confused.

"Slaves. The Slavers were constantly expanding, and you know that their style of warfare was expensive on manpower. They needed steady sources of supply, so must have had to create them. This planet was one answer. Made to order in a way. A single, lightly forested continent. With few places for the people to hide when the slave ships came. They must have planted settlements, given the people simple and sufficient sources of food—but absolutely no technology. Then they could go away to let the people here breed. After that they would return every few years and take as many slaves as they needed. Leave the others behind to replenish the stock. Only they reckoned without one thing."

Arnild's numbness was wearing off. He understood now.

"The adaptability of mankind," he said.

"Of course. The ability—given enough time—to adapt to almost any extreme of environment. This is a perfect example. A cut-off population with no history, no written language. Just the desire to survive. Every few years unspeakable creatures drop out of the sky and steal their children. They try running away, but there is no place to run. They build boats, but there is no place to sail to. Nothing works. . . ."

"Until one bright boy digs a hole, covers it up, and hides his family in it. And finds out it works."

"The beginning," Commander Stane nodded. "The idea spreads, the tunnels get deeper and more elaborate. The Slavers would try to dig them out—so they started building defenses. This went on—until the slaves finally won.

"This might very well have been the first planet to rebel

successfully against the Greater Slavocracy. They couldn't be dug out. Poison gas would just kill them—and they had no value dead. Machines sent after them were trapped like our Eyes. And men who were foolish enough to go down . . ." He couldn't finish the sentence; Dall's body was stronger evidence than words could ever be.

"But the hatred?" Arnild asked. "The way the girl killed herself rather than be taken."

"The tunnels must have become a religion, a way of life," Stane told him. "They had to be, to be kept in operation and repair during the long gap of years between visits by the Slavers. The children had to be taught that the demons come from the skies, that salvation lay below. Just about the opposite of the old Earth religions. Hatred and fear were firmly implanted so that everyone, no matter how young, would know what to do if a ship appeared. There must be entrances everywhere. Seconds after a ship is sighted the population can vanish underground. They knew we were Slavers since only demons come from the sky.

"Dall must have guessed part of this. Only he thought he could reason with them, explain that the Slavers were gone and that they didn't have to hide anymore. That good men come from the skies. But that's heresy, and by itself would be enough to get him killed. If they ever bothered to listen."

They were gentle when they carried Dall the Younger back to the ship.

"It is going to be some job trying to convince these people of the truth." Arnild said when they paused for a moment to rest. "I still don't understand, though, why the Slavers wanted to blow the planet up."

"There too, we were looking for too complex a motive," Commander Stane said. "Why does a conquering army blow up buildings and destroy monuments when it is forced to retreat? Just frustration and anger, old human emotions. If I can't have it, you can't have it either. This planet must have annoyed the Slavers for years. A successful rebellion that they couldn't put down. They kept trying to capture the rebels since they were incapable of admitting defeat at the hands of slaves. When they knew their war was lost, destruction of this planet was an easy vent for their emotions. I noticed you feeling the same way yourself when you saw Dall's body. It's a human reaction."

They were both old soldiers, so they didn't show their emotions too much when they put Dall's corpse into the necro chamber and readied the ship for takeoff.

But they were old men as well, much older since they had come to the planet, and they moved now with old men's stiffness.

# ROOMMATES

The August sun struck in through the open window and burned on Andrew Rusch's bare legs until discomfort dragged him awake from the depths of heavy sleep. Only slowly did he become aware of the heat and the damp and gritty sheet beneath his body. He rubbed at his gummed-shut eyelids, then lay there, staring up at the cracked and stained plaster of the ceiling, only half-awake and experiencing a feeling of dislocation, not knowing in those first waking moments just where he was, although he had lived in this room for over seven years. He yawned, and the odd sensation slipped away while he groped for the watch that he always put on the chair next to the bed; then he yawned again as he blinked at the hands mistily seen behind the scratched crystal. Seven . . . seven o'clock in the morning, and there was a little number 9 in the middle of the square window. Monday the ninth of August, 1999—and hot as a furnace already, with the city still embedded in the heat wave that had baked and suffocated New York for the past ten days. Andy scratched at a trickle of perspiration on his side, then moved his legs out of the patch of sunlight and bunched the pillow up under his neck. From the

other side of the thin partition that divided the room in half there came a clanking whir that quickly rose to a high-pitched drone.

"Morning . . ." he shouted over the sound, then began coughing. Still coughing, he reluctantly stood and crossed the room to draw a glass of water from the wall tank; it came out in a thin, brownish trickle. He swallowed it, then rapped the dial on the tank with his knuckles, and the needle bobbed up and down close to the Empty mark. It needed filling; he would have to see to that before he signed in at four o'clock at the precinct. The day had begun.

A full-length mirror with a crack running down it was fixed to the front of the hulking wardrobe, and he poked his face close to it, rubbing at his bristly jaw. He would have to shave before he went in. No one should ever look at himself in the morning, naked and revealed, he decided with distaste, frowning at the dead white of his skin and the slight bow to his legs that was usually concealed by his pants. And how did he manage to have ribs that stuck out like those of a starved horse, as well as a growing potbelly—both at the same time? He kneaded the soft flesh and thought that it must be the starchy diet, that and sitting around on his chunk most of the time. But at least the fat wasn't showing on his face. His forehead was a little higher each year, but wasn't too obvious as long as his hair was cropped short. You have just turned thirty, he thought to himself, and the wrinkles are already starting around your eyes. And your nose is too big—wasn't it Uncle Brian who always said that was because there was Welsh blood in the family? And your canine teeth are a little too obvious so when you smile you look a bit like a hyena. You're a handsome devil, Andy Rusch, and it's a wonder a girl like Shirl will even look at you, much less kiss you. He scowled at himself, then went to look for a handkerchief to blow his impressive Welsh nose.

There was just a single pair of clean undershorts in the

drawer and he pulled them on; that was another thing he had to remember today, to get some washing done. The squealing whine was still coming from the other side of the partition as he pushed through the connecting door.

"You're going to give yourself a coronary, Sol," he told the gray-bearded man who was perched on the wheelless bicycle, pedaling so industriously that perspiration ran down his chest and soaked into the bath towel that he wore tied around his waist.

"Never a coronary," Solomon Kahn gasped out, pumping steadily. "I been doing this every day for so long that my ticker would miss it if I stopped. And no cholesterol in my arteries either since regular flushing with alcohol takes care of that. And no lung cancer since I couldn't afford to smoke even if I wanted to, which I don't. And at the age of seventy-five no prostatitis because . . ."

"Sol, please—spare me the horrible details on an empty stomach. Do you have an ice cube to spare?"

"Take two—it's a hot day. And don't leave the door open too long."

Andy opened the small refrigerator that squatted against the wall and quickly took out the plastic container of margarine, then squeezed two ice cubes from the tray into a glass and slammed the door. He filled the glass with water from the wall tank and put it on the table next to the margarine. "Have you eaten yet?" he asked.

"I'll join you, these things should be charged by now."

Sol stopped pedaling and the whine died away to a moan, then vanished. He disconnected the wires from the electrical generator that was geared to the rear axle of the bike, and carefully coiled them up next to the four black automobile storage batteries that were racked on top of the refrigerator. Then, after wiping his hands on his soiled towel sarong, he pulled out one of the bucket seats, salvaged from an ancient 1975 Ford, and sat down across the table from Andy.

"I heard the six o'clock news," he said. "The Eldsters are organizing another protest march today on relief headquarters. *That's* where you'll see coronaries!"

"I won't, thank God, I'm not on until four and Union Square isn't in our precinct." He opened the breadbox and took out one of the six-inch-square red crackers, then pushed the box over to Sol. He spread margarine thinly on it and took a bite, wrinkling his nose as he chewed. "I think this margarine has turned."

"How can you tell?" Sol grunted, biting into one of the dry crackers. "Anything made from motor oil and whale blubber is turned to begin with."

"Now you begin to sound like a naturist," Andy said, washing his cracker down with cold water. "There's hardly any flavor at all to the fats made from petrochemicals and you know there aren't any whales left so they can't use blubber— it's just good chlorella oil."

"Whales, plankton, herring oil, it's all the same. Tastes fishy. I'll take mine dry so I don't grow no fins." There was a sudden staccato rapping on the door and he groaned. "Not yet eight o'clock and already they are after you."

"It could be anything," Andy said, starting for the door.

"It could be but it's not, that's the callboy's knock and you know it as well as I do and I bet you dollars to doughnuts that's just who it is. See?" He nodded with gloomy satisfaction when Andy unlocked the door and they saw the skinny, bare-legged messenger standing in the dark hall.

"What do you want, Woody?" Andy asked.

"I don' wan' no-fin," Woody lisped over his bare gums. Though he was in his early twenties, he didn't have a tooth in his head. "Lieutenant says bring, I bring." He handed Andy the message board with his name written on the outside.

Andy turned toward the light and opened it, reading the lieutenant's spiky scrawl on the slate, then took the chalk and scribbled his initials after it and returned it to the messenger.

He closed the door behind him and went back to finish his breakfast, frowning in thought.

"Don't look at me that way," Sol said, "I didn't send the message. Am I wrong in guessing it's not the most pleasant of news?"

"It's the Eldsters, they're jamming the Square already and precinct needs reinforcements."

"But why you? This sounds like a job for the harness bulls."

"Harness bulls! Where do you get that medieval slang? Of course they need patrolmen for the crowd, but there have to be detectives there to spot known agitators, pickpockets, purse-grabbers, and the rest. It'll be murder in that park today. I have to check in by nine, so I have enough time to bring up some water first."

Andy dressed slowly in slacks and a loose sport shirt, then put a pan of water on the windowsill to warm in the sun. He took the two five-gallon plastic jerry cans, and when he went out Sol looked up from the TV set, glancing over the top of his old-fashioned glasses.

"When you bring back the water I'll fix you a drink—or do you think it is too early?"

"Not the way I feel today, it's not."

The hall was ink black once the door had closed behind him, and he felt his way carefully along the wall to the stairs, cursing and almost falling when he stumbled over a heap of refuse someone had thrown there. Two flights down a window had been knocked through the wall and enough light came in to show him the way down the last two flights to the street. After the damp hallway the heat of Twenty-fifth Street hit him in a musty wave, a stifling miasma compounded of decay, dirt, and unwashed humanity. He had to make his way through the women who already filled the steps of the building, walking carefully so that he didn't step on the children who were playing below. The sidewalk was still in shadow but so jammed with people that he walked in the street, well away from the curb to avoid the rubbish and litter banked high there. Days of heat had softened the tar so that it gave underfoot, then clutched at the soles of his shoes. There was the usual line leading to the columnar red water point on the corner of Seventh Avenue, but it broke up with angry shouts and some waved fists just as he reached it. Still muttering, the crowd dispersed, and Andy saw that the duty patrolman was locking the steel door.

"What's going on?" Andy asked. "I thought this point was open until noon?"

The policeman turned, his hand automatically staying close to his gun until he recognized the detective from his own precinct. He tilted back his uniform cap and wiped the sweat from his forehead with the back of his hand.

"Just had the orders from the sergeant, all points closed for twenty-four hours. The reservoir level is low because of the drought, they gotta save water."

"That's a hell of a note," Andy said, looking at the key still in the lock. "I'm going on duty now and this means I'm not going to be drinking for a couple of days. . . ."

After a careful look around, the policeman unlocked the door and took one of the jerry cans from Andy. "One of these ought to hold you." He held it under the faucet while it filled, then lowered his voice. "Don't let it out, but word is that there was another dynamiting job on the aqueduct upstate."

"Those farmers again?"

"It must be. I was on guard duty up there before I came to this precinct and it's rough, they just as soon blow you up with the aqueduct at the same time. Claim the city's stealing their water."

"They've got enough," Andy said, taking the full container. "More than they need. And there are thirty-five million people here in the city who get damn thirsty."

"Who's arguing?" the cop asked, slamming the door shut again and locking it tight.

Andy pushed his way back through the crowd around the steps and went through to the backyard first. All of the toilets were in use and he had to wait, and when he finally got into one of the cubicles he took the jerry cans with him; one of the kids playing in the pile of rubbish against the fence would be sure to steal them if he left them unguarded.

When he had climbed the dark flights once more and opened the door to the room he heard the clear sound of ice cubes rattling against glass.

"That's Beethoven's Fifth Symphony that you're playing," he said, dropping the containers and falling into a chair.

"It's my favorite tune," Sol said, taking two chilled glasses from the refrigerator, and with the solemnity of religious ritual he filled them and dropped a tiny pearl onion into each of them. Passed one to Andy, who sipped carefully at the chilled liquid.

"It's when I taste one of these, Sol, that I almost believe you're not crazy after all. Why do they call them Gibsons?"

"A secret lost behind the mists of time. Why is a Stinger a Stinger or a Pink Lady a Pink Lady?"

"I don't know—why? I never tasted any of them."

"I don't know either, but that's the name. Like those green things they serve in the knockjoints, Panamas. Doesn't mean anything, just a name."

"Thanks," Andy said, draining his glass. "The day looks better already."

He went into his room and took his holstered gun from the drawer and clipped it inside the waistband of his pants. His shield was on his key ring where he always kept it and he slipped his notepad in on top of it, then hesitated a moment. It was going to be a long and rough day and anything might happen. He dug his nippers out from under his shirts, then the soft plastic tube filled with shot. It might be needed in the crowd, safer than a gun with all those old people milling about. Not only that, but with the new austerity regulations you had to have a damn good reason for using up any ammunition. He washed as well as he could with the pint of water that had been warming in the sun on the windowsill, then scrubbed his face with the small shard of gray and gritty soap until his whiskers softened a bit. His razor blade was beginning to show obvious nicks along both edges and, as he honed it against the inside of his drinking glass, he thought that it was time to think about getting a new one. Maybe in the fall.

Sol was watering his window box when Andy came out, carefully irrigating the rows of herbs and tiny onions. "Don't take any wooden nickels," he said without looking up from his work. Sol had a million of them, all old. What in the world was a wooden nickel?

The sun was higher now and the heat was mounting in the sealed tar and concrete valley of the street. The band of shade was smaller and the steps were so packed with humanity that he couldn't leave the doorway. He carefully pushed by a tiny, runny-nosed girl dressed only in ragged gray underwear and descended a step. The gaunt women moved aside reluctantly, ignoring him, but the men stared at him with a cold look of hatred stamped across their features that gave them a strangely alike appearance; as though they were all members of the same angry family.

Andy threaded his way through the last of them and when he reached the sidewalk he had to step over the outstretched leg of an old man who sprawled there. He looked dead, not asleep, and he might be for all that anyone cared. His foot was bare and filthy and a string tied about his ankle led to a naked baby that was sitting vacantly on the sidewalk chewing on a bent plastic dish. The baby was as dirty as the man and the string was tied about its chest under the pipestem arms because its stomach was swollen and heavy. Was the old man dead? Not that it mattered; the only work he had to do in the world was to act as an anchor for the baby. He could do that job just as well alive or dead.

Out of the room now, well away and unable to talk to Sol
until he returned, he realized that once again he had not
managed to mention Shirl. It would have been a simple
enough thing to do, but he kept forgetting it, avoiding it. Sol
was always talking about how horny he always was and how
often he used to get laid when he was in the army. He would
understand.

They were roommates, that was all. There was nothing else
between them. Friends, sure. But bringing a girl in to live
wouldn't change that.

So why hadn't he told him?

FALL

"Everybody says this is the coldest October ever, I never seen
a colder one. And the rain too, never hard enough to fill the
reservoir or anything, but just enough to make you wet so you
feel colder."

"Ain't that right?"

Shirl nodded, hardly listening to the words, but aware by
the rising intonation of the woman's voice that a question had
been asked. The line moved forward and she shuffled a few
steps behind the woman who had been speaking—a shapeless
bundle of heavy clothing covered with a torn plastic raincoat.
A cord was tied about her middle so that she resembled a
lumpy sack. Not that I look much better, Shirl thought, tugging the fold of blanket farther over her head to keep out the
persistent drizzle. It wouldn't be much longer now, there were
only a few dozen people ahead. But it had taken a lot more
time than she thought it would; it was almost dark. A light
came on over the tank car, glinting off its black sides and
lighting up the slowly falling curtain of rain. The line moved
again and the woman ahead of Shirl waddled forward, pulling
the child after her. A bundle as wrapped and shapeless as its

mother, its face hidden by a knotted scarf, that produced an almost constant whimpering.

"Stop that," the woman said. She turned to Shirl, her puffy face a red lumpiness around the dark opening of her almost toothless mouth. "He's crying because he's been to see the doc, thinks he's sick but it's only the kwash." She held up the child's swollen, ballooning hand. "You can tell when they swell up and get the black spots on the knees. Had to sit two weeks in the Bellevue clinic to see a doc who told me what I knew already. But that's the only way you get him to sign the slip. Got a peanut-butter ration that way. My old man loves the stuff. You live on my block, don't you? I think I seen you there?"

"Twenty-sixth Street," Shirl said, taking the cap off the jerry can and putting it into her coat pocket. She felt chilled through and was sure she was catching a cold.

"That's right, I knew it was you. Stick around and wait for me, we'll walk back together. It's getting late and plenty of punks would like to grab the water, they can always sell it. Mrs. Ramirez in my building, she's a Spic but she's all right, you know, her family been in the building since the World War Two, she got a black eye so swole up she can't see through it and two teeth knocked out. Some punk got her with a club and took her water away."

"Yes, I'll wait for you, that's a good idea," Shirl said, suddenly feeling very alone.

"Cards," the patrolman said and she handed him the three Welfare cards, hers, Andy's, and Sol's. He held them to the light, then handed them back to her. "Six quarts," he called out to the valve man.

"That's not right," Shirl said.

"Reduced ration today, lady, keep moving, there's a lot of people waiting."

She held out the jerry can and the valve man slipped the end

of a large funnel into it and ran in the water. "Next," he called
out.

The jerry can gurgled when she walked and was tragically
light. She went and stood near the policeman until the woman
came up, pulling the child with one hand and in the other
carrying a five-gallon kerosene can that seemed almost full.
She must have a big family.

"Let's go," the woman said and the child trailed, mewling
faintly, at the end of her arm.

As they left the Twelfth Avenue railroad siding it grew
darker, the rain soaking up all the failing light. The buildings
here were mostly old warehouses and factories with blank
solid walls concealing the tenants hidden away inside; the
sidewalks were wet and empty. The nearest streetlight was a
block away.

"My husband will give me hell coming home this late," the
woman said as they turned the corner. Two figures blocked the
sidewalk in front of them.

"Let's have the water," the nearest one said, and the distant
light reflected from the knife he held before him.

"No, don't! Please don't!" the woman begged and swung
her can of water out behind her, away from them. Shirl huddled against the wall and saw, when they walked forward, that
they were just young boys, teenagers. But they still had a knife.

"The water!" the first one said, jabbing his knife at the
woman.

"Take it," she screeched, swinging the can like a weight on
the end of her arm. Before the boy could dodge, it caught him
full in the side of the head, knocking him howling to the
ground, the knife flying from his fingers. "You want some
too!" she shouted, advancing on the second boy. He was
unarmed.

"No, I don't want no trouble," he begged, pulling at the first
one's arm, then retreating when she approached. When she
bent to pick up the fallen knife, he managed to drag the other

boy to his feet and half-carry him around the corner. It had only taken a few seconds and all the time Shirl had stood with her back to the wall, trembling with fear.

"They got some surprise," the woman crowed, holding the worn carving knife up to admire. "I can use this better than they can. Just punks, kids." She was excited and happy. During the entire time she had never released her grip on the child's hand; it was sobbing louder.

There was no more trouble and the woman went with Shirl as far as her door. "Thank you very much," Shirl said. "I don't know what I would have done . . ."

"That's no trouble," the woman beamed. "You saw what I did to him—and who got the knife now!" She stamped away, hauling the heavy can in one hand, the child in the other. Shirl went in.

"Where have you been?" Andy asked when she pushed open the door. "I was beginning to wonder what had happened to you." It was warm in the room, with a faint odor of fishy smoke. He and Sol were sitting at the table with drink in their hands.

"It was the water, the line must have been a block long. They only gave me six quarts, the ration has been cut again." She saw his black look and decided not to tell him about the trouble on the way back. He would be twice as angry then and she didn't want this meal to be spoiled.

"That's really wonderful," Andy said sarcastically. "The ration was already too small—so now they lower it even more. Better get out of those wet things, Shirl. Then Sol will pour you a Gibson. His homemade vermouth has ripened—and I bought some vodka."

"Drink up," Sol said, handing her the chilled glass. "I made some soup with that ener-G junk, it's the only way it's edible, and it should be just about ready. We'll have that for the first course, before—" He finished the sentence by jerking his head in the direction of the refrigerator.

"What's up?" Andy asked. "A secret?"

"No secret," Shirl said, opening the refrigerator, "just a surprise. I got these today in the market, one for each of us." She took out a plate with three small soylent burgers on it. "They're the new ones, they had them on TV, with the smoky-barbecue flavor."

"They must have cost a fortune," Andy said. "We won't eat for the rest of the month."

"They're not as expensive as all that. Anyway, it was my own money, not the budget money I used."

"It doesn't make any difference, money is money. We could probably live for a week on what these things cost."

"Soup's on," Sol said, sliding the plates onto the table. Shirl had a lump in her throat so she couldn't say anything; she sat and looked at her plate and tried not to cry.

"I'm sorry," Andy said. "But you know how prices are going up—we have to look ahead. City income tax is higher, eighty percent now, because of the raised Welfare payment, so it's going to be rough going this winter. Don't think I don't appreciate it. . . ."

"If you do, so why don't you shut up right there and eat your soup?" Sol said.

"Keep out of this, Sol," Andy said.

"I'll keep out of it when you keep the fight out of my room. Now come on, a nice meal like this, it shouldn't be spoiled."

Andy started to answer him, then changed his mind. He reached over and took Shirl's hand. "It is going to be a good dinner," he said. "Let's all enjoy it."

"Not that good," Sol said, puckering his mouth over a spoonful of soup. "Wait until you try this stuff. But the burgers will take the taste out of our mouths."

There was silence after that while they spooned up the soup, until Sol started on one of his army stories about New Orleans and it was so incredibly impossible that they had to laugh, and after that things were better. Sol shared out the rest of the Gibsons while Shirl served the burgers.

"If I was drunk enough this would almost taste like meat," Sol announced, chewing happily.

"They are good," Shirl said. Andy nodded agreement. She finished the burger quickly and soaked up the juice with a scrap of weedcracker, then sipped at her drink. The trouble on the way home with the water already seemed far distant. What was it the woman had said was wrong with the child?

"Do you know what 'kwash' is?" she asked.

Andy shrugged. "Some kind of disease, that's all I know. Why do you ask?"

"There was a woman next to me in line for the water, I was talking to her. She had a little boy with her who was sick with this kwash. I don't think she should have had him out in the rain, sick like that. And I was wondering if it was catching."

"That you can forget about," Sol said. " 'Kwash' is short for 'kwashiorkor.' If, in the interest of good health, you watched the medical programs like I do, or opened a book, you would know all about it. You can't catch it because it's a deficiency disease like beriberi."

"I never heard of that either," Shirl said.

"There's not so much of that, but there's plenty of kwash. It comes from not eating enough protein. They used to have it only in Africa but now they got it right across the whole U.S. Isn't that great? There's no meat around, lentils and soybeans cost too much, so the mamas stuff the kids with weedcrackers and candy, whatever is cheap. . . ."

The light bulb flickered, then went out. Sol felt his way across the room and found a switch in the maze of wiring on top of the refrigerator. A dim bulb lit up, connected to his batteries.

"Needs a charge," he said, "but it can wait until morning. You shouldn't exercise after eating, bad for the circulation and digestion."

"I'm sure glad you're here, Doctor," Andy said. "I need some medical advice. I've got this trouble. You see—everything I eat goes to my stomach. . . ."

"Very funny, Mr. Wiseguy. Shirl, I don't see how you put up with this joker."

They all felt better after the meal and they talked for a while, until Sol announced he was turning off the light to save the juice in the batteries. The small bricks of sea coal had burned to ash and the room was growing cold. They said good night and Andy went in first to get his flashlight; their room was even colder than the other.

"I'm going to bed," Shirl said. "I'm not really tired, but it's the only way to keep warm."

Andy flicked the overhead light switch uselessly. "The current is still off and there are some things I have to do. What is it—a week now since we had any electricity in the evening?"

"Let me get into bed and I'll work the flash for you—will that be all right?"

"It'll have to do."

He opened his notepad on top of the dresser, laid one of the reusable forms next to it, then began copying information into the report. With his left hand he kept a slow and regular squeezing on the flashlight that produced steady illumination. The city was quiet tonight with the people driven from the streets by the cold and the rain; the whir of the tiny generator and the occasional squeak of the stylo on plastic sounded unnaturally loud. There was enough light from the flash for Shirl to get undressed by. She shivered when she took off her outer clothes and quickly pulled on heavy winter pajamas, a much-darned pair of socks she used for sleeping in, then put her heavy sweater on top. The sheets were cold and damp; they hadn't been changed since the water shortage, though she did try to air them out as often as she could. Her cheeks were damp as well, as damp as the sheets were when she put her fingertips up to touch them, and she realized that she was crying. She tried not to sniffle and bother Andy. He was doing his best, wasn't he? Doing everything that it was possible to do. Yes, it had been a lot different before she came here, an easy life, good food and a warm room, and her own body-guard, Tab, when she went out. And all she had to do was sleep with him a couple of times a week. She had hated it, even the touch of his hands, but at least it had been quick. Having Andy in bed was different and good and she wished that he were there right now. She shivered again and wished she could stop crying.

WINTER

New York City trembled on the brink of disaster. Every locked warehouse was a nucleus of dissent, surrounded by crowds who were hungry and afraid and searching for some-one to blame. Their anger incited them to riot, and the food riots turned to water riots and then to looting wherever this was possible. The police fought back, only the thinnest of barriers between angry protest and bloody chaos.

At first nightsticks and weighted clubs stopped the trouble, and when this failed gas dispersed the crowd. The tension grew, since the people who fled only reassembled again in a different place. The solid jets of water from the riot trucks stopped them easily when they tried to break into the welfare stations, but there were not enough trucks, nor was there more water to be had once they had pumped dry their tanks. The Health Department had forbidden the use of river water: it would have been like spraying poison. The little water that was available was badly needed for the fires that were spring-ing up throughout the city. With the streets blocked in many places the firefighting equipment could not get through and the trucks were forced to make long detours. Some of the fires were spreading and by noon all of the equipment had been committed and was in use.

The first gun was fired a few minutes past twelve on the morning of December 21st, by a Welfare Department guard who killed a man who had broken open a window of the Tompkins Square food depot and had tried to climb in. This was the first but not the last shot fired—nor was it the last person to be killed.

Flying wire sealed off some of the trouble areas, but there was only a limited supply of it. When it ran out the copters fluttered helplessly over the surging streets and acted as aerial observation posts for the police, finding the places where reserves were sorely needed. It was a fruitless labor because there were no reserves; everyone was in the front line.

After the first conflict nothing else made a strong impression on Andy. For the rest of the day and most of the night, he along with every other policeman in the city was braving violence and giving violence to restore law and order to a city torn by battle. The only rest he had was after he had fallen victim to his own gas and had managed to make his way to the Department of Hospitals ambulance for treatment. An orderly washed out his eyes and gave him a tablet to counteract the gut-tearing nausea. He lay on one of the stretchers inside, clutching his helmet, bombs, and club to his chest while he recovered. The ambulance driver sat on another stretcher by the door, armed with a .30-caliber carbine, to discourage anyone from too great an interest in the ambulance or its valuable surgical contents. Andy would like to have lain there longer, but the cold mist was rolling in through the open doorway, and he began to shiver so hard that his teeth shook together. It was difficult to drag himself to his feet and climb to the ground, yet once he was moving he felt a little better—and warmer. The attack had been broken up and he moved slowly to join the nearest cluster of blue-coated figures, wrinkling his nose at the foul odor of his clothes.

From this point on, the fatigue never left him and he had memories only of shouting faces, running feet, the sound of shots, screams, the thud of gas grenades. Of something unseen that had been thrown at him and hit the back of his hand and raised an immense bruise.

By nightfall it was raining, a cold downpour mixed with sleet, and it was this and exhaustion that drove the people from the streets, not the police. Yet when the crowds were gone the police found that their work was just beginning. Gaping windows and broken doorways had to be guarded until they could be repaired, the injured had to be found and brought in for treatment, while the Fire Department needed aid in halting the countless fires. This went on through the night and at dawn Andy found himself dumped on a bench in the precinct, hearing his name being called off from a list by Lieutenant Grassioli.

"And that's all that can be spared," the lieutenant added. "You men draw rations before you leave and turn in your riot equipment. I want you all back here at eighteen-hundred and I don't want excuses. Our troubles aren't over yet."

Sometime during the night the rain had stopped. The rising sun cast long shadows down the crosstown streets, putting a golden sheen on the wet, black pavement. A burned-out brownstone was still smoking and Andy picked his way through the charred wreckage that littered the street in front of it. On the corner of Seventh Avenue was the crushed wreckage of two pedicabs, already stripped of any usable parts, and a few feet farther on, the huddled body of a man. He might be asleep, but when Andy passed, the upturned face gave violent evidence that the man was dead. He walked on, ignoring it. The Department of Sanitation would be collecting only corpses today.

The first cavemen were coming out of the subway entrance, blinking at the light. During the summer everyone laughed at the cavemen—the people whom Welfare had assigned to living quarters in the stations of the now-silent subways. But as the cold weather approached the laughter was replaced by envy. Perhaps it was filthy down there, dusty, dark, but there were always a few electric heaters turned on. They weren't living in luxury, but at least Welfare didn't let them freeze. Andy turned into his own block.

Going up the stairs in his building, he trod heavily on some of the sleepers but was too fatigued to care—or even notice. He had trouble fumbling his key into the lock and Sol heard him and came to open it.

"I just made some soup," Sol said. "You timed it perfectly."

Andy pulled the broken remains of some weedcrackers from his coat pocket and spilled them onto the table.

"Been stealing food?" Sol asked, picking up a piece and nibbling on it. "I thought no grub was being given out for two more days?"

"Police ration."

"Only fair. You can't beat up the citizenry on an empty stomach. I'll throw some of these into the soup, give it some body. I guess you didn't see TV yesterday so you wouldn't know about all the fun and games in Congress. Things are really jumping. . . ."

"Is Shirl awake yet?" Andy asked, shucking out of his coat and dropping heavily into a chair.

Sol was silent a moment, then he said slowly, "She's not here."

Andy yawned. "It's plenty early to go out. Why?"

"Not today, Andy." Sol stirred the soup with his back turned. "She went out yesterday, a couple of hours after you did. She's not back yet."

"You mean she was out all the time during the riots—and last night too? What did you do?" He sat upright, his bone-weariness forgotten.

"What could I do? Go out and get myself trampled to death like the rest of the old fogies? I bet she's all right. She probably saw all the trouble and decided to stay with a friend instead of coming back here."

"What friend? What are you talking about? I have to go find her."

"Sit!" Sol ordered. "What can you do out there? Have some soup and get some sleep, that's the best thing you can do. She'll be okay. I know it," he added reluctantly.

"What do you know, Sol?" Andy took him by the shoulders, half turning him from the stove.

"Don't handle the merchandise!" Sol shouted, pushing the hand away. Then, in a quieter voice: "All I know is she just didn't go out of here for nothing, she had a reason. She had her old coat on, but I could see what looked like a real nifty dress underneath. And nylon stockings. A fortune on her legs. And when she said so long I saw she had lots of makeup on."

"Sol—what are you trying to say?"

"I'm not trying—I'm saying. She was dressed for visiting, not for shopping, like she was on the way out to see someone. Her old man, maybe, she could be visiting him."

"Why should she want to see him?"

"You tell me? You two had a fight, didn't you? Maybe she went away for a while to cool off."

"A fight . . . I guess so." Andy dropped back into the chair, squeezing his forehead with his palms. Had it only been last night? No, the night before last. It seemed like a hundred years since they had had that stupid argument. But they were bickering so much these days. One more fight shouldn't make any difference. He looked up with sudden fear. "She didn't take her things—anything with her?" he asked.

"Just a little bag," Sol said, and put a steaming bowl on the table in front of Andy. "Eat up. I'll pour one for myself." Then, "She'll be back."

Andy was almost too tired to argue—and what could be said? He spooned the soup automatically, then realized as he tasted it that he was very hungry. He ate with his elbow on the table, his free hand supporting his head.

"You should have heard the speeches in the Senate yesterday," Sol said. "Funniest show on Earth. They're trying to push this Emergency Bill through—some emergency, it's only been a hundred years in the making—and you should hear them talking all around the little points and not mentioning the big ones." His voice settled into a rich Southern accent. "Faced by dire straits, we propose a survey of all the ee-mence riches of this the greatest ee-luvial basin, the delta, suh, of the mightiest of rivers, the Mississippi. Dikes and drains, suh, science, suh, and you will have here the richest farmlands in the Western World!" Sol blew on his soup angrily. " 'Dikes' is right—another finger in the dike. They've been over this ground a thousand times before. But does anyone mention out loud the sole and only reason for the Emergency Bill? They do not. After all these years they're too chicken to come right out and tell the truth, so they got it hidden away in one of the little riders tacked onto the bottom."

"What are you talking about?" Andy asked, only half listening, still worrying about Shirl.

"Birth control, that's what. They are finally getting around to legalizing clinics that will be open to anyone—married or not—and making it a law that all mothers must be supplied with birth-control information. Boy, are we going to hear some howling when the bluenoses find out about that—and the Pope will really plotz!"

"Not now, Sol, I'm tired. Did Shirl say anything about when she would be back?"

"Just what I told you . . ." He stopped and listened to the sound of footsteps coming down the hall. They stopped and there was a light knocking on the door.

Andy was there first, twisting at the knob, tearing the door open.

"Shirl!" he said. "Are you all right?"

"Yes, sure—I'm fine."

He held her to him, tightly, almost cutting off her breath. "With the riots—I didn't know what to think," he said. "I just came in a little while ago myself. Where have you been? What happened?"

"I just wanted to get out for a while, that's all." She wrinkled her nose. "What's that funny smell?"

He stepped away from her, anger welling up through the fatigue. "I caught some of my own puke gas and heaved up. It's hard to get off. What do you mean that you wanted to get out for a while?"

"Let me get my coat off."

Andy followed her into the other room and closed the door behind them. She was taking a pair of high-heeled shoes out of the bag she carried and putting them into the closet. "Well?" he said.

"Just that, it's not complicated. I was feeling trapped in here, with the shortages and the cold and everything, and never seeing you. And I felt bad about the fight we had. Nothing seemed to be going right. So I thought if I dressed up and went to one of the restaurants where I used to go, just to have a cup of coffee or something, I might feel better. A morale booster, you know." She looked up at his cold face, then glanced quickly away.

"Then what happened?" he asked.

"I'm not in the witness box, Andy. Why the accusing tone?"

He turned his back and looked out the window. "I'm not accusing you of anything, but you were out all night. How do you expect me to feel?"

"Well, you know how bad it was yesterday, I was afraid to come back. I was up at Curly's—"

"The meateasy?"

"Yes, but if you don't eat anything it's not expensive. It's just the food that costs. I met some people I knew and we talked, they were going to a party and invited me and I went

along. We were watching news about the riots on TV and no
one wanted to go out, so the party just went on and on." She
paused. "That's all."

"All?" An angry question, a dark suspicion.

"That's all," she said, and her voice was now as cold as his.

She turned her back to him and began to pull off her dress,
and their words lay like a cold barrier between them. Andy
dropped onto the bed and turned his back on her as well so
that they were like strangers, even in the tiny room.

## SPRING

The funeral drew them together as nothing else had during the
cold depths of the winter. It was a raw day, gusting wind and
rain, but there was still a feeling that winter was on the way
out. But it had been too long a winter for Sol and his cough
had turned into a cold, the cold into pneumonia, and what can
an old man do in a cold room without drugs in a winter that
does not seem to end? Die, that was all, so he had died. They
had forgotten their differences during his illness and Shirl had
nursed him as best she could, but careful nursing does not cure
pneumonia. The funeral had been as brief and cold as the day
and in the early darkness they went back to the room. They
had not been back half an hour before there was a quick
rapping on the door. Shirl gasped.

"The callboy. They can't! You don't have to work today."

"Don't worry. Even Grassy wouldn't go back on his word
about a thing like this. And besides, that's not the callboy's
knock."

"Maybe a friend of Sol's who couldn't get to the funeral."

She went to unlock the door and had to blink into the
darkness of the hall for a moment before she recognized the
man standing there.

"Tab! It is you, isn't it? Come in, don't stand there. Andy, I told you about Tab my bodyguard. . . ."

"Afternoon, Miss Shirl," Tab said stoically, staying in the hall. "I'm sorry, but this is no social call. I'm on the job now."

"What is it?" Andy asked, walking over next to Shirl.

"You have to realize I take the work that is offered to me," Tab said. He was unsmiling and gloomy. "I've been in the bodyguard pool since September, just the odd jobs, no regular assignments. We take whatever work we can get. A man turns down a job, he goes right back to the end of the list. I have a family to feed. . . ."

"What are you trying to say?" Andy asked. He was aware that someone was standing in the darkness behind Tab and could tell by the shuffle of feet that there were others out of sight down the hall.

"Don't take no guff," the man in back of Tab said in an unpleasant nasal voice. He stayed behind the bodyguard where he could not be seen. "I got the law on my side. I paid you. Show him the order!"

"I think I understand now," Andy said. "Get away from the door, Shirl. Come inside Tab, so we can talk to you."

Tab started forward and the man in the hall tried to follow him. "You don't go in there without me—" he shrilled. His voice was cut off as Andy slammed the door in his face.

"I wish you hadn't done that," Tab said. He was wearing his spike-studded iron knuckles, his fist clenched tight around them.

"Relax," Andy said. "I just wanted to talk to you alone first, find out what was going on. He has a squat-order, doesn't he?"

Tab nodded, looking unhappily down at the floor.

"What on earth are you two talking about?" Shirl asked, worriedly glancing back and forth at their set expressions.

Andy didn't answer and Tab turned to her. "A squat-order is issued by the court to anyone who can prove they are really in need of a place to live. They only give so many out, and usually just to people with big families that have had to get out of some other place. With a squat-order you can look around and find a vacant apartment or room or anything like that, and the order is sort of a search warrant. There can be trouble, people don't want to have strangers walking in on them, that kind of thing, so anyone with a squat-order takes along a bodyguard. That's where I come in; the party out there in the hall, name of Belicher, hired me."

"But what are you doing here?" Shirl asked, still not understanding.

"Because Belicher is a ghoul, that's why," Andy said bitterly. "He hangs around the morgue looking for bodies."

"That's one way of saying it," Tab answered, holding on to his temper. "He's also a guy with a wife and kids and no place to live, that's another way of looking at it."

There was a sudden hammering on the door and Belicher's complaining voice could be heard outside. Shirl finally realized the significance of Tab's presence, and she gasped. "You're here because you're helping them," she said. "They found out that Sol is dead and they want his room."

Tab could only nod mutely.

"There's still a way out," Andy said. "If we had one of the men here from my precinct, living in here, then those people couldn't get in."

The knocking was louder and Tab took a half step backward toward the door. "If there was somebody here now, that would be okay, but Belicher could probably take the thing to squat court and get occupancy anyway because he has a family. I'll do whatever I can to help you—but Belicher, he's still my employer."

"Don't open that door," Andy said sharply. "Not until we have this straightened out."

"I have to—what else can I do?" He straightened up and

closed his fist with knucks on it. "Don't try to stop me, Andy. You're a policeman, you know the law about this."

"Tab, must you?" Shirl asked in a low voice.

He turned to her, eyes filled with unhappiness. "We were good friends once, Shirl, and that's the way I'm going to remember it. But you're not going to think much of me after this because I have to do my job. I have to let them in."

"Go ahead, open the damn door," Andy said bitterly, turning his back and walking over to the window.

The Belichers swarmed in. Mr. Belicher was thin, with a strangely shaped head, almost no chin, and just enough intelligence to sign his name to a Welfare application. Mrs. Belicher was the support of the family; from the flabby fat of her body came the children, all seven of them, to swell the Relief allotment on which they survived. Number eight was pushing an extra bulge out of the dough of her flesh; it was really number eleven since three of the younger Belichers had perished through indifference or accident. The largest girl, she must have been all of twelve, was carrying the sore-covered infant, which stank abominably and cried continuously. The other children shouted at each other now, released from the silence and tension of the dark hall.

"Oh looka the nice fridge," Mrs. Belicher said, waddling over and opening the door.

"Don't touch that," Andy said, and Belicher pulled him by the arm.

"I like this room—it's not big you know, but nice. What's in here?" He started toward the door in the partition.

"That's my room," Andy said, slamming it shut in his face. "Just keep out of there."

"No need to act like that," Belicher said, sidling away quickly like a dog that has been kicked too often. "I got my rights. The law says I can look wherever I want with a squat-order." He moved farther away as Andy took a step toward him. "Not that I'm doubting your word, mister, I believe you. This room here is fine, got a good table, chairs, bed . . ."

"Those things belong to me. This is an empty room, and a small one at that. It's not big enough for you and all your family."

"It's big enough. We lived in smaller . . ."

"Andy—stop them! Look!" Shirl's unhappy cry spun Andy around and he saw that two of the boys had found the packets of herbs that Sol had grown so carefully in his window box, were tearing them open, thinking that it was food of some kind.

"Put those things down," he shouted, but before he could reach them they had tasted the herbs, then spat them out.

"Burn my mouth!" the bigger boy screamed and sprayed the contents of the packet on the floor. The other boy bounced up and down with excitement and began to do the same thing with the rest of the herbs. They twisted away from Andy and before he could stop them the packets were empty.

As soon as Andy turned away, the younger boy, still excited, climbed on the table—his mud-stained foot wrappings leaving filthy smears—and turned up the TV. Blaring music crashed over the screams of the children and the ineffectual calls of their mother. Tab pulled Belicher away as he opened the wardrobe to see what was inside.

"Get these kids out of here," Andy said, white-faced with rage.

"I got a squat-order, I got rights," Belicher shouted, backing away and waving an imprinted square of plastic.

"I don't care what rights you have," Andy told him, opening the hall door. "We'll talk about that when these brats are outside."

Tab settled it by grabbing the nearest child by the scruff of the neck and pushing it out through the door. "Mr. Rusch is right," he said. "The kids can wait outside while we settle this."

Mrs. Belicher sat down heavily on the bed and closed her eyes, as though all this had nothing to do with her. Mr. Belicher retreated against the wall saying something that no one heard or bothered to listen to. There were some shrill cries and angry sobbing from the hall and the last child was expelled. Andy looked around and realized that Shirl had gone into their room; he heard the key turn in the lock. "I suppose this is it?" he said, looking steadily at Tab.

The bodyguard shrugged helplessly. "I'm sorry, Andy, honest to God I am. What else can I do? It's the law, and if they want to stay here you can't get them out."

"It's the law, it's the law," Belicher echoed tonelessly.

There was nothing Andy could do with his clenched fists and he had to force himself to open them. "Help me carry these things into the other room, will you, Tab?"

"Sure," Tab said, and took the other end of the table. "Try and explain to Shirl about my part in this, will you? I don't think she understands that it's just a job I have to do."

Their footsteps crackled on the dried herbs and seeds that littered the floor and Andy did not answer him.

# THE GOLDEN YEARS OF THE STAINLESS STEEL RAT

W ell if it isn't Dirty Old Jim diGriz!"
The man's ugly face broke into an evil grin when he saw me standing there, handcuffed to the large policeman. He threw the door wide with unconcealed pleasure, stepped out as the handcuffs were removed, and took me firmly—a little too firmly—by the arm and hauled me forward. I tottered but kept my balance, shuffled through the door, passed under the verdigris-covered brass plate with its penetrating message:

THROUGH THIS GATE PASS THE
ANTIQUATED CRIMINAL
CROCKS OF THE GALAXY

Great stuff. That's the way with the police—always kick a man when he's down. I had to shuffle faster as the sadistic attendant quickened his pace.

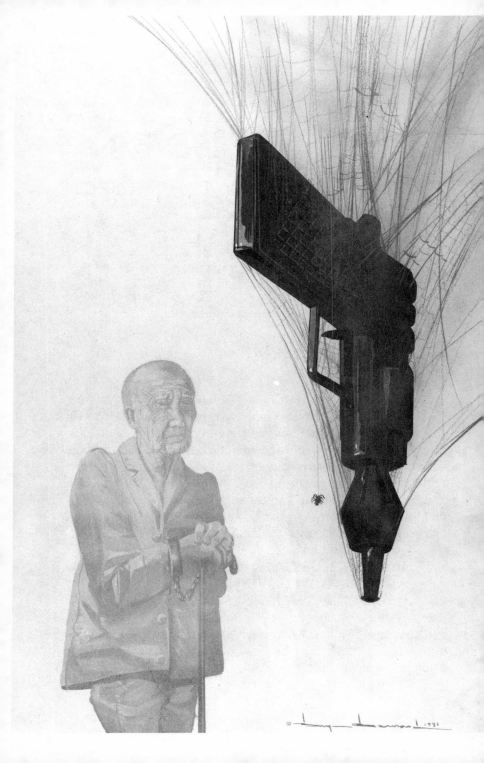

"Got to sit—" I gasped, pulling feebly at his restricting hand as I tried to sit on the bench against the wall.

"Plenty time to sit later, Pops—that's about all you will be doing. You gotta see the warden first."

I could only make feeble resistance as he hauled me down the corridor to the heavy steel door. He knocked loudly. I staggered and gasped and found myself facing a mirror on the wall with an admonitory warning over it.

> ARE YOU CLEAN?
> ARE YOU NEAT?
> WHEN'S THE LAST TIME
> YOU WASHED YOUR FEET?

"Can't remember . . ." I quavered. Looking with trembling disgust at my mirrored image. Wispy white hair tangled and matted. A white string of drool on the pendent lower lip. Skin wattled and doughy, eyes red and poochy. Not nice.

"In!" my keeper ordered as a green light flickered and the door clicked open. He pushed me forward with a meaty hand; I stumbled and fought to keep my balance. Behind me the door swung shut. Before me the warden brooded over a thick file.

"Yours," he said grimly, looking up at me. He had the face of an unshaven camel. "The file of a criminal. James diGriz, a.k.a. The Stainless Steel Rat." The rubbery lips twisted into a poor imitation of a smile. "Stainless no more, rusty if anything." He wheezed happily at his feeble joke, until smile turned to snarl.

"I get them all, Rusty Rat. In the end they all end up before Warden Sukks. They run and hide—but finally I get them. Even the smartest criminal grows old, grows dim, makes one mistake. That's all it takes to get caught and sent to Terminal Penitentiary. That's the official name. But do you know what they really call it . . . ?"

"Hell's Waiting Room!" Unwanted, the words slipped from my lips and dropped greasily to the floor.

"You got it. But that's what they call it on the outside. You come in but you don't go out. In here we don't use that fancy name. We have a better one. This is the Purgy. That's short for Purgatory if you don't know. Which is a word that means . . ."

"I gotta go to the toilet," I wheezed, legs crossed tightly. His sneer deepened.

"That's all you old crocks ever do." He thumbed a button and the door squeaked open behind me. "Bogger will show you where the heads are. Then he'll take you for your medical. We shall see that you keep fit, diGriz—so that you can enjoy our hospitality for a nice long time."

His sadistic laughter followed me down the corridor. I can't say that I was overly impressed with the reception.

Or the medical either. The burly, bored, and sadistic attendants stripped me naked, then slipped a flimsy gray smock over my scrawny bones. Then proceeded to drag me from one diagnostic machine to another, completely ignoring my mewling protests. Commenting offhandedly on the results.

"Pin in that hip. Looks kind of old."

"Not as old as those plastic knee-joints. This ancient crock has had a lot of mileage."

"The doc is really going to like this one. Spots on the lung. TB or black lung or something."

"Done yet?" Bogger asked, popping up like a bad memory.

"Done. All yours, Bogger. Take him away."

Clutching my clothes to my chest, barefooted on the cold floor, I was dragged to my cell and pushed through the door. Despite my feeble resistance Bogger pulled my clothes from me, shook the few personal objects from my pockets onto the floor, threw onto the bed an armload of coarse prison clothing and a pair of scuffs.

"Dinner at six. Door unlocks a minute before. If you're late you don't eat." His sadistic chuckle was cut off by the closing door.

I sat tremblingly onto the bed, dropped my face into my hands. Shivered. A sorry sight for anyone watching from any concealed pickups. The end of a proud, though criminal, man. A doomed nonagenarian reaching the end of his tether.

What they could not see because my hands were over my face was the quick, happy, and successful grin. I had done it!

When I raised my face the grin was gone and my lips were trembling again.

The transparent cover of my cheap plastic watch was so scratched that I could barely make out the numbers. I held it up to the light, twisted it and panted with the effort, finally made out the time.

"Dinner at six, oh deary me. Must get out when the door unlocks." I shuffled up to it just when the lock clicked open, pulled it wide, and stumbled through.

It was pretty obvious where the chow hall was, with the feeble horde of gray-clad geriatric figures all shuffling in the same direction. I joined the shuffle, took a tray at the entrance, held it out for dollops of institutional sludge. I could not tell what it was by looking at it, knew even less after I had tasted it. Well, hopefully it contained nourishment. I spooned it up with trembling hand.

"I never seen you before," the octogenarian seated beside me said suspiciously. "You a police spy?"

"I'm a convicted felon."

"Welcome to Purgy, heh-hee," he chuckled, cheered to see a newcomer. "Ever hijack a spaceship?"

"Once or twice."

"I did three. Third was a mistake. It was a decoy. But I ran out of credits, bad investments, nearing eighty and couldn't see so well . . ."

The reminiscences droned on like a babbling brook and were just about as interesting. I let them burble while I finished

my muckburger and gunge. As I was choking down the last
depressing morsel a familiar and detested voice cut through
the clatter and slurp.

"Rusty Rat. You're finished with your dinner. So rattle
your ancient bones to see the doc. Now."

"How do I find him?"

"Follow the green arrows on the wall, numbnuts. The green
ones with the little red cross. Go."

I dragged to my feet and went. There were arrows of different colors pointing in both directions on the corridor walls. I
blinked and leaned close and made out the ones I needed.
Lurched off to the left.

"Come in, sit down, answer my questions, are you inconti-
nent?" The doctor was young, in a hurry, impatient. I
scratched my head and muttered.

"Don't rightly know . . ."

"You must know!"

"Not really. Don't know what the word means."

"Bed-wetting! Do you wet the bed at night?"

"Only when I'm drunk."

"Not much chance of that in here, diGriz. I've been looking
at your charts. You're a wreck. Spots on the lung, pins in the
hips, staples in the skull—"

"I led a rough life, Doc."

"Without a doubt. And your electrolytes are all skewed. I'll
give you a couple of shots now to slow the deterioration, then
you take one of these pills three times a day."

I took the jar and blinked at the bullet-sized tablets.

"Kind of big."

"And you're kind of ill. Specially formulated for your mul-
tiple problems. Keep them with you at all times. A buzzer in
the lid will tell you when to take one. Now—roll up your
sleeve."

He wielded a wicked needle. I swear the point hit bone a
couple of times. With aching arms I stumbled around looking

for my room, got lost, got put right by passing attendants, finally found it. The door locked when I closed it and a few minutes later the lights began to dim. I fumbled off my clothes, fumbled on the sickly orange pajamas, dropped onto the bed, and was just pulling up the covers when the lights went out.

This was it. End of the line. Purgy. The purgatory before hell. Fed and healed to make the stay that much longer. The sentence with only one end.

*Oh yeah!* I said silently to myself, and permitted a wide grin to brush my lips under the cover of the blankets. My back itched under the transparent plastic patches and I scratched them happily. They were invisible to the eye, but coated with a lead-antimony alloy that blocked X rays. I had gambled on the fact that this place would not have expensive tomographs or such—and had won. On the two-dimensional X-ray plates the plastic patches on my legs looked like metal pins, on my skull dark staples. They had done their job, would dissolve and vanish the next time I washed.

I had done it! The first part of this operation was complete. Finding out about this hospital-prison had been the hardest part. It took a lot of risky work getting into planetary-government files before I managed to track it down. Risky but interesting. Guiding the twins in their successful semilegal careers had kept Angelina and me pretty busy. Now that they were successful, and rich I must add, we had been enjoying what might be called semiretirement. This suited Angelina quite well since she was happy with all those pleasure planets and luxury cruises. I, as you might very well imagine, loathed it. If I hadn't been able to polish off the occasional bank or lift a lucrative space yacht I might have gone around the twist. But it wasn't real work. Then this wonderful opportunity had revealed itself. A tiny item in the nightly news. I printed it out and brought it to Angelina. She read it swiftly, put it down in silence.

"We ought to do something," I had said.

"No" was her quick response.

"I think we owe him something—or at least you do."

"Nonsense. A grown man makes his own decisions."

"Yes, of course. I still want to find out where they have sent him."

When I had tracked him down and discovered the secret location of Terminal Penitentiary, I told Angelina of my plan. Her eyes narrowed as I spoke, her face grew grim. When I had finished speaking she nodded slowly.

"Do it, Jim. It is dangerous and looks suicidal—but you are probably the only man in the galaxy who could pull it off. With my help, of course."

"Of course. Your first task will be to find a bent but professionally competent doctor."

"Not a problem. Did you ever hear of a doctor—or a lawyer—bent or not, who could resist the continual flutter of bank notes onto a tabletop?"

"Now that you mention it—no. How is our expense account?"

"Running a little low. We could use a few million more. Why don't you knock off a really juicy bank while I line up the medic."

"Music to my ears."

But almost a year went by before the preparations were complete. There would be no rushing in, guessing or taking chances. Because if every detail were not worked out to the last decimal point I was going to be spending an awful lot of time behind bars.

Angelina came to pick me up at the clinic—and recoiled in horror.

"Jim—you look awful!"

"Thank you. It was quite an effort. Losing weight was easy enough, as well as skin aging, hair dyeing, all the usual things. It's the muscles I miss the most."

"Me too. Your gorgeous figure—"

"Wasted away with enzymes. No choice. If I am going to pass for an ancient crock I have to look like one. Don't worry, a few months of bodybuilding when this is over and I'll be as good as new."

A tear glistened in her eyes and she gave me a warm hug. "And you're doing this for me."

"Of course. But for him as well—and for Jim diGriz so I can look at myself in the mirror. Not that I really want to just now."

And that had been that. Pulling off an inept jewel robbery and getting nicked had been the easy part. I just made sure that the crime was committed on Heliotrope-2, the site of the original news report that had started this entire thing rolling.

It had rolled well. Here I was in Purgy and I had one week to acquaint myself with the layout, the alarms and videoscanners, before the operation went into phase two. It was time well spent. At breakfast next morning I looked around at all the bald heads and gray polls of my fellow inmates and found him at once. And stayed away. Time enough to renew an old acquaintance at the proper moment. As I spooned up the purple gruel I took everything in. And started with surprise.

Could it be him? Yes, it was. His hair was white now, his face tracked with countless wrinkles. But after two months together in an ice cave—well, there are things you just don't forget. I followed him after we had dumped our trays, sat down next to him in the morning room.

"Been here long, Burin?" I asked.

He turned his head and blinked at me nearsightedly—then his face lit up with a smile.

"Jimmy diGriz as I live and breathe!"

"And I'm most glad that you are living and breathing! Burin Bache, the best forger in the history of the galaxy."

"Kind of you to say that, Jimmy. And it was true at one time. Not lately—" The smile faded and I quickly put my arm around him.

"Do you still get chilblains in your ankles?"

"You bet I do! You know—I still can't put ice into a drink. Hate the sight of it."

"Yes, but the ice cave was only a hiccup. . . ."

"Some hiccup! But you're right there, Jimmy me lad. After what we hauled down on that job I didn't have to work for ten years. You were young but you were a genius. Hate to see you ending up here like me. Never thought they would get you."

"Happens to the best of us."

As I spoke I had my stilo concealed in my cupped hands, printing a quick message on my palm. Then I rubbed my chin with the back of my hand and waited until Burin had looked at it, his eyes widening.

"Got to go now," I said as I blurred the message with a saliva-dampened fingertip. "See you around."

He could only nod shocked and silent agreement as I left. I couldn't blame him. Since his incarceration I am sure he never thought he would ever read those words.

WE'RE GETTING OUT OF HERE.

The immense bribe that Angelina had paid to the city official had been well worth it. The building permission floorplans had not been complete—but they sufficed. I got close to the room we had selected on the second day, stuffed my stilo into the keyhole on the third. After being held in my armpit for an hour, the memory plastic of which it was made had softened to the consistency of clay. A moment after being pressed against the cold metal it had hardened into a perfect mirror image of the lock's innards.

We were permitted an hour in the garden every day and I had found a bench that was well away from any sites that might have held videoscanners. I sat there, apparently dozing over an open book. You would have to stand very close to see what I was doing.

That morning I had stripped off part of the plastic covering of my battered wallet. And chewed it well. It had not tasted as bad as some of the meals we had consumed. It had reacted with my saliva and had softened to a nice doughy consistency. And had remained that way in the darkness of my pocket. Now I pressed it against the mold of the lock's interior. It should be shaped to duplicate the key that would open it. When I was satisfied with the effort I held the plastic in the warm sunshine. The catalyst it contained reacted with the light and it hardened instantly.

Logically I should have waited for the right moment to try to open that door. But I had to make a dry run. Get any problems out of the way so I could move quickly and smoothly at the decided time.

Burin was more than happy to help. We synchronized watches and at the precise moment I reached the door he stumbled and fell onto the table where the card game was in progress. There was a great crashing, shouts of anger and dismay as I slipped the homemade key into the keyhole. Turned and pressed.

Nothing happened. I took a deep breath, held it—then used every iota of skill acquired during a lifetime of lockpicking.

It grated slightly—and the door opened.

I was through in an instant, closing and locking it behind me. Listening for footsteps, shouts of alarm.

Nothing. Only then did I look around me. I was in a small storeroom piled high with reams of paper and mounds of forms so dear to the bureaucratic heart. There was enough light from the small window to see clearly. I memorized the layout of the room, then moved one box that blocked a direct path. Enough. Time to go. I was too close to D Day, H Hour, M Minute to get into any trouble now. Silence in the hall. Through the door, lock it, stroll back to the morning room, where a sort of antique fistfight was going on. I was sorry we had to spoil their game. No, I really wasn't. Burin glanced in my direction and I flashed him a sort of conspiratorial wink, or tic, then passed on.

Angelina and I had agreed on absolutely minimum contact
this first meeting. And the timing was crucial. It had to be after
dark for concealment—but not so late that we had been
packed off beddy-byes. On the selected evening I was first
through the door after dinner, stumbling swiftly in the direction of the heads. Past that door and up the stairs. I had cut
it too close, only seconds left. Lock and relock the door, tread
quickly the few steps along the memorized path—my watch
ready in my hand.

Grasped in both hands so I could draw the watch strap back
and forth across the window lock with a quick sawing motion.
This stripped away the surface plastic that covered the far
harder plasteel of the flexible saw inside. It rasped noisily until
there was a sharp click. I stuffed the watch into my pocket,
seized the window, and pulled it open.

Angelina, all in black, black gloves and blackened face, was
outside. She pushed the package into my hands. Despite our
agreement she could not resist a softly hissed "About time!"
as I pushed the window shut.

I retired at once, the bundle concealed in my clothing,
pushed under the pillow as I got into bed. I left it there after
I had worked the detector out of it.

Soon after the lights were out I began to toss and turn.

"Can't sleep," I moaned. "Insomnia and arthritis got me
down. Groan."

I thrashed a bit longer, then rose and stumbled about the
room rubbing my leg. Rubbing the controls on the detector as
well with gratifying results. There was only a single detector
over the door. Which left at least two blank spots in the room
out of its field of view. A good night's sleep was now in order,
because there was plenty to do on the morrow.

It was almost noon before I went looking for Burin Bache,
sat down next to him in the sun porch. He raised his eyebrows
quizzically but I did not respond until I had moved about a bit
with the detector.

"Great," I said. "Just don't talk too loud. Contact has been made."

"Then you have everything?" He was trembling with excitement.

"Everything. Most of it hidden where they can't find it. Let's go out into the garden in exactly twelve minutes."

"Why?"

"Because concealed in my mouth is an optical laser communicator." I opened my lips to reveal the lens. "I can hear through my hard palate."

"Hear what?" He was mystified.

"The dulcet tones of my dear Angelina, who even now is making her way to the upper floors of that office building that you can just see peeking over the wall in the distance. Untappable communication. Let's go."

I leaned back in the deck chair and at the proper moment smiled in the direction of the distant building. My aim didn't have to be too precise since she would have opened up a two-meter receiving lens.

"Good morning, my love."

"Jim, I'm sorry we ever got involved with this insane plan," her voice said squeakily through my head bones.

"Only way out now is full steam ahead."

"I know that. And I didn't enjoy climbing your building— even with molecular grappling gloves and boots."

"But you did it, my love. You are strong and skillful—"

"If you dare add—for a woman of my age—I will skin you alive when you get out!"

"The farthest thought from my mind. What I wanted to ask is—do you think we can take out two instead of one? I have found an old acquaintance here who, truthfully, saved my life once. In an ice cave. I'll tell you about it one day. How about it?"

She hesitated a moment and I could imagine her sweet little

frown of concentration. My Angelina does not speak until she is certain.

"Yes, of course. I'll just have to change transportation."

"Good. If you are changing transportation make sure the vehicle is big enough."

"For four?"

"Not really. What I had in mind was well, a figure a little closer to sixty-five. . . ."

"Message breaking up. Repeat last. It came through as sixty-five."

"Right! Bang-on! That is correct!" I tried to sound cheerful and not smarmy. She was not fooled.

"Don't try it on, diGriz—I know you. Sixty-five—that must be every inmate there."

"Correct, my love. Exact number. I would suggest a tourist bus. I did this kind of thing once before and it worked. Locate the bus and I'll get back to you same time tomorrow with more details. Must go—someone coming." I clicked off. We were still unobserved but I wanted Angelina's justified wrath to have twenty-four hours to cool before I talked to her again.

"What happened?" Burin asked. "I could hear you mumble a bit, that's all."

"Gears meshing like clockwork. Couldn't be better. My dear wife is filled with wild enthusiasm for the plan. Particularly its new dimension."

"What—?"

"Details later. Let's go in to lunch now. Don't drink the water."

"Why not?"

"I tested it this morning. Laced with pacifiers, saltpeter and brain-scrambling drugs. That's why the inmates mumble and stagger around so much. I think almost all of them are in far better shape than what we see."

Angelina's anger had cooled when we talked the next day. More than cooled. Her voice, even vibrating buzzily through my ear bones, had a positive chill that brought back memory of the ice cave.

"I have the bus. Bought legally. What else will I need?"

"A bus driver's uniform for yourself to explain your graceful presence behind the wheel. And, well—a few other items—"

"Like what?" Temperature of liquid nitrogen. When I had dictated the list her voice was approaching absolute zero.

"This is the most insane, harebrained, impossible plan that I have ever heard. I shall make every effort to see that it does not fail, that you are not injured and escape in one piece. So I can then personally kill you myself."

"My love—you jest."

"Try me." She clicked off.

Maybe it wasn't such a great idea. But now that I had started down this path I had to go all the way. For the first time I was more depressed than excited. Too much of the drinking water maybe. Then I remembered the medicine I had put into the bundle for just such a moment as this.

Out of sight of the pickup above my door I opened the wall grate and removed the plastic bottle labeled DANGER—HIGH EXPLOSIVE. In a way it was. One hundred and ten proof and twelve years in the barrel. My good humor returned in a surge.

For six more days Angelina and I had our daily chat by laser. Formal and brief no matter how I tried to be friendly and crack the occasional joke. All this was ignored. My darling was in a temper. With good reason, I sighed. Only thing to do was get on with it.

On the seventh day our conversation was most one-sided. She spoke a single word and disconnected. I turned off the transmitter with my tongue and turned to Burin—who looked much more alert now that he wasn't drinking water with his meals.

"The date is set."

"When?"

"I'll tell you after dinner."

He started to speak—then clamped his mouth shut. Appreciating the wisdom of my decision. The fewer that knew the less chance of any slipups. A maximum of one keeps a secret a secret.

That evening when the rattle of spoons on metal had slowed and the slurping of the jellied gray dessert had replaced it, I took my tray into the kitchen, came out without it, and closed the door. Was watched by some of the slurpers with bleary-eyed interest as I slipped a tiny metal packet over the cable to the pickup on the wall.

"May I have your attention," I called out, hammering on the table with a spoon. I waited until the hum of voices had died down—then pointed to the side door.

"We are all going to leave now by that side door. The gentleman who is now opening it, Burin Bache, is your guide. You will follow him." I had to raise my voice to be heard over the babble of voices. "You will shut up now and ask no questions. All will be revealed later. But I can tell you now that the authorities will definitely *not* like what we are going to do."

This drew nods of approval since every inmate was here because of flouting the law and thumbing the nose at authority. This, plus all the hypnotics in the drinking water, had them trooping out quietly following my orders. I stood by the door, smiling and patting an occasional shoulder as they went by, working hard not to show any impatience.

With each passing minute there was a growing chance that the mass escape might be discovered. The kitchen staff and two guards were sleeping quietly in the storeroom; the wall pickup was transmitting a recording of happy diners munching away. And the two other doors were locked. That was the weak spot in the plan. Normally no one came into the dining area during a meal. But there were exceptions. I crossed my fingers behind my back hoping that this wasn't one of the exceptional days.

As the last bent shoulder moved by in front of me I sighed with relief, stepped through, and locked the door behind me. Followed my shuffling colleagues down the stairs to the service corridor, closing and locking each door after going through it. I did the same thing as we passed through the cellar, to the boiler room at the far end. The fire door here was heavier and slid closed with a satisfactory thud.

I turned to look at my colleagues, wringing my hands with pleasure.

"What's happening?" one of them called out.

"We are leaving here," I looked at my watch, "In exactly seven minutes!"

As might very well be imagined that caused no little stir. I listened to the voices then shouted them to silence.

"No—I'm not mad. Nor am I as old as I look. I had myself arrested and incarcerated in this place for only one reason. To crack out. I will now pass through you, that's it, move aside, thank you, to the far wall. You may or may not know that this prison is built on a hillside. Which means that while the other end of the building is deep in the earth and rock—this end is level with the road outside. Will you all kindly move to the far side of the room, that's it. As you can see I am placing a shaped charge of macrothermite on the wall. When ignited this not only burns but penetrates and keeps on burning until it reaches the other side."

They watched in tense silence as I patted into place a rough circle of the doughy substance, then sprayed it with sealant and pushed in an igniter.

"Push close together—get as far away as you can," I ordered, looking at my watch. When there were five seconds to go I pushed the igniter button and hurried to join them.

It was most dramatic. The igniter flared and a ring of fire sprang out from the wall. It crackled and flamed and smoked;

there was a lot of coughing as the smoke spread and the vent fans labored to clear it. Then I pulled the hose from the reel and opened the valve to spray water on the wall. There were cries of fear and more serious coughing as clouds of steam added to the discomfort.

The hissing and crackling died down and I turned off the water, strode forward. I raised my foot and gave a good push against the circle of wall. It obliged me by falling outward with a rumbling crash.

"Lights out!" I ordered, and Burin threw the switches.

A streetlight lit up the ground outside, revealed the roll of carpeting. This began to rotate and the flexpowered end crept in through the opening. The carpet was red as I had ordered.

"Let's get out of here! One at a time. No talking and don't touch the wall or the ground. Stay on the carpet, which is heatproof. Burin—over here."

"It's working, Jim—it's actually working!"

"Your faith is touching. Make sure they are all out before you leave."

"Will do!"

I joined the line of shambling figures, hurried along the carpet, and jumped off to join the neatly uniformed figure of my wife.

"My love—"

"Shut up," she suggested. "There's the bus. Get them aboard."

There it was indeed. Engine idling, coachwork gleaming. A large banner on the side bore the message—

### RETIREES MYSTERY TOUR

"This way," I said and turned the nearest man in the right direction and led the way to the door. "Go to the rear and find a seat. Put on the clothes that you will find on the seat—and the wig as well. Go."

I repeated this until Burin appeared. He took over the message muttering while I herded the remainder aboard. Angelina climbed in as well and sat in silence in the driver's seat.

"That's the lot," I said as cheerfully as I could.

"Door closed and we're away! I did this once before, years ago, only with bicycles." I turned and nodded approval at the gray wigs and dresses, at what appeared to be a busload of old ladies.

"Well done," I shouted. "Very well done."

And that was very well that. Other than my wife's cold silence everything was just about perfect. We rolled merrily into the night and were well out of the city before we saw a police checkpoint ahead. I struggled into a dress, popped on the wig, then led all the assembled ladies in a sing-song of "Row, row, row your boat—"

The bus had barely rolled to a stop before we were told to move on. There was many a high-pitched shriek of joy and a flutter of waved handkerchiefs as we left.

It was almost midnight before the headlights lit up the sign BIDE-A-WEE RETIREMENT HOME FOR GENTEEL LADIES. I jumped out and opened the gate, then closed it behind the bus.

"Inside, ladies," I called out. "Tea and cakes waiting—as well as a self-service bar."

This last drew shouts of hoarse pleasure as they streamed inside, dresses and wigs now cast aside. Angelina signaled me over and I hurried to her side.

"What do I say to him?"

"I thought you were angry with me?"

"That's long past. It's just . . ."

He stood aside from the others, saw us talking. Walked slowly over to join us.

"I must thank you both—for what you have done for all of us."

"It just worked out that way, Pepe," I said. "The truth is we set the whole thing up to spring you out of that place. The operation sort of, well, grew a bit after that."

"Then you still remember me, Angelina? I recognized you at once." He smiled warmly and his eyes grew damp.

"It was my idea," I said quickly, before things got out of hand. "I saw this item in the news and felt obligated to do something. For old times' sake at least. Since I was the one who arrested you for stealing the battleship."

"And I was the one who led you into a life of crime," Angelina said firmly. "We felt a certain—responsibility."

"Particularly since we have been happily married for years and have two fine sons. If you two had not been partners I would have never met the light of my life," I added to make sure all the ground rules were known. Pepe Nero nodded and knuckled his eye.

"I guess about all I can say is . . . thanks. So it all comes out even in the end. I think I was always suited for crime, Angelina. You just set my foot on the right road. Now I am going to have a really large drink."

"That is a really great idea," I agreed.

"A toast!" Burin called out. "Jim and Angelina—our saviors. Thanks for life!"

Cups and glasses were raised—as well as a hoarse cheer from all present. I put my arm around her waist and this time it was I who had the tear in my eye.